CHRISTMAS FOR JULIET

A Christmas Novel

By

Elyse Douglas

COPYRIGHT

Christmas for Juliet
Copyright © 2013/2021 by Elyse Douglas
All rights reserved.

This is a work of fiction. Names, characters, places and incidents are either the product of the author's imagination or are used fictitiously. Any resemblance to actual persons, living or dead, events, or locales is entirely coincidental. The copying, reproduction and distribution of this book via any means, without permission of the author, is illegal and punishable by law.

ISBN – 13:978-1492854531

BROADBACK BOOKS USA

"Change is the hardest at the beginning, messiest in the middle, and best at the end."

—Robin S. Sharma

For Jay, who loves Christmas stories.

CHRISTMAS FOR JULIET

PROLOGUE

It was hate at first sight. Indifference at second sight. Love at third sight and then, finally, in hindsight, hate again. Juliet Sinclair sat at her desk, cellphone in hand, listening to her attorney. Her divorce from Evan, which she had initiated seven months ago, was finally over. With no children and no property, it had been an easy process, except for the humiliation she'd felt for ending a marriage of only six months' duration.

Juliet tried not to relive, for the millionth time, her shock and embarrassment when she finally realized he'd been lying to her. He had *not* ended his affair with the actress in L.A. he'd dated when they were doing a show together in Cleveland. He had *not* ended the affair with the "just a friend" actress in New York, who had two kids. When she finally put the pieces together, from friends' hints and credit card bills, she hated him as much as she'd hated the Casanova, he played the first time she saw him in an off-Broadway production. Furious, she confronted him.

"Sweetheart, just let me explain," Evan had said, rushing to caress her cheek the way she loved. "Let me tell you what happened…"

"Don't you touch me!" she'd yelled, backing away. Then she'd stormed out of the apartment, deliberately slamming the door behind her.

He texted her. *"You're over-reacting. I love you. They didn't mean anything."*

She texted back. *"If they didn't mean anything, then our marriage didn't mean anything! You're a liar! A cheat! Leave me alone! It's over!"*

The next day, Juliet moved out of their one-bedroom apartment and lived with a friend for six weeks before finding her own place, a studio apartment on the Upper West Side of Manhattan.

As soon as Juliet said goodbye to her attorney, she grabbed her coat and bag and snuck out of the office.

"I'm meeting a client," she told a co-worker. She hurried into the elevator and punched the lobby button. As the elevator descended, she struggled into her full-length chocolate-brown leather coat with a faux fur collar, a gift from her father last Christmas. The coat made her feel elegant and sophisticated, and since it had been present from her father, it also made her feel loved and protected.

The elevator doors slid open. She exited toward West 57th Street, her heels clicking across the marble floor of the lobby. She pushed through the revolving doors. She had to get some air.

It was 3 p.m. on a cool, November day. Juliet inhaled and looked around Columbus Circle, suddenly knowing exactly what she needed: a chocolate croissant and mocha cappuccino from The Petrossian Café. After she'd found a table and ordered, she called her mother in Ohio.

"Why did this happen, Mom? I really thought he'd be like Dad; he was funny and romantic. How could I have been so stupid to fall for such a liar? Why are men such liars?" she asked.

"They're not *all* liars," Anne Sinclair said. "You just fell for a particularly bad one. Look, you have a right to be upset, but you'll find the right person, eventually. You just need time to get over this."

"I feel like such a fool. You and Dad tried to warn me; you told me to slow down. So did most of my friends. You all said Evan was a jerk. Why didn't I see that? Why didn't I listen to you? Why don't you see anything clearly when you think you're in love?"

"We didn't say he was a jerk," Anne said in a soothing voice. "We said he was a very handsome man who seemed to be more in love with himself than he was with you."

"I thought he'd grow up," Juliet said quietly. "That was my first mistake."

"People don't generally change very much."

"Oh, God, I don't think I'll ever meet anyone I can trust. The whole dating, relationship, love and marriage thing is just so messed up. It's impossible!"

"Give yourself some time, Juliet."

"I'm thirty years old, Mom. I want to get married and have a family, and I'm not getting any younger."

"You're still young. You'll find the right guy."

"At least I didn't get pregnant. Thank God for that. Thank God we both wanted to wait a couple of years."

Juliet drained the last of her cappuccino as the café filled with tourists, who were pointing at the dessert display cases that featured freshly baked breads, cookies, muffins and brioche.

"I wanted to have a relationship like you and Dad have. Playful. Romantic."

"Our marriage hasn't all been roses, you know. We've certainly had our ups and downs. Your father and I have had to work hard at our marriage, just like you'll have to."

"I thought I was working hard at it. I was trying to be understanding when he didn't come home until dawn... and when he didn't even remember my birthday and... Oh, forget it! I'm tired of thinking about it. How did you know Dad was the right guy when you married him?"

"I didn't know at first," Anne said. "Every girl I knew was in love with your father. All but me. I turned him down the first three times he asked me to marry him."

"What? You never told me that. Why?"

"I don't know. I guess because I'd just been involved with another man... and he broke my heart. I was like you: confused and angry."

"You know you're going to have to tell me *that* story someday," Juliet said.

"It's not worth talking about. It was a hundred years ago. Have you talked to your father recently?"

"I called him this morning. He said he was going to be busy the rest of the day. He said he's working for one of the most difficult clients he's ever had."

"Oh! That woman. Yes. She wants him to redesign her kitchen again, for the fourth time, and she already signed off on the third plan. She's driving him crazy. But you know how patient he is. He said as long as she pays him, he'll keep redesigning and placating the contractors."

"I could never be an architect," Juliet said. "I don't have his patience."

"No, Juliet, you don't. I'm afraid you inherited my impatient genes."

Juliet paused. "Mom, thank you for being there during this ordeal. I'm so grateful I have you and Dad."

"You know we love you very much, and we always will."

After Juliet hung up, she changed from heels to walking boots and left the café, shouldering her new Michael Kors tote bag, something she treated herself to a few weeks before. The sun had dropped below the skyline, bringing a sudden chill, and so she turned up the fur collar. Juliet walked aimlessly, fighting depression and low energy. She caught a glimpse of herself in a shop window and lingered a moment to study her reflection. She was 5' 7" and had a good figure, though her hips were a little wide and her breasts were a little on the small size. She had a pretty face, with high cheek bones, a narrow nose and a well-formed mouth. Her straight auburn hair was cut in a bob, and her cool green eyes "always seemed to be searching for something." That was her father's description.

"Where did you get those gorgeous green eyes?" he'd often ask. "Not from my side of the family, and not from your mother's. They all have dark hair and eyes."

"Maybe you adopted me and you're keeping it a secret," Juliet teased.

Her father laughed. "Oh, no, Juliet. We wanted you, we planned for you, and we dreamed about you. My darling girl, you are all ours and always will be."

That was her father, the romantic; the most romantic man she'd ever known. He spontaneously bought her mother flowers and candy. He always stopped at antique stores, searching for the Victorian porcelain figurines Anne loved and collected. At dinner, he insisted on music and wine, special labels he surprised her with: California Cabs, French Pinot Noirs and Argentinean Malbecs. His movie choices often surprised Juliet because he loved girlie movies like *An Affair to Remember*, *A Walk in the Clouds* and *The Notebook*. But he also loved sports, fast cars and *The Three Stooges*. He once told her that any time he felt the least bit depressed, he grabbed his DVDs of *The Three Stooges*. They were his therapists.

"Works 'most every time," he said. "If that doesn't work, and if it's winter, I go ice skating. Nothing like it to clear the mind."

Juliet turned from the store window, smiling at these memories, and merged back into the crowd. She considered cabbing it home to watch *The Three Stooges* on YouTube, but continued strolling and window shopping instead, allowing the steady flow of the crowds to nudge her along toward 5th Avenue.

At 51st Street, traffic was heavy. Taxi horns blared and pedestrians bloated the sidewalks. There was already a holiday spirit to the City, even though Thanksgiving was more than a week away.

Juliet moved on, still with no particular destination in mind, bumped and buffeted by the curious, the anxious and the aggressive. She edged along, observing the faces that hurried by. Where were they all going? Where were they from? Why had they come to New York?

As her eyes turned east, she saw him—her father! He was approaching from about forty feet away, his six foot three-inch frame striding straight toward her, smiling. He wore the camel cashmere overcoat and the red silk scarf she'd bought him last Christmas. The wind tousled his long salt-and-pepper hair as he waved.

On reflex, Juliet lit up, went to tip toes and waved back.

"Dad!" she shouted. "Dad!"

Then the impossibility of the moment struck. She froze. Blinked. When her eyes refocused, he was gone. Juliet stood rigid, staring, as people streamed by, looking strangely at her. She darted looks around, ahead and behind. She scanned the streets. He wasn't there.

She exhaled trapped breath. Her heart pounded. And then, in the blowing cold wind, she shivered, suddenly aware that darkness was descending. The shop lights and street lights gleamed, changing the quality of light and mood. She lifted her tight shoulders and dropped them, taking small uncertain steps. As she advanced toward Rockefeller Center, she forced a tight smile.

"Well, that was weird," she thought.

Obviously, she'd seen a man who resembled her father, but she'd been mistaken. And how *could* she have seen him? He was in Ohio. She walked for a while, accepting the experience with nervous reluctance.

Then she had an idea. She was near the world-famous ice rink at Rockefeller Center. Why not go skating? She'd call her father later and tell him about what had happened. He'd say something like "I have a doppelganger. You should have taken a picture." They'd have a good laugh and that would be that.

She walked through the Channel Gardens, edging her way through the crowds. She hurried down the stairs, and at the promenade, turned right to the Skate House.

Twenty minutes later, she was gliding easily across the ice with fifty or so other skaters, recalling Skater's Pond back in Ohio, where her parents had taken her when she was a girl. The world of lights, towers and flags whirled by as she circled the rink, gazing up now and then at the famous gilded statue of Prometheus and the crowds of spectators looking down from the plaza above.

Fifteen minutes later, as she skidded to a stop, she saw him again. Her father! He was above, gazing down at her from the plaza, waving. It *was* her father! There was no doubt about it. Her eyes sharpened on him. She called out to him, her voice full of force.

"Dad! What are you...?"

He waved once more, flashing a splendid smile. Then he turned and disappeared into the hectic, merging crowd.

In desperation, Juliet shot away toward the locker room.

Inside, at her rented locker, she grappled with the lock. Just as she flung open the locker door and reached for her phone, it rang. She seized it. It was her mother. Her throat tightened, pulse quickened.

"Mother, what is it?" Her voice held alarm.

"Juliet..." her mother said, voice cracking with emotion. She made a gulping sob. "Your father has had a heart attack. He's dead."

CHAPTER 1

More than fifty flower wreaths and floral bouquets were displayed in the foyer, and at the altar, an easel held a 24 x 36 photograph of Rad, taken by Juliet two years before. She'd caught her father by surprise at his drafting table. He'd glanced up, horn-rimmed glasses perched on the end of his nose. His thick salt-and-pepper hair was long, his face lean and open. One could feel the impact of his unique and exceptionally intense projection of interest, warmth and humor. Even in surprise, there was a playful gleam in his soft brown eyes; a sincere, frank expression of strength and expectant adventure on his face. Juliet had selected the photograph because it was neither cloying nor sentimental. It simply revealed the inimitable spirit of her father that everyone had loved.

Rad had specified in his will that he wanted to be cremated. No open casket. "No weeping and gnashing of teeth," he'd often said, quoting the Bible. He also specified what two hymns he wanted sung at a memorial service: *Abide with Me* and *Amazing Grace*. Rad loved *Abide with Me,* which had been one of his mother's favorite hymns. She'd often sung it around the house when Rad was a boy growing up in Kentucky.

With bowed heads and misty eyes, the congregation listened as Margaret Dale sang *Abide with Me* with reverence and majesty, her warm, sonorous voice filling the church with graceful melancholy. She was a chorister at the church and a college friend, who had studied architecture with Rad at the University of Cincinnati.

Anne and Juliet Sinclair sat in the front pew, absorbed in sorrow and memory. Anne was fifty-eight, a slim 5' 7", with medium black hair streaked with grey. Her eyes were swollen from tears and lack of sleep. She kept a handkerchief balled-up in her right fist so she could weep quietly into it. They both wore black: black dresses, black shoes and black coats. They sat in dejected silence. Juliet was stoically erect, holding her mother's hand, a dazed, faraway look in her eyes, her lips trembling.

Eulogies were read, prayers were said, and then, finally, Margaret ended the service with *Amazing Grace.*

Anne had never been particularly religious. She had seldom joined her husband when he occasionally attended Sunday morning services at the church, but she was aware that, in his own way, Rad had been a deeply religious man.

Juliet listened to the moving hymn, feeling deep misery and rising anger. She knew it was an irrational anger—everyone has to die—but as she wiped the tears from her burning eyes, she knew that without her father's light, love and guidance, she would never be the same again. Part of her had died when he died. Part of her was broken. Part of her wanted to die, too. The pain of his loss was nearly debilitating.

She shut her eyes against the poignant hymn and against her thoughts, and then the tears came flooding out. She hated life, and she hated God. What was the point of living? What was the sense of it? Her father was still a young and vital man. He had so much to live for. He was such a bright spark in an often dark and confusing world.

"Life is a big ole' adventure, Juliet," he'd told her the last time she'd been home, right after she filed for the divorce. "Whatever comes at you, accept it and seek the adventure in it. If you can do that, you'll never be bored and you'll never be defeated. You'll always stay young and curious." He'd wrapped his arms around her, offering one of his famous bear hugs. "You'll be okay, honey, I know you will. You're better off without him. You'll find someone who *really* appreciates you next time, I'm sure."

In the half gloom of the morning light, Juliet bowed her head, feeling the beat of contradictory emotions: hate and love. They battled away in her like two medieval knights charging, their lances poised, ready to strike.

With great effort, she mustered the strength to thank God for giving her a good and loving father. She offered this gratitude only because her father would have wanted her to. She prayed to God that He accept her father— that He open the gates of heaven and let her father in so that he could live in paradise forever.

After the service, it was an agony to stand near the altar to watch the sad, gloomy faces as they streamed by Rad's photo, bidding him a last farewell. Old friends tenderly touched Anne's arm and whispered supportive phrases. Some nodded sympathetically to Juliet. Some high school and college girlfriends and boyfriends who'd known her father well, wept and hugged Juliet, offering support. They encouraged her to call and to come for a visit.

The lines of mourners seemed endless. They inched forward unhurriedly, lingering, absorbed by memories and the energy in Rad's photograph. And then, even more people arrived—people Juliet and Anne didn't know and had never seen. People Rad had known as a boy in Kentucky. Clients who'd hired him and loved his work. Contractors, car mechanics, a pizza parlor manager, County Sheriff Tim Hansel, Rad's barber, a cashier at the local supermarket, and even the UPS man, Henry Gonzalez. Rad Sinclair had touched them all in some way, with his enthusiasm and his warm, personal touch.

With blurry vision, Juliet met them and listened as they offered their condolences and briefly shared their admiration for Rad. The lines stretched to the rear of the church and outside, as far as the front lawn.

Juliet had lost track of time. At some point, she noticed an attractive woman in her early fifties standing alone in the right rear of the church. She was quietly weeping, a tissue blotting her eyes. Juliet didn't recognize her and, as far as she knew, she'd never seen her before. The woman stared intently at Rad's photo, her shoulders slightly hunched in grief. She started forward, then hesitated, turning to stare at a stained-glass window, the light filtering through the glass, bathing her in a kind of angelic glow.

Juliet wiped the dazed mist from her eyes and refocused on the woman. She saw fatigue in her soft, miserable face. She saw uncertainty in her posture, as if she were caught between advancing and indecision. The woman was slim and elegant, wearing a stylishly long belted dark winter coat and a white silk scarf. Her dark hair was cut in a conservative, mid-length style, with sweeping bangs that suited her face perfectly.

Juliet stared, as if trying to understand something. There was a quality about the woman that was both attractive and disturbing. The longer Juliet watched the woman, the more she felt an ineffable feeling of a threat. She shook it off, turning her attention back to the approaching mourners, but then the uncomfortable feeling returned and persisted.

Juliet did not see the man seated in a pew about midway down, watching her attentively. His flashing dark eyes held melancholy and curiosity. He was dressed in a dark suit and tie, long curly hair combed back, revealing a broad forehead and strong handsome face. This was Paul Lyons. He was thirty-four years old. First, he stared at Rad's appealing photo, and then he shifted his focus to Juliet. He followed her gaze, aware that she had observed the grief-stricken woman at the back of the church, standing by the stained-glass window. Paul took it all in, sitting absolutely still.

Juliet allowed her gaze to return to the woman's restless eyes, watching her with suspicion and speculation. Then their eyes met. The woman offered Juliet a sweet, sad smile. Juliet struggled to read the woman's face.

When the woman finally turned to leave, Juliet, on an impulse, left the altar and started up the right aisle. She was vaguely aware of her mother calling after her. But by the time she had worked through the crowd, arriving at the back of the church, the woman had exited out the front door. Juliet followed, gently acknowledging friends and family with a demur nod.

She brushed by the waiting crowd and stepped through the glass doors, lingering on the front steps. A cold morning breeze stirred across her and quickly fell back to stillness. Wearing only a long woolen dress, Juliet crossed her arms for warmth while scanning the area. People were gathered on the lawn, the steps and the parking lot. Juliet's eyes moved and probed until she finally spotted the woman striding purposefully across the parking lot to a late model gray Prius. Juliet wouldn't be able to reach her in time. She glanced about, realizing suddenly that she must have looked a mess, because the faces looking back at her were filled with sympathy and concern.

Juliet didn't have her cellphone, or she would have snapped a photo of the car and license plate. She quickly descended the steps and hurried off toward the parking lot. By then, the Prius had backed up, its red taillights glowing. Juliet waved at the car, but either she was not seen, or she was ignored. The Prius rolled to the edge of the lot, moving toward Maple Street. Juliet waved again, more dramatically. No response. Just as the car turned and drove away, Juliet caught a glimpse of the license plate. She squinted, focused, and memorized it.

Juliet turned to a group of people nearby. Paul Lyons was standing near her, but she didn't notice him.

"Do you know who that woman is?" Juliet asked.

Paul didn't speak. The others shook their heads sorrowfully.

Juliet inhaled a deep breath and went back inside.

CHAPTER 2

Juliet missed her 6:20 morning plane back to New York. It was Thursday, two days after the memorial service, a week before Thanksgiving. When her cellphone alarm had pulsed and played Garth Brooks' *The Dance,* Juliet had shut it off and turned over. Then Anne came in to wake her, but Juliet told her she wasn't leaving. She couldn't move. The pillow was soft and deep; the white down comforter was warm and protective. Anne shrugged, rubbed her sleepy, swollen eyes, and left the room to go back to bed.

Outside, it was raining. Juliet lay on her back, staring at the ceiling, listening to the rain drum on the roof and strike the windows. Fragments of memories danced by, bringing fugitive emotions that kept her from returning to sleep. Though she'd blink them away, they'd swiftly return. And always there was the continuo of deep sadness that made her body numb and heavy. Her father was gone.

She'd have to call the office and tell them she wouldn't be in until Monday. It had been insane to think she could return to work before then. Of course, the "big" boss, Max West, would throw some things and call her some names, because he always did whenever anyone called out for any reason, but Juliet didn't care. She could reschedule her meetings for the week after Thanksgiving, and work from home and accomplish as much as if she were in the office.

She laced her hands behind her head, recalling what her father had said about her being hired as PR and Marketing Manager for DevelopIT Communications, a software development and infrastructure support company, whose clients included companies in telecommunications, healthcare and biotechnology.

They were eating breakfast at Cora and John's Diner, her father's favorite breakfast spot on Saturday mornings. Seated in a yellow booth across from each other, he had ordered a second pot of coffee and was munching on a crisp piece of bacon.

"So, this DevelopIT Communications got lucky," he'd said. "I'm sure hiring you will be the best decision they ever made." Then he'd scratched his head, gazing up inquiringly at the ceiling. "What exactly will you be doing there, honey?"

Juliet sat up a little more erect. After having gone through three intense interviews and many nights of restless sleep, she was proud of herself for landing the job. The competition had been stiff.

"I'll be in charge of branding, developing social media and marketing. It's rumored that the company may go public within the next year and my job would expand dramatically if it did. I'll be meeting with designers and project managers on direct marketing ideas. It's a lot of responsibility. There'll be a lot of production coordination meetings with upper management, and a lot of hand holding and politics."

Her father had stopped eating, facing her, staring hard into her eyes. "I have to ask you another, even more important question here, Juliet." He'd swallowed, allowing the moment to build in anticipation. "Are you really smart enough to do all that?"

Juliet had reached over playfully and slapped him on the arm. They'd laughed.

THERE WAS ANOTHER ROLL of thunder, and the rain sounded like static. Juliet pushed up and reached for her phone. It was after 9 a.m. She dialed Max in New York. He was always in the office by 7:30.

"Hey, Juliet. What's up?" his boyish tenor voice asked.

Juliet could picture him seated behind his militaristically organized desk, a laptop glowing numbers, two iPhones at the ready, a large Starbucks coffee half drunk and a yellow doodling pad nearby, because Max always doodled. His stiffly moussed dark hair was carelessly styled, and his brooding eyes were narrowed for accusation. He'd probably just finished eating a bowl of Sugar Pops.

"I didn't make my flight, Max."

He paused. "Did they cancel it?"

"No. I couldn't get out of bed."

Juliet waited for the expected explosive outburst.

Silence. And then more silence.

"Max? Are you there?"

"Yep. You know what, Juliet? Don't worry about it. You only have one father. You just stay in bed and take it easy. Can you get here Monday?"

Juliet blinked about the room in surprise. This wasn't the bad tempered 27-year-old-tech-boy wonder who yelled and ranted that nobody-ever-takes-off-under-any-circumstances-no-way-no-how Max, whom she knew.

Juliet threw back the comforter, swung her feet to the floor and stood. "Max... that's so nice of you."

"Hey, I'm really a nice guy. I'm just misunderstood by everybody, and that's why they hate and fear me. Of course, we both know that's just bullshit."

Juliet went to the closet and grabbed her blue flannel housecoat. "I can work from here."

"Forget it. Just relax. You must have a thousand details to take care of. Can you push your meetings until Monday or Tuesday? Wednesday's no good. Everybody escapes from their offices and flees for Thanksgiving."

"Yes. I'll put some calls in after I hang up," Juliet said, struggling into the housecoat.

"Okay. So will you be back on Monday then?"

"Yes, Max. I'll be there." She paused. "Max... please thank everyone for the beautiful flowers and card. My mother and I really appreciate it. And so many clients emailed and sent flowers and cards."

"Yeah, well, that's cool. Now if those same clients would just pay their freakin' invoices, I'd love 'em like family, and you know how much I don't love my crazy family. And we both know that's why I'm not in PR, sales and marketing."

"You should take some time off too, Max. It would do you good."

"You know I'm a hopeless workaholic, Juliet. If it ain't work, it ain't fun. Hey, but we're all thinking of you. You kick back now and rest, okay? Are you coming in Monday?"

"For the third or fourth or fifth time, yes, I'll be there."

"Good. Later then."

He hung up.

JULIET FOUND HER MOTHER in the kitchen, hunched over a mug of coffee and a half-eaten slice of cinnamon toast. They mumbled out "good morning" as Juliet poured a mug of coffee and sat beside her mother at the breakfast bar.

"You want eggs?" Anne asked, still in her pajamas and cotton housecoat.

"No..." Juliet said, staring out the broad kitchen window through the beaded glass into the morning fog.

Juliet sipped the coffee. "I forget how crazy Ohio weather can be in November."

Anne nibbled on the toast. "Temperature's supposed to drop tonight. Go down into the high twenties. People always get sick this time of year."

Juliet took in the kitchen—her father's design. The breakfast bar was nine feet long and featured a two-inch-thick, dark-stained walnut top on a forty-two-inch-high raised counter, which comfortably accommodated stools. Raised breakfast bars were his specialty, even though most people ended up choosing bars with standard height. Behind the bar was a thirty-six-inch-high work counter with extra work sink, covered by green Costa Esmeralda granite. Juliet knew the measurements because Rad was all about numbers and measurements, and she and Anne had discussed the five different designs Rad had presented them with before he chose this one.

He'd redesigned the entire house several times. It was a modern L-shape ranch, with deep overhanging eaves and a gabled roof. He'd used a combination of wood and brick, with wood on the upper half and brick on the lower half. Rad loved windows and there were five large picture windows that looked out into a long belt of woods and a duck pond. There were three sliding glass doors. All the common areas had glossy wood floors and a minimum number of walls, something Anne never liked and repeatedly called impractical.

In the living room was the masonry fireplace Rad had fashioned from field stones he'd collected from old stone walls in Massachusetts and New Hampshire when they'd visited Anne's relatives. He'd had the stones shipped back to Ohio, and the fireplace was his pride and joy. The fireplace had also given him some notoriety when it was featured in two national architectural magazines, along with accompanying articles about Rad and his work.

Juliet remembered all this as she turned toward her mother and noticed, for the first time, that she looked older than her fifty-eight years old. She was ashen, exhausted, and stooped. The lines around her mouth and eyes had deepened; the skin under her neck was sagging. Anne had never been a beauty, but she had a voluptuous figure and a pretty face, with high cheek bones and lively dark eyes. Men found her attractive. According to her father, "I chased your mother from Kentucky to Indiana, out past Ohio to many points west, as far as Utah, Montana and El Paso, Texas, before I finally captured her."

Anne simply looked beaten. Juliet knew she must be feeling indescribable misery and despair.

"I'm sorry I've been so selfish," Juliet said.

Anne looked up. "What do you mean, selfish?"

"I was going back to New York and leave you with everything. I guess I just wanted to get back to work so I could forget it all."

Anne lifted a weak hand and let it drop. "It doesn't matter. I'm the one that has to go through your father's things... sort them all out. Find places to give away his clothes. There are so many people in need. I guess I'll give most of it to the Salvation Army. There are other groups that do good work, too, but..." She let the thought drop. "And then I've got to go see, what's his name? Payton... what's his last name?"

"Dad's financial adviser?"

"Yes."

"John Payton, isn't it? You told me his name the other day."

Anne nodded sadly. "Oh, yes, right, John Payton. We'll have to sort out the finances. Your father had good insurance. I don't remember how much life insurance he had. Well, we'll learn about all that. And then I'll have to see Dan Marcus, too. The attorney. He's going to help me with the will." They sat silently, staring into their coffee. They listened to the rain and a hoarse wind circling the house.

Juliet looked down and away. "Mom, did Dad ever talk about Jimmy?"

Anne stared ahead. "Yes, sometimes. But most of the time neither of us talked about him. I'm not sure your father ever fully recovered from his death. I guess I didn't either. I guess that's when I lost my faith in God or religion or whatever. I also lost my love for Rad for a time. Truth was, I hated him."

Juliet kept her attention on her mother's face.

"Ironically, after Jimmy was gone, Rad started going to church every Sunday, and he did for a long time. That's how he dealt with it. He said that without the church, he wouldn't have made it. I thought, what good is religion or the church? God didn't protect little Jimmy. God didn't save our precious little boy."

Anne's eyes drifted into a reverie. "I had so many dreams and wishes for him. Of course, you do for your children. You love them more than you love your own life."

Anne lifted her chin in defiance. "So what good is it to believe? To believe in anything other than what's in front of you? You go on with your life and you do the best you can."

Anne sat perfectly still, while old emotions returned and wounded her again. It took her minutes to recover. She finally turned to Juliet. "Do you think about Jimmy often?"

Juliet smiled thoughtfully. "Yes. I think about him. Sometimes I have dreams about him; a little 5-year-old running around the house chasing after Dad. I was just thinking about him the other day, wondering what it would be like to have a little brother to talk to and share things with. He'd be twenty-four now."

Anne nodded, with a sad smile. "Your father worshiped him, and he loved his father. You could see the joy in Jimmy's eyes when Rad came home from work."

Anne lowered her head. "God, the things humans have to go through."

Neither spoke for a long time. They stared, allowing old memories to rise and fall, while the sound of the rain slowly died away.

Anne finally spoke. "I'll get your father's ashes sometime early next week, and then my world, as I knew it, will be over. I suppose, a new one will be born, but I can't imagine what that might be."

CHAPTER 3

Anne and Juliet spent the next few days in various states of grieving, finding little jobs to keep them occupied. Juliet cleaned the house; Anne cooked, answered emails, and fielded phone calls. Though some of Juliet's high school and college classmates called or texted, she realized she needed to be alone and spend time with her mother. Her three best friends had moved away long ago to Oregon, Chicago and Florida and she hadn't contacted any of them yet. She'd wait until she could talk about it with more composure.

She offered to help with the sorting of Rad's papers and the boxing up of his clothes, but Anne wasn't ready for those painful chores, lacking the strength for any prolonged work. There were times throughout the day when both women just closed themselves off in their rooms and wept. The home was empty and lifeless, without the playful exuberance of Rad's energy.

Sunday was a bright, cold day. Anne drove Juliet to the Port Columbus Airport, about forty miles away. Juliet regretted leaving her mother and dreaded returning to a stressful job that was growing less and less rewarding. At the entrance to security, Juliet hugged her mother. She still looked weary and sad.

"Will you be okay?" she asked, holding her at arm's length.

"Of course. I'm meeting with Dan Marcus tomorrow... and I may even try to teach my Tuesday class this week..."

"Are you sure you're ready to face Fairpoint Community College? They don't deserve you. They cut your salary."

"They cut everyone's salary... and benefits. Enrollment is down."

"You've been there for ten years, Mother, and they still haven't given you tenure."

"I can't talk about this now, Juliet. I need to be busy doing something. And I received so many wonderful cards from the faculty. President Boswell and his wife sent a beautiful arrangement and card. He said to take as much time as I needed. I thought that was thoughtful and kind."

"Are they still discussing dropping the music and art departments?"

"There are rumors. They want to go after the engineers and business types. They think they can bring in more money. Maybe they can. I don't know. Well, anyway, it would do me good to get back to work. I could teach my music history class at least."

"Wait a few weeks, Mom. Go back after Thanksgiving."

"I suppose you're right, although it's no great challenge to teach music history. The students sleep through it, anyway. Maybe I could shock them and play Led Zeppelin or something." She brightened with a thought. "No, you know what I'll do? I'll play Samuel Barber's *The Reincarnations* and then I'll wake them up with Led Zeppelin. Which one do you think they'll like the best?"

BACK AT HER JOB ON MONDAY, Juliet struggled to keep up with the workload: the early morning meeting, the rapid decisions, the emails from project managers, the employee gossip, the attitude and arguments, and, of course, Max's temper.

During what should have been her lunch "hour" (more like fifteen minutes, usually, when she gobbled down a sandwich delivered from the local deli), Carla Gomez, Head of HR, dropped into her office to offer condolences, then spent a good half hour complaining about Max's belligerent behavior. Carla was thirty-five years old, and according to most who saw her, she looked like the quintessential Maria from the musical *West Side Story*.

"I keep telling Max he's got to learn to control his temper," Carla told Juliet. "I know at least eight people who are looking for another job. I spend all my time trying to calm everybody down and keep them from walking out and suing the company."

Just after Carla left her office, Max flew into a rage when he learned that two employees had called in sick. Juliet happened to be passing his glass-enclosed office when he emerged, face alive with fury. He stood like a little general, hands on his hips, body rigid.

"What the hell's the matter with you, Juliet!?" he yelled. "I've got deadlines before Thanksgiving and you're walking around like you've swallowed two Ambien and had a shot of whiskey! Carla just spent an hour in your office bullshitting. Come on, girl! Get off your pretty little ass and get with it!"

Juliet faced him, her eyes burning, her cheeks hot. Today, of all days, she couldn't take this bullshit. "Stop it, Max. Just stop it!" She took a deep breath and lowered her voice. "First of all, my pretty little ass has nothing to do with it! You can't talk to women employees like that! What's the matter with you? Do you want me to sue you for sexual harassment? Second, you've got everybody in this office nervous and stressed out! Now, just stop it! We will all do our best to meet our deadlines. We always do. But, if for whatever reason we miss one, the world will not come to an end."

The room fell into a quivering hush. Computer chatter ceased. Talking stopped. Heads periscoped down from the tops of cubicles. Colleagues lowered their cellphones, ducked away and fled, as if a bomb were about to go off.

Max's inflammatory face was scarlet. "You don't tell me to do anything! Nothing, do you hear me?!"

"Well, I'm telling you this. I'm taking the rest of the week off, starting right now!" Juliet said.

"What!?"

"You heard me, Max."

"Nobody gets a vacation now. Nobody! Do you hear me? I have deadlines coming out of my ass!"

"Then *your* pretty little ass will have to make sure you make those deadlines. I'm taking the weeks' vacation I didn't take last summer or last fall because we had deadlines then. You said I could take those vacations later. *This* is later."

Max shook his head, struggling with rage. His voice dropped. "I'm disappointed in you, Juliet. I mean, I really am. You're supposed to be a leader. Employees look up to you. Do you know that I've got three vacation requests sitting on my desk right now? Three *other* people want to take vacations right now. This week! They all want to take vacations the same freakin' week as Thanksgiving. What does that tell you?"

"It tells me there's a crisis in this office. People are unhappy, and sick of the stress and your bullying them around. They want to get the hell away from you. That's what it tells me."

"I'm not getting into this conversation, Juliet. I don't have the time and I don't give a shit about everybody's silly complaints. I'm not here to hold people's hands. We're all hired to do a job. We're all paid good money to do a job. And, frankly, most of our employees are lucky to have jobs, being the lazy, whiny and incompetent slobs they are. Now do you want your job or not?"

Juliet felt a gush of competitive anger. "I'm going to take a week's vacation so I can take care of some pressing family business."

"Okay, Juliet. Okay. You know what? Here's my answer. NO! I already gave you time last week. And nobody gets a vacation right now, okay? I'm not giving you or anybody else a friggin' vacation the week of Thanksgiving. Not one person. Not you. Nobody. No way! It's not going to happen. Is that clear and understood!?"

Juliet stood firm, her chin jutting out. "You are such an arrogant little jerk. You can't even see that you're killing this company. Look at the employees who have left in the last two months. Look at the clients they've taken with them. Look at the bottom line for the last two months. We're down twenty percent! Why?"

He ignored her, looking beyond her at the far wall. "Do you want the job or not? That's all I want from you. I don't give a shit what you or anybody else thinks of me. Do you want the damn job or not?"

Juliet turned and started off. She stopped abruptly and pivoted toward him. She was trembling. "Max... I hope you have a Happy Thanksgiving."

"What the hell does that mean?"

"It means I'm leaving, and I won't be coming back."

He started after her, jabbing his finger. "You'd better think about this, Juliet. I mean, you really need to think about this!"

Juliet folded her arms, as if to block his attack. "I'll call the people on my team and make sure there's a smooth transition."

"NO!" Max bellowed. "Don't call anyone. Don't do anything. You are history. You are out of here. Don't ever come back to this office. Never! You're done, girl. I mean, you are really done here. Get your stuff now and get your ass out of here. I'll make sure your name is poison wherever you go, okay? Poison!"

Juliet had heard all this before, when he'd fired others. How had she stuck it out for almost two years?

"Do you hear yourself, Max?" she said calmly. "Do you really hear what you're saying? No wonder business is down by twenty percent. Nobody wants to work here. Nobody wants to be around you."

He pivoted and stormed off.

LATER THAT NIGHT, propped up on her couch, Juliet sipped a glass of white wine while scrolling through her emails and texts. Most were from her colleagues, offering support and threatening to quit, too. She'd given everyone courage to speak out. Clients were dissatisfied with the company because Max was constantly alienating them and then expecting his project managers to smooth things out. Everybody was unhappy. Co-workers were suggesting they form their own company. Carla apologized for spending so much time with her, thinking she had caused her to get fired. Juliet felt exhausted and blunted.

After she'd booked a flight to Columbus for early Tuesday morning, she closed her laptop, dropped her phone on the floor and shut her burning eyes. Moments later, she fell into a light sleep and began to dream.

She was standing alone in a forest under a gentle snowfall. Fresh, glistening snow blanketed the ground. It was twilight. She was cold and confused. Off in the distance, she heard the cry of an animal. A low moaning sound. It scared her. She wanted to run, but she couldn't move. Her feet were frozen to the ground. Suddenly, through the scrim of falling snow, she saw an approaching figure. Juliet squinted into the cold, blue night. In dazed astonishment, she recognized the figure as the same woman she'd seen at the funeral, standing in the back of the church! Dressed in an electric red dress, she seemed to glide forward, her bare feet gently skimming the ground.

Juliet swallowed. A raw evening wind came in, scattering her hair. She trembled. The woman drew close, nearly face to face with Juliet, her burning eyes wide and sinister. She stopped.

"You are such a fool," she said in a low, threatening voice. "You are such a pretty little fool. You'll never know the truth. Never!"

Juliet shot up, awake and trembling. Shaken, she arose from the couch and stepped to the window that looked out on West 104th Street. A light rain was falling.

Her cellphone rang. Startled, she turned and hurried to pick it up. It was her mother.

"Mom, it's after midnight. What's the matter?"

"Juliet... I got your father's ashes today. Are you coming home soon? I hate being alone. I'm so sad. I can't stand it, being here all alone with his ashes."

"I'll be home in the morning."

"You can leave your job?"

"Yes... Are you all right?"

"... Something has come up. We need to talk."

CHAPTER 4

Tuesday morning was cold and clear, a perfect day to fly. Juliet said good-bye to the New York skyline, then took out a notepad and began re-working a poem about her father she'd started a few days before.

By the time they landed in Columbus, there was a softness to the light, crisp air. An inch of snow had fallen the day before; most of it still covered the ground and lay in the crooks of trees. Juliet knew it was the kind of winter day Rad would have loved. He'd leave the house early, walk the worn path through the trees and circle the duck pond, pausing to skim stones or watch the ducks beat across the water, rise and disappear over the trees. He would lock his hands behind his back, and he'd present his face to the wide close sky, allowing the crystal wind to wash his face and whip up the red in his cheeks.

Anne picked Juliet up at the airport and they drove home, making low conversation. Rad had often told Anne that he wanted his ashes to be sprinkled across the duck pond, and Anne wanted to scatter them right away.

Juliet agreed. She didn't tell her mother that she'd actually quit her job. This wasn't the day for it.

About 2:30, they left the house and stepped along a flat stone path through some trees, and then up a broad lawn to their neighbor's house. They'd made plans to borrow Bob Wheeler's rowboat. He accompanied them down to the pond, prepared the boat and pushed them off, waving, his heavy face set in sadness.

With an aching nostalgia, Juliet recalled the walks she and her father had taken together, strolling along the edge of the water. After Jimmy died, she'd always tried to be both daughter and son to him, instinctively trying to fill the gap left by his death. Whenever Rod suggested a tramp through the woods, she'd drop whatever she was doing and go along.

These had been quiet times. Loving moments of peace and contentment. Neither father nor daughter needed words. They just sauntered together, enjoying the simple magic of singing birds, rippling water, and an open sky. It seemed so long ago.

Juliet rowed them to the center of the pond. At a solemn moment, she rested the oars. The boat glided for a time, allowing each of them a personal reverent silence. Juliet took in the deep ocean of blue sky, feeling the sting of the cold wind on her face. She watched the wind wrinkle the water and saw her mother fighting tears.

Juliet reached into her pocket and drew out a folded piece of paper. It was the poem she'd written on the plane. She gently opened the page and began to read aloud, as little clouds of vapor escaped her mouth and vanished like ghosts.

You who sang with bricks and stone,
You who loved with walls and floor,
You who danced with plans and pen,
Who opened hearts and opened doors,

Find rest in Heaven with your son,
And never more know loss or gain.
Live on in joy and perfect love,
Far from sadness, far from pain.

Live on in brightest day, great soul!
In all that's right and good and true.
We know that we can join you when
Our hearts are full of love for you.

Juliet knew the poem was no masterpiece, but the words were sincere and from her heart. Anne's and Juliet's eyes filmed with tears as Anne lifted the golden urn, opened the lid and tenderly sprinkled Rad's ashes across the gray moving surface. Sunlight glittered on the water and, in the distance, a songbird's melody echoed, as if nature were blessing the sacred moment.

In timelessness, the two women sat watching the afternoon ripen; watching clouds drift over hills; watching the clouds throw dark swimming shadows across the water; watching the ducks descend, splash down, and waddle onto shore. As the sun warmed their faces and shoulders, Juliet wiped her eyes, gathered the oars and started back toward the dock.

THAT EVENING, JULIET AND ANNE sat next to each other on the chocolate brown leather couch in the living room, facing Rad's generous fireplace that was alive now with a flashing and gleaming fire. Shadows played on the walls and ceiling of the wide and warm living room, which enveloped the women in a cocoon of privacy. A restless wind moaned eerily outside. Snow was predicted. "Up to four inches is possible," said the perky meteorologist.

On the glass top coffee table sat a Chinese peach blossom tea set, a Christmas gift from Rad four years before, when he and Ann had taken a Far East cruise from Beijing to Shanghai. Anne had fallen in love with it when she'd learned that peach blossoms, also known as Prunus Persica, symbolize both eternal beauty and lasting paradise. Her mother used the tea set only for special occasions, and it pleased Juliet that her mother had taken it out that night, in her father's honor. She studied the calligraphy on the back of her tea cup. "It means 'live in a dream of paradise,'" Anne said.

Juliet studied her mother, noticing again the heavy fatigue, as if the effort of the recent events were aging her. Her eyes, in the dim firelight, seemed far away, focused on recently awakened, distant memories.

"Mother," Juliet said, in a tender voice, "I know you wanted to talk tonight, but can it wait until tomorrow? I'm really tired and you look exhausted."

Anne lifted her head a bit, awakened by her daughter's words. Her eyes cleared and she tugged her lavender shawl more snuggly up and around her shoulders.

"No, dear, I want to get it over with." She gathered herself up. "Juliet... yesterday, I met with our financial adviser, John Payton." Anne took a deep breath and exhaled. "It seems that I—we—don't have as much money as I thought we did. Your father liquidated most of his investments in stocks, mutual funds and bonds a little over a year ago. His business account is all but gone and, in fact, there are some outstanding bills I'll have to pay. Mr. Payton doesn't know what happened to the money after your father closed those accounts. While I was there, I called Dan Marcus to see if your father had drawn up any legal documents, and he said there were none. Your father had mentioned certain additional projects that needed to be completed and said that he was going to invest some of the money in those projects, but Dan said there's no paper trail, at least not that he knows of, so we don't know what those projects were or where the money went."

Juliet gave her mother a long look, then stood and went to the fireplace. With folded arms, she stared into the fire, watching the dance of the yellow flames, feeling the heat on her body and face. "Well somebody must know what those projects were," Juliet said, turning to face her mother. "What about Tom Baker, Dad's old partner?"

"You know they went their separate ways over a year ago," Anne said.

"Yes... but have you called Tom?" Juliet asked.

"Yes. He said Rad had met someone... he didn't say who. He said Rad got involved in some "thing", but he didn't know what. Tom said he didn't like not knowing. Rad said it was something he had to do. Tom told me that during their conversation, Rad had a changed look about him. When Tom mentioned it, Rad just waved him away and said, 'Life is short, Tom. Life is way too short.'"

"Did Tom give you any names? I mean there has to be someone who knows what's going on," Juliet said.

Anne nodded. "Dan Marcus is going to look into it. He said he'd get back with me next week."

Juliet considered her mother's words. "Didn't you and Dad talk about any of this?"

"You know how secretive your father could be when it came to his work. That's one reason Tom broke off the partnership. He said your father was just too secretive or he just got lost in his enthusiasms and would throw reason to the wind. If he wanted to do something, explore something or build something, he always tried to find a way to do it. Sure, your father and I discussed his projects and, yes, he mentioned he was working on a couple of things that were out of town, but he was never specific."

Juliet stepped forward. "But didn't you know about him liquidating the investment accounts?"

"We always kept our money separate. It's just something we did before we were married, and we never changed. Most of it was in retirement accounts, anyway, and so I didn't have control over his. I do remember him saying he was going to draw some money from his SEP IRA, but he never told me how much or why. I assumed he needed it for the business."

Juliet looked out into the dim light of the dining room. The whistling wind crescendoed, and then died away. She walked casually to the large picture window and peered out.

"It's snowing a little... how much did they say we'd get?"

Anne reached for her teacup, went to take an absent sip, and then realized it was empty. She made an ugly face and replaced the cup on the saucer with irritation. "I don't know. Maybe three or fours inches."

"Mom, that thing Tom mentioned, about how Dad said life is short. Had he been to a doctor? Did he have his yearly physical?"

"You know he wouldn't always have his yearly physical. He said it was a waste of time. But he was always healthy. He seldom ever got sick."

Juliet toyed with the ends of her hair. "Did you notice a change in him during that time?"

"What do you mean, a change?"

"I don't know. Something must have happened to cause him to take that money from his retirement accounts and just... I don't know, put it into something or spend it or..." she stopped talking, shaking her head.

"Your father was very impulsive, Juliet. You know that."

Juliet strolled back to the couch. She stood for a time, suddenly feeling exhausted. Her phone was on the coffee table. She picked it up and checked the time and her messages.

"It's after eleven," Juliet said.

"Yes, and you've had a long day," Anne said softening her voice. "You must be tired."

Juliet eased back down on the couch, scrolling through her messages. She finally looked up. "How much did Dad take out?" Juliet asked.

Anne paused, noticeably nervous. "Over four hundred thousand."

Juliet shut her eyes for a moment, processing the amount and the mystery. When she opened her eyes, she spoke with surprise, confusion, and irritation. "That's a helluva lot of money, Mother!"

"I know it is! Don't you think I know it's a lot of money?" she answered heatedly.

Juliet backed down. A very long moment later she dared to ask, "And his life insurance policy was for a hundred thousand?"

"Yes."

Juliet massaged her forehead, avoiding her mother's face. "That's not much these days. Will you have to sell the house?"

Anne waited. "Yes, I might have to. I'm just so confused. I don't know if I can afford to live here. I still have my salary and retirement, but I can't afford the mortgage and taxes and upkeep. I can probably find someone who'll love the house. Your father made a good name for himself and it's a beautiful house. On the other hand, the real estate market isn't great, and we don't exactly live in a thriving town."

To distract herself from the awful thought, Juliet glanced down at her phone. She saw a text message from Evan, who still refused to accept the fact that the marriage was over. It read "how's ohio? how's your crazy mom?"

Irritated, Juliet deleted the text. What had she ever seen in him? He was charming, he was charismatic. When they met at a party, he was in a Broadway play and had just finished a national commercial. A few months later, he was signed to do an independent film with Chris Cooper and Amy Madigan. All her friends said he'd be a star someday. He had talent and looks. Unfortunately, he had little else, like self-control, fidelity, or honesty.

Juliet had never told Evan that her mother was crazy. Maybe she'd called her difficult, but then whose mother was not difficult at times? Juliet placed the phone on the coffee table and faced her mother.

"Mom, aren't you curious to know how Dad spent all that money?"

Anne looked away, lowering her voice in controlled anger. "Of course, I'm curious. I told you, Dan Marcus is looking into it. That's all I need to know right now. I can't think about it, and I don't want to talk about it anymore. I knew I had to tell you, and I did. That's enough."

They sat in an infinite silence as the fire hissed and snapped. Juliet wanted desperately to ask her mother if she'd noticed the ash blonde at the church, but she didn't. So she stared, estimating the mood and the pulse of emotion.

"Mom... Something kind of strange happened the day Dad died. I didn't tell you because I wasn't sure how you'd respond... But I saw him."

"What do you mean, you saw him?" Anne asked sharply.

"I saw him in New York. Twice. The first time he was walking toward me on the street. The second time I saw him at Rockefeller Center—at the skating rink. Right after I saw him, you called and told me he was dead."

Anne glanced over at Eaton, her 7-year-old Siamese, who was curled inside a woolen blanket on the leather recliner. He lifted his sleepy head, yawned, blinked around and settled back into sleep.

Anne readjusted herself on the cushion, eyes blinking rapidly, as if trying to understand.

"It's late, Juliet. We should both get some sleep."

"Don't you believe me?" Juliet asked.

Anne dropped her head wearily. "I don't know what to believe. If you say you saw him, then I guess you did.

But what does it matter? He's gone. He left us. And he didn't bother appearing to me to say good-bye."

Her mother's bitterness surprised Juliet. She softened her voice. "It must have been hard to get the call from Joe," Juliet said, imagining how wrenching it would have been to hear the news from a contractor you didn't even know.

Anne sat motionless. "Yes, it was hard, and your father left that morning before I woke up." Her voice cracked. "I didn't even get to say good-bye to him."

Anne fought to control her tears, and then turned to Juliet, taking a tone of reconciliation and patience. "So, you think you saw him?"

"I did see him."

"You didn't dream it?"

"No, I didn't dream it. It was the middle of the day. He was smiling and waving. I haven't been able to get it out of my head. I just keep seeing him smiling and waving."

Anne stared into the fire. The wind came and made a hollow, lonely sound.

AFTER ANNE HAD GONE TO BED, Juliet lay sprawled on the couch, staring deeply into the fireplace. She knew she'd have to try to find the woman who'd stood in the back of the church. The woman who had not come forward to meet Anne or Juliet. The woman who'd driven off abruptly, without uttering a word. The woman who had surely known Rad and who probably held secrets behind those beautiful, sad eyes.

Where had Rad's money gone? Not that Juliet wanted any of it, but her mother certainly needed it. Her mother couldn't lose the house. The house she loved. The house

Rad had loved. The house Juliet had loved because her father had designed and built it.

She rolled onto her back and stared up into the ceiling. She was certain that if she found this woman, she'd learn the answers to a lot of questions. On the other hand, Juliet had the odd feeling that she was betraying her father's trust. The question was, what had happened to her father a little over a year ago that had caused him to withdraw so much money?

CHAPTER 5

Juliet slept late on Wednesday, and then spent most of the day on the phone, calling old friends, and sending and receiving emails from colleagues and friends in New York.

At dinner that night, Anne opened a bottle of Rad's Cabernet. They nibbled on meatloaf, mashed potatoes and peas, both lost in thought. Beyond them lay a deep silence. The house seemed to grow larger and quieter every day.

"Are you going to tell me why you came home on Tuesday?" Anne finally asked.

Juliet raked a strand of hair from her forehead. She pushed peas around her plate, staring unfocused and numb. "I quit my job."

Anne stopped chewing. "... Okay... Shouldn't we talk about this?"

"I have some savings. I'll look for something else after Christmas."

"Is that all?"

Juliet nodded. "I wasn't very happy there anyway. My boss, Max, was crazy. It's amazing how one person can make such a difference in a place, for good or for bad."

Anne reached for her glass of wine. She sipped, studying her daughter. "So the good news is that you'll be here until Christmas."

"Yes."

"It's good you're taking the time, Juliet. I know how much you loved your father. And he adored you."

Juliet felt tears spring into her eyes. She looked up.

"What's the matter?" Anne asked softly.

"Why didn't you know about Dad's other life?"

"What other life?"

Juliet looked away. "He spent four-hundred thousand dollars on something, or on someone, and you know nothing about it?"

Anne set her wine glass down and leaned back. "Juliet, your father and I loved each other very much, but we weren't what you'd call 'soul mates.' He could be very secretive. And, by the way, so can I. Did I ask him about those secrets? Yes. Did he always tell me? Sometimes. Sometimes he was evasive, or he'd just make some cryptic comment. Sometimes he'd just smile. Over a year ago, when I asked him why he'd decided to break with Tom and go his own way, he said, 'Anne, I'm having a kind of midlife crisis.'"

Anne reached for her wine glass again. "That's all he said. I could have gotten angry at him for not telling me—well, actually, I got angry. But I knew he'd tell me when the time came. He always did. I had the feeling the time was coming, soon."

Anne turned reflective. "He was working too many hours. I told him he should slow down. He just laughed and said..." She hesitated. "He said, 'I'll sleep when I'm dead.'"

After dinner, Juliet went outside into the large dark night. A swirl of cold, glittering stars looked back at her. Where had her father gone? Was he up there somewhere watching her—thinking of her—as she was thinking of him?

Tomorrow was Thanksgiving. The holidays would be so empty without him. He had always expanded every holiday moment with happiness and celebration. Thanksgivings had been filled with parade-day excitement, with a house pulsing with the laughter of friends and family. Her mother had participated too, of course, preparing the food and acting as the perfect hostess, but it was her father who had glowed, and around whom everyone else orbited.

During the Christmas season, the stately tall fir tree was a celebration of light; the garlanded mantel with white Christmas lights, dazzled, and a stack of artfully wrapped Christmas presents beneath the tree brought childlike anticipation.

The sweet smells of clover and pine filled the air, and there was always music playing: Bing Crosby, Nat King Cole, Arthur Fiedler. Seated at the piano, her mother played carols and they, along with Rad's many friends, sang noisily and mostly off key, while sipping her father's famous thick and creamy eggnog. How lovely it had all been. How festive. How perfect. How she missed him. How Juliet ached for him. Her big and tall, loud, handsome and generous father.

This Thanksgiving would be simple, quiet and empty. It would just be her, her mother and her mother's older sister, Aunt Carolyn—quiet and whispering Carolyn, a retired secretary who had never married and lived in an apartment in Cincinnati. None of them felt much like cooking, but when one of Anne's friends invited them over, they realized they weren't ready yet to socialize. So Juliet went shopping and bought a small Butterball turkey, some vegetables and a pumpkin pie.

What would Christmas bring?

Juliet strolled into the frosty night, kicking at the snow. Rad's enthusiasm for everything was contagious. He had more enthusiasm for life than she and her mother put together. He had more zest for Christmas and the spirit of Christmas than Santa Claus himself.

Juliet turned in place, staring up into the sky.

"Dad... where did you go?"

.

CHAPTER 6

Thanksgiving came and went without much energy or celebration. They watched the Macy's Thanksgiving Day Parade on TV, put the turkey in the oven, spoke on the phone with friends and family and, when Aunt Carolyn arrived, they opened a bottle of sparkling wine, a high-quality Prosecco Rad always served on Thanksgiving.

Carolyn, a slender woman of sixty-three with short, grey, bushy hair, was 5' 6" and weighed one hundred and twenty pounds. She spoke in a quiet voice and moved like a shadow. Since her energy was soft and healing, Anne loved having her around. They sipped Prosecco slowly while Carolyn made stovetop stuffing and Juliet cooked potatoes and broccoli. Anne opened a can of cranberry sauce, making a feeble joke about how much work it was. She and Carolyn reminisced about childhood Thanksgivings, and how their mother always insisted on making fresh cranberry sauce with orange rind and pecans. Juliet thought of Rad's special recipe, with ginger, and wished she'd thought of making it herself this year. They ate their pumpkin pie, struggling to find conversation, and after dinner they all fell asleep while watching an early airing of *It's a Wonderful Life*.

That night, as Juliet passed her mother's bedroom door, she heard her crying. What did Juliet have to be thankful for? Her parents. They had always been there for her, supported her, and loved her. Juliet made a vow: it was her turn to take care of her mother. She needed to find out what happened to those four hundred thousand dollars.

ON MONDAY MORNING, Juliet drove to the other side of town to see Tim Hansel, the County Sheriff. She found his office easily. It was a two-story square structure, built of red brick and rusticated stone, that formerly housed the town library. Like many libraries in small towns, a wealthy patron, Cyrus Burnett, had built it in 1906, in memory of his mother. During the economic hard times of 2007 and 2008, it lost support. Because of that and the emergence of digital books, the library had been moved to a more modest building near the town square. Amidst protests, the county took over the building and moved the Sheriff's and Clerk Recorder's offices there.

Juliet exited her car, climbed the five cement steps, passed two formidable concrete Corinthian columns, and entered through the heavy oak door. Inside, she took in the spacious room with its vaulted ceiling and large windows, through which it bathed the space in clear morning light. There were several metal desks, arranged at angles, some filing cabinets and a holding cell. This was not the room she'd remembered when she and her father had roamed the aisles, searching for books, lounging at the heavy wooden tables, leafing through magazines and old newspapers. Ironically, this room seemed to have more warmth to it. More life.

She strolled across the wooden floor, hearing her boots echo in the quiet room, and then drew up to the Sergeant's desk and waited while he stared into a computer screen with heavy eyes. His face was soft, his body pudgy and his round stomach straining the buttons on the tan uniform shirt. Juliet continued to wait, glancing about at the two deputies behind desks, one on a cellphone and the other looking boldly back at her. He was about her age, though not especially attractive. He winked. She dropped her eyes to the floor as the Sergeant looked up.

"Yes?"

"I'm here to see Sheriff Hansel. I have a ten o'clock appointment."

"Your name?"

"Juliet Sinclair."

The Sergeant chewed gum, sniffed, and didn't seem in any hurry to move. He chewed some more then pushed up, grudgingly, buzzed her in the glass security door and beckoned her to follow him. She did, past more metal file cabinets and the still persistent hungry gaze of the blunt-faced deputy.

They came to an oak door with a brass nameplate screwed into it: **Sheriff Tim Hansel**. The Sergeant knocked lightly.

"Yep," came the Sheriff's low-pitched voice from inside.

The Sergeant opened the door and leaned in.
"Sheriff, there's a Juliet Sinclair here for a ten o'clock appointment."

The Sheriff nodded and stood. "Yep. Come on in, Miss Sinclair," he said, coming from around his desk, flashing an easy crooked smile. "Come right on in."

He shook her hand. "Nice to see you again, Miss Sinclair. And, again, my condolences. Your father was a fine man."

"Thank you, Sheriff," Juliet said, suddenly noticing a big, white, overweight dog in the corner of the room, sound asleep on an old checkered red and black dog bed. He was snoring like an old man. She couldn't pull her eyes from him.

Sheriff Hansel followed her eyes. "Oh, well, that's ole' Puffy. He's thirteen years old going on eighty," the Sheriff said, apologetically, with a slight southern accent. "I've had him since he was a little ole' pup. When I got him, he was just a white puffed-up ball, so I named him Puffy. Shouldn't have him here, I know, but he just gets all unhappy and morbid if I leave him home."

The Sheriff's office was large but cozy, with high windows, a polished parquet floor and old black and white photos on the walls depicting Fairpoint as far back as the 1930s: snow mounds on sidewalks and cars in winter; happy faces and fishing poles in summer; grinning children gathered around bushel baskets of apples and pumpkins in autumn.

The gray metal desk was piled with papers, a laptop computer and a color photograph of Tim with his wife and two grown sons. Juliet noticed a white coffee mug that had THE COFFEE MUG printed on it in bold black letters. She glanced at a coffee maker on the windowsill behind the Sheriff's desk. She could smell the coffee.

Sheriff Hansel directed her to a straight-backed oak chair about five feet from his desk. She removed her coat as he rounded his desk and went to the coffee maker.

"Would you like some coffee, Miss Sinclair?"

"I'd love some," Juliet said. "You can call me Juliet."

He reached for a paper cup, poured the coffee and nodded. "Okay, then you call me Tim. Cream? Sugar?"

"Black."

"Just like your father." He approached Juliet and handed her the cup. "Now I know it's not as good as The Coffee Mug's coffee, but it ain't bad either."

"Thank you, Sheriff." Juliet took it, gratefully, then sat back down and took a careful sip. "It's good. Really good. Hits the spot."

The Sheriff returned to his desk and sat, folding his big, freckled arms across his barrel chest. He was a sturdily built man, a bit overweight, with a broad and ruddy pleasant face and gray vigilant eyes. His hair was a short wire brush gray that gave him a militaristic bearing. He had, in fact, been a sergeant in the Army, and had retired some twelve years ago.

He studied Juliet for a minute, nodding. "Did your father ever tell you how we met?"

"No, he didn't."

He leaned back, still nodding. "Well, it was about ten years ago. I was a patrolman then. I had left the Army about two years before that. Anyway, I'm just sort of driving around one night on patrol and all of a sudden, I see this car just shoot by me. I mean it had to be going fifty miles an hour in a thirty-five mile an hour zone."

Puffy snored raggedly. Sheriff Hansel glanced over, annoyed.

"Puffy, stop that now. Stop it!"

Puffy shook awake, startled, half-hooded eyes struggling to focus.

"You stop that snoring! You're messin' up my story."

Puffy lifted his head with a great effort and yawned.

"The D.A. doesn't like Puffy much, but then I don't think Puffy likes the D.A. all that much either."

Puffy settled back down, grunted, and went to sleep.

"Okay, anyway," the Sheriff continued. "Your father was going fifty miles an hour. So, I started after him, my dome light flashing, siren wailing. Well, I finally caught up to him because he had slowed down some. He pulled over to the side of the road, and I pulled in behind him. I punched his license plate number into the computer to see if the car was stolen and then I climbed out with my partner. He stood at the rear of your Dad's car and I walked up to the driver's window. I shined my flashlight on him, and he was looking back at me, smiling. Not a smart-ass smile, exactly. It was a real friendly smile. Your mother, Anne, was with him and she wasn't smiling. She seemed a little intimidated and irritated."

"'Good evening, officer,' your dad said.

"I asked him for his driver's license and registration. He produced them and I looked them over. Everything was fine. I said, 'Mr. Sinclair, you were traveling at fifty miles an hour in a thirty-five mile an hour zone.'

"'Well,' he says, 'Yes, I was, officer, and the only thing I can say in my defense is that I knew I was going fifty miles an hour.'

"Well now, that set me back a little. So, I says, 'Mr. Sinclair, I don't see that as a defense of anything. That just means you were willfully breaking the law.'

"He said, 'Not willfully, officer, but anxiously. You see, my daughter is flying in from college for the

Christmas holidays and we're late. Our dog got sick, and we had to take him to the vet.'"

Juliet lit up. "Yes, I remember. Dad and Mom were over an hour late picking me up at the airport because they said they had to take Frank to the vet, and then they got pulled over for speeding."

Sheriff Hansel nodded. He reached around for the coffee pot and poured himself a half a cup. "Okay, so I'm a sucker for dogs. I love dogs more than I love most people. So I asked him what kind of dog he's got. He says some mutt, and then I tell him about Puffy, who was only about two years old then. I mean, I'm talkin' away like there's no tomorrow. Then I realize, your dad is glancing nervously at his watch and your mother is shifting uncomfortably in her seat."

The telephone rang, and Sheriff Hansel answered it. Juliet drank her coffee while she waited. After the Sheriff hung up, he turned his attention back to her.

"Okay, so you know what I did. I didn't give your dad a ticket. I just let your parents go, free and easy. I said, 'Merry Christmas folks.'

"Well, you should have seen my partner's face. He got real mad at me. I thought he was going to report me, but he never did. So, along about a week later, I'm at my desk down at the Courthouse and I get two packages from UPS. I look at the sender and it's the local pet store, but I know they're really from your dad."

Sheriff Hansel smiled at the thought. "One box was filled with dog food and biscuits and the other was a dog bed." Sheriff Hansel pointed to Puffy. "See that bed Puffy's sleeping on? That's the bed your dad sent me. Puffy loved it from the first day and even though that damn thing is old and stinky, Puffy won't let me toss it out."

Juliet crossed her legs, grinning. She looked at Puffy. "Yeah, that sounds like my dad."

"After that, we got to be good friends. He'd bring Frank over and I'd bring Puffy and we'd go out for coffee and a donut over at the diner. We spent most of the time talking about our dogs and sometimes... well, most of the time, he'd talk about you. How proud he was of you, working in New York. How he hoped you'd find the right guy some day."

Juliet looked down reflectively, causing Sheriff Hansel to pause. He suddenly remembered Rad's skepticism when Juliet had married the New York actor, and then some mention of a divorce.

"Well, you know, things like that," he added, flicking a hand.

Juliet was momentarily lost in deep sadness for having disappointed her parents, and then for Rad. She still couldn't believe her father was gone.

"On the phone, you said you needed to ask me for a favor."

Juliet's gaze lifted. Her eyes were restless. "Yes."

She reached into her purse and drew out a piece of folded pink paper. She handed it to the Sheriff.

He took it and unfolded it. He stared at it for a time. "A license number?"

"Yes."

"Somebody you're trying to locate?" he asked, evenly.

Juliet hesitated. "Yes. She was at the funeral, but she left before I could ask her who she was."

Sheriff Hansel kept his attention on the paper. "I see. And... she's the only person you didn't know at the funeral?"

Juliet didn't speak.

He lifted his eyes and focused on her for long, alert seconds. "She's the only person whose license number you took the time and the trouble to write down?"

She averted his gaze. "Yes."

"I suppose you want me to trace the license number?"

"Yes. If it's not too much trouble."

"Well, Juliet, it's not that it's much trouble. The DMV keeps records of all license plate numbers and their owners, but we don't usually do this kind of thing for the public. It's done for businesses or government officials or by the police in connection with an investigation. People need to verify the legal reason why they need the information."

Juliet nibbled on her lower lip. "Yes... I learned that online."

"So, is there a legal reason why you need this information?" the Sheriff asked.

When Juliet spoke, there was an edge of anxiety in her voice. "I wish I had one, but I don't, Sheriff. It's just that, my father had a... well, a kind of secretive side. He took a lot of money out of his account about a year ago and neither my mother nor I, nor anybody else, knows why he did it, or what he did with the money."

"Rad had a partner, didn't he?" the Sheriff asked.

"Yes, Tom Wheeler. He was at the funeral, but we didn't know about the money then. I've tried to reach him in the last couple of days, but he's in Europe and hasn't called me back. My mother's not sure he'd know anything anyway, but I'm going to keep trying to reach him."

Sheriff Hansel exhaled and made a steeple of his hands. He tucked them under his chin and squinted at her, as if trying to read her inner thoughts.

"Juliet, I've been in law enforcement for a while now. I'm not going to get all fatherly here or act like some wise, old sage who has all the answers. The older I get the less I seem to understand anything or anybody. But..." He dropped his hands on the desktop and shifted back and forth in his swivel-backed chair. "But... sometimes it's best to let things be. Just let them be as they are. Sometimes it's best to let secrets—if that's what they are—stay secrets."

Juliet stared out the window into sunlight. "Sheriff... Tim. There was something about that woman. The way she looked at my father's photo. It was... well, as much as I hate to say it, her expression was intimate. It was filled with pain and loss. There was no one else in that church, except my mother and me, who had that particular kind of look. At least no one I noticed."

They sat in stillness for a moment. There was a knock on the door and the same blunt-faced deputy who'd eyed Juliet, entered diffidently, ignoring her. He handed Sheriff Hansel a stack of papers and left.

Sheriff Hansel stood staring down at his desk.

"Sheriff, I promise you I will not harass this woman in any way. I just want to know who she is."

"But when you find out who she is, you'll approach her?"

Juliet's eyes dropped to the floor. "I just want to know the truth."

The Sheriff arched an eyebrow. "Oh, the truth," he said, cynically. "Such a noble thing, the truth. So lofty. So sought-after and prized. Well, Juliet, in my opinion, you've got to be real careful when you go off trying to find the truth. I've seen the truth do a whole lot of damage. I've seen the truth destroy people. I have seen the truth turn into lies. In one way or the other, I deal with trying to find the truth every day and I've got to tell you, I think the truth is a whole lot overrated." Then as an aside, he added, "But don't tell anybody else I said that, otherwise I might not get re-elected."

Juliet waited, watching him.

Sheriff Hansel came around his desk and hitched his right hip on the edge. He looked directly into her face.

"I've got to think about this, Juliet. Give me a couple of days. I'll get back to you."

Juliet stood. "Thank you, Sheriff."

He jerked a nod.

Outside, Juliet walked aimlessly. The snappy morning wind chilled her, and she tightened the burgundy woolen scarf around her neck. She strolled to a nearby playground and watched the children swing and bounce and play. A little blond girl sitting on a green belt swing was alone, looking dejected. Her mother was talking on her cellphone twenty feet away, unaware and preoccupied. Juliet went over, looked at the mother and indicated toward the girl and the swing, seeking permission to talk to her. The mother nodded, flashing a quick, perfunctory smile. Then she turned away, fully engaged in her conversation.

Juliet stepped up to the girl. She was about five years old, dressed in blue pants, a blue parka, a red and white scarf and red tennis shoes. She was a pretty girl, with long blond curls, a pug nose and button mouth.

"Hi. What's your name?"

"Amy."

"Hi, Amy. I'm Juliet."

"That's a big name," Amy said.

"Really? You think so?"

"Yeah..."

"Do you want me to push you?" Juliet asked.

The girl looked up, squinting through sunlight. "I guess so."

"I can push you while your mother talks on the phone."

"She's not my mother. She's my babysitter."

"Oh, is your mother at work?"

"No... she's gone."

"Gone?"

"Yeah. Daddy said she's with angels in heaven."

Juliet masked her surprise. "Oh... I see. Well. Do you want to swing, Amy?"

Amy nodded. Juliet shouldered her purse and took hold of the swing. She gave Amy a gentle push. "Do you know how to swing?"

"Yes. My daddy taught me."

"Okay. Hold on tight, Amy. And kick with your legs."

Juliet gave her another gentle push, and there was the first squeak of the swing as Amy used her arms, chest and legs to gain height.

Juliet pushed a little harder. "That's good, Amy! You're doing real well! WEEeee!"

Amy giggled and climbed higher. "Yeah... I'm good."

Amy glided up and back and Juliet stood aside, watching, smiling and remembering when she, her mother and her father all went swinging together one cold winter afternoon, after Juliet finally recovered from a bad flu that had kept her housebound for a week. It had been her father's idea, of course.

"You're doing great, Amy. That's right, legs out, body back…legs in, body forward. Are you having fun?"

Amy kept swinging and laughing. "I'm flying."

"Are your ears cold?" Juliet asked.

"No... I'm higher. Look how high I can go."

"Not too high, Amy."

Juliet fell into playful animation, coaxing, clapping and forgetting, for a time, her father, her failed marriage, her lost job and the mysterious woman. Would Sheriff Hansel tell her who the woman was? Probably not. That was alright. She'd find another way.

CHAPTER 7

Tuesday morning, Juliet planned to drive her father's Audi to Cora and John's Diner. Anne was teaching two morning classes, and they'd agreed to meet at noon to do a little shopping before going home and continuing the seemingly endless task of sorting through Rad's clothes and papers.

This was the first time she'd been in his car since his death. As she pulled open the driver's seat door, she suddenly had the strong sensation that her father's hand was on top of hers. She stopped, startled, allowing a little girl's love and adoration to fill her body. How many times had she watched her daddy open the car door before turning and lifting her up onto the seat? Every outing with Rad was such an adventure!

She slid behind the steering wheel and was comforted by the smell of his Polo aftershave, which still hung in the air. "Ah, Dad, I miss you so much!" she whispered.

When she backed out of the driveway, she remembered his patience when he was teaching her to drive. When she pulled out of their street, she recalled the talk they'd had her freshman year in college. "Have fun, but study hard. You're deciding your future during these four years." When she pulled onto the highway, she relived the last conversation she'd had with him in person when he was driving her to the airport, and she'd hinted that things with Evan weren't going so well.

"If he doesn't treat you the way I treat you, then don't put up with him," he said. "It's as simple as that."

Later, at the airport, he'd taken her by the shoulders and fixed his eyes on hers. "No matter what you ever do, you can always count on me. I will always love you and support your decisions. You're an intelligent and beautiful girl. Don't settle for less than you deserve."

THE DINER WAS CROWDED, so Juliet sat at the counter on a black swivel stool, vaguely aware of the rattle of dishes, the muffled conversations and the combination of oldies and Christmas music coming from the overhead speakers. While waiting for the waitress, she reached for her phone and scrolled through text messages and emails. More questions at work, more words of sympathy from friends. She was about to start answering a few when a former high school classmate, Karen Tiggs, approached her from behind the counter, wearing a blue nylon dress. Juliet looked up, surprised.

"Karen! I didn't know you worked here."

"How are you, Juliet? I was so sorry to hear about your dad. I couldn't get to the funeral because both my boys were sick. But Cora and John went."

"Yes, I saw them, and the beautiful flowers from the Diner staff. I guess I didn't focus in on everybody's name on the card, or I'd have noticed yours. Anyway, thank you. How are your boys? Are they better?"

"Oh, yes. They're back in school, raising hell as usual. You want some coffee?"

"Yes, thank you. How long have you been working here?"

Karen poured coffee into Juliet's white mug and Juliet watched the wreaths of steam arise from it.

"A little over three months now. Working double shifts two nights a week."

Karen was a sturdy woman, with big brown eyes and long, dark brown hair, which she tied into a ponytail. She'd lost her girlish figure and peaches-and-cream complexion, and Juliet noticed lines forming around her tired eyes and mouth. Karen had always been cheerful and enthusiastic, so she'd been voted most friendly in high school. She'd been a cheerleader, a member of the school chorus, and vice-president of the senior class.

"How's Dave?" Juliet asked, sipping the coffee. Karen and Dave had been high school sweethearts who were always together. People believed they were soul mates who'd live happily ever after.

Karen slumped a little. "We got a divorce, like everybody else."

Juliet's face fell. "Oh, I'm sorry. I didn't know."

Karen shrugged. She looked down and away, a little embarrassed. "You know, it happens. After he lost his job, things just went bad for us. We still stay in touch but...and then there are the kids..." Karen let the rest of the sentence drop.

To fill the awkward silent, Juliet ordered eggs, bacon and rye toast. Karen hurried away to other customers and Juliet went back to her texting, pushing away sudden sadness about Karen's and Dave's divorce. They'd been so happy together. So right for each other. Juliet's eyes suddenly glazed over as she thought, "If they can't make it, who can?"

Minutes later, Karen arrived with Juliet's breakfast.

"So you're living in New York?" Karen asked.

"Yeah. Just divorced my husband and quit my job. So I'm single, unemployed and I have no idea what I'm going to do next."

"You'll find something. In high school you were always lucky. Besides, there must be more jobs and available men in New York than there are here. You'll find the right guy."

Juliet shook her head. "Oh, I don't know. At this point, I don't really care about finding the right guy. It occurred to me just the other day that maybe I met the right guy and didn't know it. Then again, maybe I'm all wrong for the right guy. Maybe he came along, but I just wasn't the right girl for him."

"Hey, I've thought about that, too!" Karen said, laughing. "Maybe Mr. Right Guy sat down at the counter this morning—the perfect guy for me—but I was too busy, didn't notice he wanted to ask me out, and after bacon, eggs, hash browns and coffee, he left my life forever, never to return. He went back home to Montana or Alaska or..."

"... Paris," Juliet said, her playful eyes widening with the possibility.

"Or Rome," Karen said, joining in on the fun.

"Or... let's see... what about Capri?" Juliet said.

"Where's that?" Karen asked.

"It's an island, near Italy."

"Yeah! Or Hawaii, or the Caribbean or Australia."

"Or Dayton, Ohio," Juliet said.

They laughed much too loudly; heads turned toward them.

"Oops," Karen said as the two ladies lowered their heads and voices. Karen turned serious, resting the coffee pot on the counter.

"It's hard being single," Karen said. "Especially after Dave, who I loved since high school."

"Where is he now?" Juliet asked.

"Somewhere north of Columbus. He comes for the boys, and they do things together. He's working again. Got a job as a bartender at some restaurant. He doesn't talk about it though. I don't think he likes it much."

Karen moved away to pour coffee and take orders while Juliet ate her breakfast.

When Karen returned, she refilled Juliet's mug and took away her empty plate. Minutes later she was back, her eyes alert with questions.

"Juliet, have you ever tried those on-line dating services? I was tempted once, but I just couldn't seem to get myself to do it."

"I tried it twice," Juliet said. "One guy looked really good on paper. He was handsome and rich. Then I met him. Unfortunately, he was also arrogant and obnoxious, and he seemed to love talking about himself and *only* about himself. He didn't ask me one question. The other guy was nice enough, but he just wasn't my type. The whole experience made me nervous and uncomfortable."

Karen scratched her nose. "Well, having two boys who act like wild animals is probably a turnoff for most men anyway, don't you think?"

Juliet thought about it and concluded that Karen was probably right, but she wasn't about to tell her so. "I don't know. There are plenty of guys who love boys,

Karen. Men who fantasize about playing sports with their sons, taking them fishing. You know, that kind of thing."

"You think so?"

"Yeah, maybe you should try the online thing. One of my girlfriends in New York met her husband online and they seem happy."

Karen turned contemplative. She rested her chin in the palm of her hand as she thought about it. "You never know where your life's going to take you, do you, Juliet? I mean, five years ago my life was going along, and I was happily married with a new baby and then, I don't know, you wake up one morning and it's all messed up."

Juliet took a breath. "If I thought about it for very long, it would scare me," she said. "Anything can happen at anytime, anywhere."

After they'd exchanged phone numbers and said their goodbyes, Karen dropped the check and rushed away to take care of other customers.

Juliet retrieved a twenty-dollar bill from her wallet and laid it on the counter under the sugar dispenser. Christmas was coming, and she knew Karen could use a little extra tip to help buy presents for the boys. She waved goodbye to her and then stepped over to the cashier to pay her check.

As Juliet was leaving through the double glass doors, a man approached, climbing the steep concrete stairs. It was Paul Lyons, but Juliet didn't know him. He smiled at her—a warm smile. It gently startled her. She immediately found him attractive, causing her to blush.

"Good morning," he said, smiling.

Juliet nodded and smiled as she passed him, staring at him for much too long. "Good morning."

He slipped inside, and Juliet turned ever-so-slightly to catch another glimpse of him. He was tall, dark and handsome, just like in the movies.

AFTER DRIVING AROUND TOWN and doing some errands, Juliet met her mother at the mall, hoping the expedition would lighten their spirits. They browsed through Macy's, picking through a few racks of clothes, but every time Juliet showed any enthusiasm for a garment, Anne just nodded. She was clearly too distracted and preoccupied to participate in their usual shopping rituals. At one point, Juliet received a text from Karen: *"You shouldn't have. Too much tip!"*

She texted back. *"The service was great. Fun conversation."*

After they browsed a few more shops, Juliet proposed they grab a sandwich somewhere, but Anne finally admitted she wasn't feeling well and just wanted to go home to bed. As they walked to the parking lot, Juliet was concerned by her mother's slow, heavy energy.

"I'll pick up the groceries we need," Juliet said, closing the door to her mother's car for her.

"Thanks," Anne answered. And then Juliet headed for the Audi.

Back at the house, she noticed that Anne hadn't eaten any lunch. The door to her room was closed. She decided to fix her mother a cup of chai vanilla, her favorite tea. She placed the cup on a tray, along with a plate of chocolate chip cookies and a freshly peeled tangerine.

She knocked softly on her mother's bedroom door and entered quietly. The room had beige walls, a king-size bed with olive leather headboard, two floor-to-ceiling windows with beige and olive draperies and two bleached oak fretwork-framed mirrors. Juliet walked across the walnut wood floor leading to the thick area rug near the bed and set the tray on the nightstand.

Anne lay on the bed, the white down quilt pulled up to her chin. She smiled at her daughter.

"Aren't you sweet?" She patted the edge of the bed. "Sit with me for a minute."

Juliet did. "Do you have a cold?"

"Oh, I don't know. I just feel overwhelmed and exhausted. I could hardly get through my two classes. Maybe everything is finally hitting me. Maybe because Christmas is coming, and I dread it. Maybe I finally realize that your father's never coming home."

Anne looked at her daughter with steady, sad eyes. "He'd be gone for a week here and there when he was working on a project, and I got used to that. Sometimes he was gone longer. Once he was gone a month. I'd wait for the sound of the front door opening and hear his booming voice call out to me that he was home."

Juliet reached under the quilt for her mother's hand. She held it gently. Anne sat up and used a pillow to prop her back against the headboard.

"Did you hear from Dan Marcus?" Juliet asked, softly.

Anne reached for the mug of tea and blew across the steamy surface before taking a careful sip. "Yes, I did. He hasn't learned much. He thinks your father probably invested the money in something. He said he paid over twenty-thousand dollars in estimated taxes when he took the money out."

"But why?" Juliet asked. "Did he find out why he did it?"

Anne sighed. "He said he didn't want to speculate, but when I insisted he speculate, he said that's when spouses hide money from each other, it usually has to do with an extramarital affair... or to keep from sharing it in a divorce."

Juliet screwed up her lips in sudden anger. "Well, we know he wasn't having an extramarital affair."

Anne stared down at the tea.

"We know that, don't we?"

"I suppose. I don't know."

"Well, I do," Juliet said, defiantly. "What else did he say?"

"He said Rad may have put the money in a safe-deposit box or set up a secret online brokerage account."

Juliet shot up and turned away. "It just doesn't make any sense." She turned back to her mother. "Was he really that secretive with you?"

"Well, we all have our little secrets."

"This is not a little secret, Mother."

Anne reached for a cookie. "Have one," she said.

Juliet stood with her arms crossed. "Is that all Mr. Marcus said?"

"He said I could check your father's web-surfing history and social networks to try to find traces of hidden bank accounts and business deals. His laptop is in his home office. It's password protected."

"So, you tried to get in?"

"Not really. I don't have the stomach for it. I looked at his phone... at some of his old texts and emails, but I didn't see anything unusual, not that I'd know usual or unusual anyway. I knew some of his clients through the years, but I didn't recognize any of them. I called some of the names I didn't know on his list."

"And?"

"Vendors. Subcontractors. A designer."

Juliet straightened, dropping her arms to her side. "A designer? A woman?"

"No, a man. They all expressed their condolences. They all said what a great guy he was. Then I just got more depressed, and I stopped."

"Did Marcus say anything else?"

"He said I could check digital bank statements and credit-card bills. Finally, he said I could hire a private detective."

The room fell into a cold silence. Juliet grew nauseous at the thought of spying on her father. At the thought of some private investigator prying into her father's history—into their history. She lowered her head. "Mother, do we really need to know? I mean, maybe it's better not to know what happened to the money. Maybe it's best not to know what Dad was doing."

Anne nibbled on the cookie. "It's a lot of money, Juliet. It's not that I'm mercenary or greedy, but I'm not getting any younger. I'll be retiring soon, if I can. I just wish that... I just wish that Rad had..." her voice trailed off.

Juliet sat back down on the edge of the bed. They both stared into the middle distance, lost in thought.

A few minutes later, Juliet reached into her jeans pocket and drew out a little black jewelry case. She presented it to her mother.

"What's this?" Anne exclaimed.

"Just a little something I bought in town today. Thought you might like it."

Anne took the case and lifted the lid. Her face opened with happy surprise at the sterling silver, treble clef earrings.

"Oh! How nice."

She lifted one out of the case and held it up to the light. "I love them!" She tilted her head to the side and slipped one on.

Juliet looked on, smiling. "They'll look great on you."

Anne reached and gave her daughter a kiss on the cheek. "Thank you... that's so thoughtful of you. So nice."

"I thought you could use a little lift," Juliet said.

Anne attached the other earring and leaned back against the pillow with a sigh. She looked at her daughter, her eyes misting with tears. "Okay, I know. I get all sentimental. But there's just the two of us now, Juliet, and this was such a thoughtful thing to do."

Juliet gave her mother a hug and sat with her until she fell asleep. Then she left the bedroom quietly, closed the door gently and padded off into the living room to build a fire. As she stacked the wood, she felt a sudden heaviness and dread. She stopped, eased down, and sat in a cross-legged position, staring at the carpet.

When her phone rang, she glanced over to see who it was. Sheriff Hansel. Did she really want to know about the woman and her father's past?

CHAPTER 8

Paul Lyons sat at a back table in The Coffee Mug. Before him, on the white marble top, lay a half-drunk mug of coffee and a glass of water. Linda, a thin, loose-limbed red-headed high school girl, was sweeping up. It was after 8 p.m. on Tuesday night, and the café was closed.

"How did you do on your math test?" Paul asked.

Linda stopped, leaning on her broom. "Better, I think. We get our tests back on Thursday. I just don't think geometry is my thing."

"You have lots of homework tonight?"

"Yeah. Social studies, which I hate, and I have to write a book report."

"What's the book?" Paul asked, leaning forward with interest.

"*The Old Man and the Sea.*"

"Hemingway," Paul said, knowingly. "Did you like the book?"

"Not really. I mean, so this old guy is trying to catch some fish." She shrugged. "It didn't really thrill me or anything."

Paul smiled. "Well, maybe it's more of a man's book. You finish up sweeping and I'll take out the garbage and do the close."

Linda brightened. "Really?"

"Yeah, you get home and write your book report."

Linda swept with renewed vigor, moving chairs and tables, while Paul fell back into his thoughts. His eyes wandered the room, taking in the light blue walls and the framed color photos by a local photographer, who'd captured various scenes: coffee mugs and donuts, coffee cups and croissants, spilled black coffee pooling around a fallen yellow daisy, and a trio of college girls toasting with coffee cups.

The Coffee Mug was a modest coffee café, just eight tables and four stools at a five-foot Formica counter. In the center of the room stood a glass display case with muffins, cakes and sandwiches and, of course, there were many types of coffee on the blackboard menu: cappuccino, espresso, mochaccino, latte, café au lait and frappuccino.

Paul had opened the place a little over three years ago. The first year, he'd lost money; during the second year, just when he was about to close because he was nearly broke, Rad Sinclair changed his life. Rad, one of his best and most frequent customers, had learned that Paul was about to shut the place down.

"Why, Paul?" he'd asked. "It's a great little place and a great little location."

"I'm losing money, Rad."

Rad had looked around. All the tables were full. There was a line of people waiting to be served. Rad opened his hands as if to say, "I don't get it."

Rad immediately made a phone call to a woman he knew, who specialized in helping small businesses not only survive, but thrive.

She agreed to help. After completing a thorough analysis of Paul's operation, she made several recommendations that Paul swiftly implemented. He negotiated lower prices with his suppliers and changed his Point of Sale system to one that was both cheaper and more efficient. He placed ads online and in local papers, and found a woman who baked bread, muffins and cakes for half the price of his Columbus, Ohio supplier. He also found another talented cook who made outstanding soups and pies.

Paul's sales jumped. Suddenly, local book clubs rented the space, as did the local community college faculty and church groups. Requests for parties and private events nearly overwhelmed him. His sales shot up thirty-five percent, and he hired more help.

Time passed. Paul had never received a bill for the restaurant consultant's services. When he called her to ask why, she told him it had already been paid.

"Paid? By who?" he asked.

"Anonymous," she said. "It was paid by anonymous."

The next time Rad came by for a coffee and muffin, Paul confronted him.

"How much was it?" Paul asked. "How much was the consultant fee?"

"What consultant fee? I don't know what you're talking about," Rad said, nosing toward the display case glass, examining the pastry and donuts.

"Rad, I know you paid that woman consultant. I want to pay you back."

Rad shrugged. "Paul, I like you very much, but I have no idea what you're talking about. Do me a favor."

"Sure. Anything, Rad."

"Give me that chocolate donut. It looks absolutely sinful."

And that was that.

From then on, they were the best of friends.

IN LATE JULY, Rad came by and Paul joined him at a back table. They drank coffee and talked.

"I'm thinking about taking over that little ice cream shop/burger place that just closed," Paul said.

"You mean Dreamer's Drop In, right down the road from here?"

"Yeah, that's it. I've got to move fast, though. Rumor has it there's a lot of interest in the place."

"Are you going to move The Coffee Mug over there?"

"No. I want to open a restaurant. Nothing fancy or anything. Something simple and basic. Tracy wanted to open a little restaurant after she left the military. She was going to call it Mama's Little Kitchen, or something like that. We'd serve only comfort food, like mac and cheese, fried chicken, hamburgers and meatloaf. The desserts would be apple pie, chocolate cake, pumpkin pie, you know things like that."

Rad considered it. He lifted an approving eyebrow. "I like it. Maybe we should go have a look at the place. Make sure the roof doesn't cave in while I'm munching on my fried chicken. I can draw up some plans."

Paul smiled. "I hoped you'd say that. I can get a loan. I already talked to the bank. The Mug's doing well now, but I can only make so much here. I'm thinking it's worth the risk. And it's something Tracy always dreamed of."

"Of course, it's worth the risk," Rad said. "Go for it, Paul. Anne and I will be your best customers."

Paul gave him a firm nod.

During the end of their conversation, Rad extracted his phone, tapped out a photo, and handed the phone to Paul.

"My daughter, Juliet," he said proudly. "You don't know her. She left town after college."

Paul looked at it. He would never forget the startling rush of warmth and excitement he felt, as though he'd been touched by an electric current. How could a mere photograph do that?

"She's pretty, isn't she?" Rad asked, sitting up a little straighter. "That was taken about a year ago."

Paul was mute, still studying the photo. Juliet stared back at him with dancing green eyes, lustrous auburn hair and full red lips. Her expression was one of remote invitation, as if she held secrets but she'd never let you in on them. That made her exceptionally attractive and mysterious.

Rad grinned. "I can see you agree."

Paul stared at Rad over the top of the phone. "Yes, she's very pretty. Married?"

Rad threw up a hand. "Don't get me started on that. She used to date this one, that one and the other one and she always found something wrong with all of them. Even when she was in high school, she never went steady with any guy for very long, not that I minded *that* so much. I didn't trust most of them, anyway. Truth be told, I was always happy when she broke up with those guys. That's the father in me I guess, or it's the memory of being 20 something, when I was trying to date every pretty girl I saw."

Rad turned pensive, sliding his mug around on the tabletop as if he were trying to find the right spot. It would rest for a while and then he'd move it again.

"But now, you're worried about her?" Paul asked, handing him back the phone.

Rad considered the question. "Worried? Well, I don't know," he said, adjusting his horn-rimmed glasses. Then his expression changed. "Yes. I am worried. She's married to a... well, I'd better be nice. He's an actor, in more ways than one. She's not happy with him, at least that's what she tells her mother. He's a good enough looking guy, and he has all the right manners, but I never trusted him. He talked her into getting married in New York a few months ago, in Central Park. One of his friends got a license to perform marriages, I guess, and Evan wanted to be the first to hire him."

Paul rubbed his chin as Rad continued.

"It was Valentine's Day, freezing cold, and there we all were, about ten of us, standing on a dock near a little pond. Juliet hadn't even told us she was getting married until we got to New York. We tried to make the best of it, but we'd always hoped for a big church wedding for our only daughter… but then again, maybe it's best we didn't bother this time around. I don't know what Juliet saw in him. I guess he was just so different from anyone in Ohio. She won't talk to me about it, but I really don't think the marriage will last. So now, she's up there in New York, unhappy with her job, unhappy in her marriage, and just unhappy with life in general. The last time I saw her, she just wasn't herself. Juliet always laughed easily and took things pretty much in stride. She's kind of like me in that way."

Paul scratched his head. "So you'd like to see her come home for good?"

"Oh, I don't know, maybe." Rad stared Paul directly in the eye. "I'd like to see her happy, Paul. That's what I want. I know I sound like every other father on the planet, but there it is. She's not happy and I want her to be."

Paul began sliding his mug from side to side. "I don't use the word elusive very often," he said. "Are you being elusive, Rad?"

"It's a good word," Rad said. "Maybe I am, and maybe you know what I'm trying to say. I think a lot of you, Paul."

Paul took a drink of his coffee and then crossed his right leg over his left. "When is she coming home again?" Paul asked.

"I never know with her. Her job keeps her busy. Probably Thanksgiving, if not some weekend before that."

"And her husband comes too?"

"Unless she's ditched him by then. I hear rumblings she might."

Rad narrowed his eyes on him. "I like you and I trust you, Paul."

PAUL WAS DRAWN BACK into the present when Linda approached with her usual floppy walk. She reminded him of a puppy. Her coat was buttoned, her hat pulled down over her ears and her hands gloved.

"Okay, Mr. Lyons. I'm leaving. I took the garbage out. No problem."

Paul smiled. "Thanks, Linda. Good luck on your book report."

After she left, Paul got up, ran his nightly report, and counted the register. He placed the money and credit card receipts in his wall safe, checked the lock on the back door, and wandered into his closet-like office to shut down his laptop and get his coat.

He checked his phone for messages and saw that it was after 9 o'clock. He had a text from his mother-in-law, Donna Webber. She'd put his daughter, Amy, to bed. He twisted up his lips in annoyance at himself. He'd meant to call before 8:30 and say goodnight to his little girl.

Paul called anyway, speaking briefly to Donna, who was harsh and critical as she often was. But Amy was fine. Paul told Donna he'd be home in a half hour.

After Paul switched the light off, he paused, again distracted by a thought.

During a subsequent conversation with Rad, he'd noticed that his friend seemed more tired than usual. A couple of times, while there was a lull in the conversation, he'd even turned philosophical.

"Life is so short, Paul. I was your age only a couple of years ago, at least it seems that way. What are you, about thirty-three or thirty-four?"

"I'm thirty-four," Paul said.

Rad turned reflective. "There was so much I wanted to do with my life, Paul. So many things I wanted to build. I wanted to have another son. Did I ever tell you that I lost a son?"

Paul shook his head. "No, Rad."

"He drowned. We were fishing on the edge of the river. I thought I was watching him. I was a good and careful father but... I could get lost in the moment of doing things, I guess you could say. I focus too much on one thing and let other things kind of fall away. It's a blessing and a curse."

Rad's eyes filled with remorse and tears. "Little Jimmy was only 5 years old. Just five. It was all my fault. I got all absorbed in trying to catch that damn fish. Anyway, the little fellow had wandered off. I could still see him from the corner of my eye. He was climbing on rocks and suddenly he slipped and fell in. He hollered to me, but he was pulled under before I could get to him. There was a strong current that day…. I hadn't made him put a life vest on because we were on shore. We weren't anywhere near a damn boat."

Rad sank and wiped his wet eyes. "What a sad thing, Paul. What an awful and sad thing."

Paul lowered his head. "I'm sorry, Rad. Truly."

Rad quickly recovered, finding a little smile. "Well, you've got to move on, don't you, Paul? No matter what. No matter what hits you or hurts you, you've got to move on. That's right, isn't it?"

Paul saw wretched pain in Rad's face. He stared back at Paul as if he were seeking absolution.

"Yes, Rad. That's right."

Rad shook away his grief and reached for his coffee. "Well, anyway, there were places I wanted Anne and me to go; so many things I wanted to see, but life just gets away from you, you know? I didn't do most of what I wanted to."

"You still have time," Paul said.

Rad smiled enigmatically. "Oh, well, I hope so, Paul. I sure hope so."

Paul had remembered that smile and the strange look. Maybe Rad had sensed something. Maybe he'd known he didn't have long to live.

The last time Paul had seen him, just three weeks back, Rad had said "Juliet's coming for Thanksgiving. You know she's filed for divorce now."

"Yes, Rad. You've told me about five times."

"Well, I'm warning you. I'm going to play matchmaker, Paul, so don't be surprised when I call you to say that Juliet and I are on our way to The Coffee Mug."

That was the last time Paul had seen or spoken to his good friend. And then he was gone. His very good friend was just gone.

Paul remained in the darkness of his café for a long time. In the deep stillness, his ears rang, and thoughts crowded in. He heard a distant siren. He felt the emotion of losing his friend: his very good friend, Rad Sinclair, and his eyes closed at the start of tears. Paul was tired of tears. He was tired of loss.

He drove home in a light snowfall along quiet roads. He did want to meet Juliet, but Rad's death had changed all that. Now the timing was all wrong. Had Rad talked to Juliet about him? He'd never said he had, and Paul thought not, because as he passed Juliet at the diner the previous morning, she hadn't seemed to recognize him. She'd smiled at him—an alluring smile that lit up her entire face and her green eyes—but he could tell from her expression that she didn't know him.

What had Rad said to him after one of their last conversations? "Paul, if anything happens to me, check in on my family now and then. Check on my daughter and make sure she's okay. I trust you, Paul. Maybe it's because of what you've gone through, or maybe I've always been able to read people and I know I'll always be able to count on you."

Paul's father had died when he was 7 years old. Conrad Sinclair had become a kind of surrogate father, and Paul loved him deeply. When Rad had asked him to look after the Sinclair family, Paul thought it was a great honor and privilege.

Paul had told him, "You can always count on me, Rad. Always."

CHAPTER 9

The next morning, Anne was sick in bed with a cold. Juliet sat at the kitchen table, huddled over hot oatmeal, a poppy seed bagel and a mug of coffee. Her phone lay before her, staring back like a live thing, reminding her that she had a decision to make. In her head, she again played back the conversation she'd had with Sheriff Hansel the day before.

"Is this a good time to talk, Juliet?"

"Yes, Sheriff."

"I've got the information you requested. I assume you still want it?"

Juliet paused. "Yes... I still want it."

"You've got a pen and paper handy?"

While she hurried into the kitchen for the scratch pad and pen, the Sheriff continued. "Before I give you this, Juliet, I want you to promise me something."

"...Okay."

"Don't say okay until you've thought about it. I'm only giving you this information because you're Rad's daughter, and I had great respect for him. I'm also giving it to you because I think I can trust you."

Juliet had the pen point pressed into the pad, waiting.

"But...I don't really know what you'll do if you find out some things that disturb you. I suspect you don't really know yourself. I tried to think if Rad would want me to give you this information, and I came to the conclusion that I just don't know. But that's neither here nor there. Here's what I want you to do. I want you to promise me that when you find this woman and when you talk to her, as I know you will, you'll call me and let me know what transpired. Will you promise me that?"

Juliet had leaned against the counter, lightly tapping her lips with the pen as she processed his words. "Yes, Sheriff, I promise to call you."

Then, and only then, did Sheriff Hansel give her the woman's name, address, and telephone number.

Juliet scooped the oatmeal, held it to her mouth, paused, and then spooned it in. The warmth of it comforted her. She nibbled the bagel, sipped the coffee, and stared deeply into the dull morning light, feeling hopeful and fearful. She had not called the woman. She had not called Cindy Evans. That was her name, Cindy Evans. She had checked her father's phone. Cindy Evans was on his contact list.

No, Juliet did not call. As tempting as it had been, Juliet had not even done an internet search. She'd spent a mostly sleepless night wrestling with anxious thoughts, images and possibilities. Finally, at dawn, she'd swung out of bed and checked on Anne. She was sleepy, hungry and achy, so Juliet brought her tea and toast. Anne soon drifted back to sleep and Juliet lingered, stroking her hair. Finally, she kissed her mother's warm forehead and left.

In the kitchen, Juliet prepared breakfast while staring at the blue note paper that held Cindy's information. Juliet stared with intensity, as if it were some fragment torn from an old biblical scroll and, through persistent careful study and keen analysis, Juliet would be able to decipher its true meaning. Through her tired eyes, she'd be able to comprehend and understand its mystery. And what was the truth about Cindy Evans? What was the answer to the mystery? Just this: Cindy Evans was a Conrad Sinclair admirer, just as Sheriff Hansel was an admirer. Just as all the people at the funeral were admirers. That was the truth. At least that was the truth Juliet wanted to believe and hoped was true.

But was it the truth? What had Sheriff Hansel said? "The truth is overrated."

The truth was, Juliet had built an elaborate fictional world around this woman, and it was probably just that: fiction. Nothing more. As her father had often said, Juliet was making a mountain out of a molehill.

While Juliet stacked dishes into the dishwasher, she paused, glancing about distractedly. The truth was, she was also scared—scared of the ticking time bomb note that held Cindy's information. Scared of not finding the truth and scared of finding it, and being hurt and devastated by it. Juliet was scared to death that she'd discover some dark secret about her father and it would threaten to destroy all the love and respect she had for him, her dear father whom she'd always admired and worshipped.

She leaned back against the kitchen island, cradling the warm mug of coffee in both hands. She knew herself well enough to know that it was just a matter of time before she'd be on her way to Holland Grove, to learn who Cindy Evans was and why she hadn't come down to the altar to meet Juliet and her mother. Juliet knew she'd have to go. Otherwise, she'd always wonder.

Why was Cindy on her father's contact list? Had their relationship been strictly work-related, or had it been something more? Did Cindy know what had happened to the money? Had her father given her some of the money? Money that was rightfully her mother's? At the funeral, what was it that Juliet had read in Cindy's expression? Anguish? Fear? Guilt?

AT 10:20, JULIET SET HER LAPTOP onto the kitchen counter and turned it on before preparing a salad and a tuna sandwich for her mother. She'd put them in the frig and leave her mother a note, saying she had some shopping to do and wouldn't be home until early evening.

While she chopped and mixed, Juliet did an internet search for Holland Grove, Ohio and learned that the town was named after General Thomas Holland, who'd served with distinction in the Spanish American War, and later settled in the little town of Crooked Creek, about thirty miles north of Dayton. By 1902 the town's name was changed to Holland Grove, as Thomas Holland's influence expanded. He became known for his many apple orchards as well as his conservative politics. According to the article, Holland exported his Cortland, Golden Delicious, Ohio Red Delicious and Ohio McIntosh apples throughout the Midwest.

Juliet also learned that in 2010, Holland Grove had a population of about 19,000, the estimated median household income was $47,000, and the estimated median house or condo value was $196,000. Males were 47.8% of the population and females were 52.2%.

Next Juliet did a *Google* Map search to locate Cindy Evan's address. From the aerial view, she could see that Cindy lived on a side street in a condo that lay nestled in trees, not far from a golf course.

As she was writing her mother a note, her phone rang. She didn't know the number.

"Hello?"

"Juliet, this is Tom Wheeler." Her father's former partner.

"Hey, Tom. How are you?"

"I'm back in the U.S. Actually, I'm only about five minutes away. Do you still want to talk?"

"Yes... Yes, I do."

TOM WHEELER HAD COME FOR DINNER at the Sinclair house many times during the years he and her father were partners. He was a short man in his fifties, about 5' 6", well-built, with broad shoulders and chest. His thinning blond hair was combed back, showing light gray around the temples and over the ears. There was an air of quiet authority about him; a sense of easy confidence in his smile and pale gray/blue eyes. Rad had often described Tom as having both feet and both hands on the ground, adding that Tom worked in a kind of practical coma. What he lacked in imagination he made up for in research, attention to detail and a smooth, disarming personality.

Juliet was happy to see him, for his association with her father and the memories they had shared. She welcomed him in and took his coat. He was wearing a royal blue cashmere sweater, crisp white shirt and pressed jeans. Her father had once commented on Tom's pressed jeans, proof that he was a detail man. After a few moments of small talk, he leaned down and pet Eaton, who was once again ensconced and purring in his woolen blanket.

"How's your mom?" Tom asked.

"Actually, she's in bed with a cold. I think she's been pushing herself too much." She paused. "Can I get you some coffee?"

"That would be great," he said, settling into the other brown leather recliner. Juliet brought him a mug of coffee and they talked briefly about the weather and Tom's recent trip to France. Finally, Juliet broached the subject she found most pressing: her dad.

She stood by the fireplace, arms folded. "Thanks for coming over, Tom. I guess I just wanted to know more about your relationship with Dad," she said. "I was so caught up in school and career that I never knew much about Dad's work."

Tom smiled, kindly. "He was a guy I thought would live forever. He had the ability to energize everyone and everything. He got people excited and passionate and involved. People just loved being around him. And he could do it all. He could sell, design, and bridge the personality gaps between designers, contractors and clients. Long after I'd lost patience with someone, Rad was right there, in the middle of it, smoothing the waters. And in the end, nearly everybody was happy about the outcome. There were always a few impossible people, of course, but overall, Rad just had the magic of being liked, respected, and even loved."

Juliet listened attentively. "Why did you two split up, Tom?"

Tom took a drink of the coffee. He grinned. "Good coffee. It's dark roast, Rad's favorite." Tom set the coffee mug on a side table and pushed both sleeves up to his forearm, as if he were getting down to work.

"A little over a year ago, Rad changed. I asked him about it."

"How did he change?" Juliet asked.

"He came into the office one day, sat down in front of my desk and said he wanted to go off on his own. Just like that. I was shocked, of course. When I asked him why, he said it had nothing to do with me. He said he wanted to go off on his own for personal reasons. I'd noticed he'd been more subdued, and you know Conrad Sinclair was never subdued. He told me something had happened, and he needed a change. He'd need to decide on something, and it wasn't easy."

Juliet eased down on the couch opposite Tom. "Did he say what had happened?"

Tom hesitated. He didn't look at her. "Juliet... this is difficult."

"Just tell me," Juliet said, a knot forming in her stomach. "I'm a big girl."

"Rad said he met someone."

Juliet shut her eyes.

Tom hung his head.

"Did he say who it was?" Juliet asked, with an awful expectation.

"No. He didn't say. He said it was a personal thing, but he said it made him see his life in an entirely different way."

Juliet tensed up. "Did he say if this someone was a man or woman? Did he give any indication at all what happened or what specifically had happened to change him?"

Tom lifted his regretful eyes. "No, Juliet. He just got up, came over to me, gave me a big Rad bear hug and said he loved working with me and maybe we'd work on some things in the future. That was it."

Juliet turned away. "Did you and my mother ever discuss this?"

"No, Juliet, I never said anything to anyone. Rad didn't ask me to keep it to myself, but he knew I *would* keep it to myself."

Juliet stood up, looking toward the back hallway to make sure her mother wasn't there. She paced a little then turned to face Tom.

"Do you think he was having an affair?"

Tom was still. He met her eyes. "Juliet, I don't know. I do know that he loved you and your mother very much. I know he was proud of you both and he treasured you both. That I know for sure. The other thing..." His voice trailed away.

"Tom, my father sold off four hundred thousand dollars of investments and we don't know where that money went."

Tom's eyes expanded in surprise. "That doesn't sound like Rad. He was always impulsive and generous, but not reckless. Maybe he invested it somewhere."

They let the question hang in the air.

Juliet pulled an uneasy breath. "Did you talk to Dad or see him after you split up?"

"We met for lunch once a few months back and I asked him how things were going. He said things were going good. Those were his words. Life is good. That's all he said about it."

Juliet decided to ask what was really on her mind. "Tom, do you know a woman named Cindy Evans?"

Tom considered the question. "Name sounds vaguely familiar but I don't know her. Why?"

"She was at the funeral. I'd never seen her before. That's all."

Tom left a few minutes later. At the front door, as he slid into his coat, he turned back to Juliet. "Rad had a touch of the dramatic, Juliet. But you know that. He also had his secrets, but all that just added to his charm and likeability."

Juliet nodded, but her mind was wandering somewhere off in Holland Grove.

"Did you and your mother have a good Thanksgiving?" Tom asked.

"Yes. Simple and quiet."

Tom took her arm and gently squeezed it. "Just give it some time, Juliet. It was such a shock to lose him like that. Just give it a little time and remember all the people who loved and admired your father. Remember those things."

Juliet nodded and thanked him for coming.

After Tom left, Juliet went back to check on her mother. She was still sleeping.

It was 12:10 when Juliet climbed into the gray Audi and started toward Holland Grove, seventy miles away.

CHAPTER 10

Fifteen minutes from Holland Grove, the sun burst through the clouds and Juliet slipped on her sunglasses. As she traveled, she worked on a plan: she'd call Cindy, tell her who she was and say she'd received her phone number from a friend at the funeral. She would causally say that she was just passing through town and would love to meet for a snack or a drink. Her choice.

If Cindy asked why Juliet wanted to meet, Juliet would say, again casually, that she wanted to thank her for attending the funeral. She and her mother were touched by the support of so many family and friends.

What if Cindy grew suspicious? Juliet was sure she could sound sincere and be disarming without being threatening. After all, she *was* in PR. Manipulative? Maybe, but for a good cause. Her mother needed that four hundred thousand, and Juliet needed to eliminate Cindy Evans as a party to this mystery.

She took the Holland Grove exit off I-75 South and followed the signs until she entered Holland Grove proper, driving past renovated nineteenth-century buildings, a courthouse with a tower clock, an ice cream shop, antique stores, galleries, upscale women's specialty stores and quaint restaurants.

She found a parking place in front of an electronics store and parallel parked expertly, just the way her father had taught her. After she shut off the engine, she glanced about, noticing signs in shop windows announcing Christmas sales. She lit up. There was nothing more exciting than twenty-five percent off everything, especially things she needed and could buy her mother for Christmas: sleepwear, slacks, sweaters and jewelry. She explored the shops after she met with Cindy.

She pulled her attention from store signs, sales banners and retail discounts and refocused on why she'd come. She gathered herself, reached for her phone and did a quick internet search for Cindy Evans. She was ready now. Ready for a quick biography. She entered the name and waited. While her phone chugged along, searching, Juliet saw heavy gray clouds had covered the sun. Wind gusts blew across the streets and people shouldered their way against them.

As Juliet had expected, there were many listings for Cindy Evans. She quickly scrolled through each one until she found a listing for Holland Grove, Ohio. With her heart beating in her ears, she selected it and waited. When the screen refreshed, she expanded the listing and looked back into the attractive face of the woman she'd seen at the funeral. It was an open, friendly face. The smile was genuine, but there was a savvy coolness in the eyes. The hair was a bit longer, and she looked younger in the photo than in person. Juliet stared for minutes, feeling a new burning curiosity.

Cindy Evans was a real estate agent with a company called Holt/Springer Real Estate. She had twelve years of experience. One comment read:

Cindy is awesome! She knows the loan process backwards and forwards! She knows the streets, the houses and the obstacles you have to get through to make home ownership happen!"

Juliet dialed Cindy Evan's cellphone number.

At the first ring, Juliet felt the rise of nerves. She nibbled on her lower lip, counting one ring, two rings, three rings, four rings.

"Hello, this is Cindy Evans." It was a light, airy voice. Appealing.

Juliet froze. She couldn't find her voice.

"Hello..." Cindy said, inquiringly, her voice dropping a little into mild suspicion.

Juliet forced out, "Hi, Cindy?"

"Yes, this is Cindy."

Juliet swallowed away a dry throat. "Cindy... my name is Juliet."

"Yes, Juliet. Can I help you with something?"

"You don't know me," Juliet said, suddenly feeling foolish.

"Okay... Juliet. Is there something I can help you with?"

Juliet fortified herself by grabbing a breath and sitting up. "Cindy, I saw you at Rad Conrad's funeral. A friend gave me your number. I wanted to know if we could meet. Maybe meet and talk. I mean, I want to thank you for coming to... for coming to the funeral."

Juliet shrank. She heard her strained and uncertain voice.

There was a long pause before Cindy spoke. "You're Rad's daughter, aren't you?"

This startled Juliet. She hadn't expected Cindy to know her. Juliet struggled to think. She stammered. "I...I... Well, I... yes, I'm Juliet Sinclair."

There was another long silence.

"Are you in town, Juliet?" Cindy asked calmly.

"Yes. I was just passing through and..." Juliet stopped. "Actually, that's not the truth. The truth is I drove down because I want to meet you."

"...I see..."

"Can we meet?" Juliet asked.

Juliet heard a little sigh on the other end.

"I won't take up much of your time."

"Okay, Juliet. I can meet you at 3:15, at a little restaurant on West 5th. It's called Baker Street Inn. Do you need directions?"

"No, I'll find it."

"Okay. See you then."

After hanging up, Juliet sat in a long, chilly silence. She checked the time. It was a quarter to three.

JULIET EASILY FOUND THE RESTAURANT and a space in the parking lot, which was near a hardware store and a bank. It was just after three by the time she entered the restaurant, a dimly lit room with heavy oak tables and red leather dining chairs. The music from the speakers was early rock, but subdued. On the wall were old photos of freshly baked bread, cast iron ovens and late nineteenth century mustached bakers, standing proudly by their oven-fresh products. A lean, tall, artificial Christmas tree blinked with red lights.

The young leggy hostess, dressed in black tights and black top, greeted her with a menu. Juliet pointed toward the bar and started over. The bar was spacious, with a dark marble top, backless dark mahogany bar stools, and seven draft beer handles. She sat near the beer handles, the only person at the bar.

The female bartender was a buxom, stocky redhead with long bangs and short curls. She was older than Juliet, maybe late thirties, and there was a sense of purpose in her dark eyes and sharp nose. She, too, was dressed in black.

"Hi," she said in a raspy voice that suggested many nights of shouting to be heard. "Can I get you something?"

"I'm waiting for someone. I'll just have a cranberry and club soda."

The bartender delivered the drink and drifted away into the kitchen. Juliet sipped and waited, her right foot nervously tapping the bronze foot rail.

At 3:15, Juliet kept glancing back over her shoulder to see if Cindy was there. Two men in suits, ties and black overcoats entered together and were ushered to a table. Three women entered, struggling with shopping bags, purses, hats and coats.

At 3:25, Juliet's phone rang. It was Cindy.

"Hello, Cindy?"

Cindy's voice sounded tense and low. "Juliet... I'm really sorry, but I'm not going to be able to make it. Something has come up."

Juliet sank. "I can wait for you."

A pause. "No... I have to leave town. It's a business thing. It just came up. I'm so sorry."

"Can I see you again? You name the day and time," Juliet said.

"Yes. We'll set up a time. Look, I really have to go now. Take care."

And then she was gone. Juliet sat with the phone at her ear, deeply frustrated and worried. Juliet didn't believe Cindy. Something had happened. Maybe after thinking about it, she got scared. Maybe she'd called someone, and that someone had advised her not to come. Not to meet Rad Sinclair's daughter.

Juliet had the impulse to march out of the restaurant and show up at Cindy's workplace and demand a meeting. After a minute's reflection, Juliet knew Cindy wouldn't be there. She'd left. She'd run away and Juliet would never have the chance to see or talk to her again.

The bartender returned and must have seen the distress on Juliet's face.

"Are you okay?"

Juliet dropped the phone into her purse. "...Yes. Yes, I'm okay."

But she wasn't okay. She felt a low, dragging depression creep over her. Her worst fears were seeping into her body like a cold fluid. She needed a drink. She needed to blot out the experience. She had to distract herself so she could think.

"I'll have a glass of cabernet."

The wine was poured, and Juliet took a grateful sip. Moments later she felt its welcomed soothing buzz, as it helped cool her agitated thoughts and emotions. And then Juliet had a sudden thought. If Cindy had recommended this place, maybe the bartender knew her.

"Do you happen to know Cindy Evans?" Juliet asked.

The bartender's face opened in recognition. "Yeah, sure, I know Cindy. She comes in for lunch about once a week. Sometimes she just comes to the bar and has a glass of wine."

Juliet's eyes shined with interest. "Is she married?"

"Cindy?" The bartender thought about it. "She was, I think. Yeah, we talked about it once a long time ago. I think she said she'd been married, maybe a couple of times."

Juliet reached into her purse and tugged out her phone. She quickly scrolled through her photographs until she found a clear shot of her father. She held the phone up to the bartender. "Did this man ever come in here?"

The bartender squinted a look. Her face widened again with happy recognition. "Yeah! That's Rad!"

"You know him!?" Juliet exclaimed.

"Sure I know him. He's the best. The Rad Man! He used to come in with Cindy. They used to order food and wine and laugh. Rad was so much fun. Everybody liked Rad. I know Cindy was crazy about him. She said she'd marry him in a minute. They were a great looking couple."

Juliet opened her mouth to say something, but nothing came out. It was as though she'd been stabbed in the chest. She sat like a cold, dead thing.

The bartender's eyes narrowed in on her. She grew uneasy and suspicious. "Why do you want to know about all this?" she asked, even more suspicious. "Who are you?"

Juliet retrieved her wallet, found her credit card, and handed it over. "I need to go."

The bartender hesitated.

"Please, just run the card," Juliet said, turning away. The bartender reluctantly took the card and went to the computer. She swiped the card and waited nervously for the print out. Juliet was standing, with her coat on, when the bartender presented the slip for signature. Juliet signed it, leaving a ten-dollar tip. She thanked the bartender, turned, and left the restaurant.

Juliet seemed to wander aimlessly across the lot. It took a great effort to focus enough to find her car. She was not drunk. The buzz from the half-consumed glass of wine had long since faded. She was more clear-headed than she wanted to be. It was the truth that had stunned her. Weakened her. Damaged her. In a kind of intoxicated agony, she slid behind the wheel of the car, shut the door and started the engine.

Juliet did not want to go home. She did not want to face her mother. She did not want to face the world. She wanted to fly away somewhere—anywhere, away from her angry, punishing thoughts.

How could he have done it? How could her father have betrayed them like that and then just disappeared into death, leaving them to suffer, hurt and hate. Because at that moment, as she pulled out of the parking lot into afternoon traffic, staring through a screen of tears, she hated him. She hated him for his betrayal, for his lies, for his total destruction of her love for him. She hated the cheery, faithful persona he had created and slung out into the world like so much confetti. The generous friend. The religious man. The good and loving father and husband.

Juliet turned on to I-75 North and started for home. Home? How could she face her mother? She could never tell her the truth. She could never share the truth with anyone. That meant she'd have to live with the secret, and with her hate, for the rest of her life.

Go home? What home? To that damned house he'd built for them? Suddenly she hated that too! Thank God her mother would have to sell it. The sooner the better! The sooner they could throw away all his things, the better. The sooner she could erase him from her mind, the better. The sooner she could get out of that town and away from any memory of him, the better. The Rad Man! What a stupid, silly name. Is that what Cindy had called him?

Juliet struggled to contain her pain and fury.

The faster she drove, the faster hatred consumed her. It was a hate that blazed. It was a poisonous hate that pumped through her veins.

Juliet drove on, nearly blind from tears, as darkness descended. She drove on, unaware of a ragged tear of light that broke through distant purple clouds. She drove on, unaware that she'd missed Junction 5, the road that would lead her back to Fairpoint, Ohio.

CHAPTER 11

At the coffee mug, Paul Lyons, and Linda worked feverishly. Paul made coffee drinks while Linda took orders, ladled soup, snatched pastry, swiped credit cards and took cash. At 5:10 in the evening, every table was full, and still there was a line of people waiting. This was the after school/after work rush. Students hovered at tables, staring into phones, laptops and notebooks. Employees from the mall, the law office, Ostterman Electronics Warehouse, and the Fairpoint Community College pushed in, all chatty and twitchy.

"The last thing some of these people need is more caffeine," Paul thought to himself.

But he wasn't complaining. His place had become a kind of community center. It was a cozy, conveniently located hangout, where no one had to worry about consuming too much alcohol and being stopped for a breathalyzer test by one of Sheriff Hansel's deputies.

In the three years since Paul had opened the place, two couples had met in his café and subsequently gotten married, events which prompted the local newspaper to publish an article entitled *Hot Coffee Brews Hot Love at*

The Coffee Mug. The opening line read: *"At The Coffee Mug on North Main, what is Paul Lyons putting in his coffee? Love potion number Nine?"* Paul and the two couples were featured in the article, and the free publicity both in the newspaper and on-line had helped business even more.

A little after six, The Coffee Mug began to empty, as people left for home or other evening activities. Paul was wiping down the tables when Juliet entered. He saw her from the corner of his eye and turned sharply toward her. And suddenly there it was, the rise of heat to his face, the impossible vocabulary to describe an attraction so immediate and intense that it made him dizzy and shy.

She lingered by the door, and he noticed she was shivering. She looked weary and sad. Paul froze. Linda was cleaning behind the counter and didn't seem to notice her. Finally, Juliet stepped forward, got Linda's attention, and ordered a cappuccino. Paul hurried over, slipped behind the counter and began steaming the milk while Linda tamped the ground espresso into the steel head. Paul indicated that he'd take it from there, and Linda went back to cleaning.

Paul poured the steaming foam over the espresso, sprinkled cinnamon and handed the cup to Juliet, whose eyes were filled with vague distractions. She reached for her wallet.

"That's on me," Paul said.

Juliet awoke and focused on him.

Linda shot him a curious glance.

"You're not charging me?" Juliet asked, with mild surprise.

"No. It's on the house. Would you like a pastry? A sandwich? The soup's good. We have split pea and mushroom barley," Paul said eagerly.

"We're out of the split pea," Linda said over her shoulder, as she wiped the surfaces of the display case.

Juliet managed a thin smile. "... No... Thank you. Just the coffee."

She took the cappuccino to a table and sat with her back to Paul and Linda. Minutes later, she was the only guest, sitting slumped, head down.

A few customers came in for takeout coffee and, as Paul worked, he kept a watchful eye on her. Around 6:20, he glanced over to see Juliet quietly weeping, her body shuddering in anguish.

Concerned, but not wanting to intrude, he drifted to a nearby table and waited until most of the emotion had worn itself out. Then he moved closer. In a soft voice he said, "Are you all right?"

Juliet had a tissue crushed in her right hand. She didn't look up. She nodded. "Yeah..."

"Can I get you anything?"

Juliet slowly lifted her pale, miserable face. She blinked a few times and seemed to see him for the first time. Yes, this was the handsome guy who'd passed her at the diner. He looked down at her with concern. The force of his compassion opened her; she felt vulnerable, threatened. She stopped breathing, tears flooding her eyes.

"I need to go now," she said, lowering her head and reaching for her purse.

She started for the door. After a few steps, she stopped, keeping her back to him. "Thanks for the cappuccino. It's one of the best I've had in a long time."

"Sure you're okay?" Paul asked.

She nodded and left.

Paul watched her wander across the lot to her car. He remembered Rad's words. "Check on my daughter and make sure she's okay. I trust you, Paul." She was definitely not okay.

Paul turned to Linda. "I'll be back in a half hour or so. Call me if you need me."

Linda's head periscoped up over the counter. "Yeah. Cool."

Paul walked briskly to his office, snatched up his brown leather jacket, and pushed out the back door. He climbed in behind the steering wheel of his 2003 black Toyota, started it up and shot away around The Coffee Mug, just in time to see Juliet's Audi pull out, heading south. He followed.

JULIET WAS EXHAUSTED, physically, emotionally, and spiritually. She'd been driving for hours, lost for a time and not caring, driving back roads through little towns she'd never been to or heard of. She dreaded going back to the house. Her mother would be worried, because Juliet had not answered her calls or texts. She couldn't. She needed to recover some before facing Anne. Juliet had the kind of face that was easy to read: what you saw was what you got. She was a terrible poker player. She always lost. She could not, under any circumstances, tell her mother what she had learned. She could not show it on her face.

Juliet scarcely noticed it had begun to snow. She was thinking about her life; about her own naiveté. At thirty years old, what did she think the world was? A pretty little dream world where bad things don't happen, where people don't lie, and where you wish upon a star so all your dreams can come true? Evan wasn't an anomaly; he was like all men, including her father.

She recalled a psychology seminar she'd attended in Minneapolis about two years before. It had some relationship to PR, but she couldn't recall what that relationship was. The speaker, a white-haired, wise-looking woman in her sixties, had said, "Expecting the world to treat you fairly because you're a good person is a little like expecting the bull not to attack you because you're a vegetarian."

Streetlights faded away as she left the town proper and drove on into the darkening night. The house was only eight miles away. She'd driven it many times. She could probably drive it in her sleep. Snowflakes attacked and crashed into the windshield. She turned on the wipers.

Another sickening thought struck. How would she get through Christmas? All the old warm memories of family, friends and good times now seemed foolish and pointless. Can anyone really be thankful for pain and heartache? Can anyone really celebrate the magic, love and mystery of Christmas when you feel like your insides have been kicked out?

"Get hold of yourself, Juliet," she said aloud. "Stop feeling sorry for yourself. Do you think you're the first person who's been hurt because someone you loved lied to you?"

There was a curve ahead. Not a very sharp curve. But snow had covered the two-lane highway. There were DEER CROSSING signs posted every few miles, but Juliet didn't see them. Her mind was on other things.

She was exceeding the speed limit of thirty-five. She was going forty-two.

There were tall, arching trees on both sides of the road. In the darkness, they were vague and large, but in the sweep of headlights, and in the swift wind, their branches shook and seemed to reach for her as she approached the curve.

Juliet was remembering a family Christmas trip to New York City when she was ten years old. Jimmy must have been four. For some reason, she remembered his big hat with earmuffs attached.

They went to Radio City Music Hall to see the Rockettes and the Christmas show. Rad was like a child, clapping and laughing with Jimmy, hoisting Juliet up to see the high-kicking Rockettes and the dancing Santas.

Afterwards, as they'd wandered the festive streets, her mother and dad held hands and gave each other furtive, playful pecks on the lips, as they explored the department store windows and the towering Christmas tree at Rockefeller Center. It had been magical and fun. Her parents had seemed deeply in love.

Now alone, driving in the snowy night, Juliet exclaimed, angrily, "Why did you do it, Dad!? Why?!"

A deer jutted out from the darkness onto the road. Juliet's headlights framed it. There were seconds of shock, fear, and reaction. Juliet jerked the wheel left. The terrified deer leapt and darted off into darkness. Juliet's tires lost traction. They slid away. Juliet fought for control, but the car was lost in a chaos of motion.

There was a clearing of trees. A drop-off into a ravine. Juliet braced as the car shot off the road and plunged sideways down a five-foot embankment. The car struck the ground, right wheels first. Off-balance, it leapt and flipped, grazing a tree trunk, slinging Juliet about like a rag doll. The car, miraculously, righted itself, coming down hard on all four wheels. With a terrible bounce, it settled into brush and newly fallen snow.

Paul witnessed the accident in horror. When he saw Juliet's Audi slide away and sail over the embankment, he shouted, "No!"

He muscled his car to the right shoulder and flipped on his emergency flashers. He shoved open his door and burst out, scanning both sides of the highway. No cars! He sprinted across the road, vapor puffing from his mouth. Bracing with his right hand, he slid down the slope, fighting for balance, and staggered over to Juliet's battered, silent car.

The blowing snow and sharp, cutting wind punished him as he swiftly inspected the area. He didn't smell gasoline. That was good. He didn't think the car was in danger of catching on fire.

In the hollow darkness, he grabbed for the driver's side door handle. He yanked it hard, but it wouldn't budge. It was locked or jammed. He swung out of his jacket, wrapped it around his right fist and forearm, with maximum padding at his fist. He cocked his arm and punched the window hard. He repeated the blows until the glass gave way, shattering. He carefully cleared the glass and peered in.

"Juliet... Juliet!"

He dropped the coat, reached in and from inside, unlocked the door.

In the dim light, he could see she was leaning right, unconscious, the seatbelt still around her waist, but the air bag only partially deployed. Paul groped for the inside door handle, found it and, with a straining effort, forced the door partially open. Grabbing the door frame with both hands, he tugged and pulled until the door gave way.

He leaned in. "Juliet!"

She didn't respond. He saw blood leaking from her left scalp, flowing down her face. He fumbled for his phone and dialed 911. He calmly communicated the situation and the location and then went to work. Having been a Marine Corps Special Operations soldier, he'd had medical training; he'd used it in Iraq and Afghanistan. He knew he shouldn't move her. She could have neck or spine injuries and any movement could make the injuries worse.

Paul stuck his fingers into the side of her neck.

"Give me a pulse," he said. "Juliet, stay with me. Stay with me. Come on, give me a pulse!"

But there was no pulse. Juliet was dead.

.

CHAPTER 12

The darkness felt smooth, silky and warm. There was no wind, no pain, no sound. It was deathly quiet. And she felt at ease. Comfortable. At peace. A peace she'd never experienced before. Where was she? What had happened?

At that moment, she realized she was floating up near the tops of the trees. What!? How? She looked down. She saw her car. She saw a man, and she recognized him. He was the guy from The Coffee Mug. He was pressing on her chest—applying CPR. Trying so hard! She watched in disoriented wonder.

Then the sweeping red lights of an ambulance approached. It stopped. Two EMS workers emerged. The man started waving both arms, shouting, "Over here. Over here!" Why was he crying?

What *was* all this? She saw the blue dome sweep of a police car as it skidded to a stop near the ambulance. She saw a stretcher and the two EMS men struggle down the hill to where she lay. She saw it all while floating in a calm, pleasant peace.

The violence of what had happened came gradually, as Juliet watched the dynamic scene below. At first, it stunned her. Saddened her. When she saw her lifeless body being lifted onto the stretcher and hauled up the embankment to the ambulance, she lingered, watching in disbelief.

She had been in a terrible accident and her body was down there! Who was she, then? Who was up here, watching? It was strange and weird! What was going on!? Was she dead? Was she having some kind of nightmare?

Then the peace returned, washing her in a warm liquid serenity. She relaxed. As she did, she heard the distant sound of wind chimes. She glanced about, trying to locate the source. It seemed to be everywhere and nowhere. It was soothing and comforting.

Suddenly, she thought of her mother. If all this was true, and if Anne learned of the accident, she'd fall apart. She'd never survive another death.

In an instant, Juliet was transported to her house. She stood in the living room next to the fireplace looking at her mother, who was curled up on the couch, reading a book and sipping tea.

"Mom," Juliet said, in a tentative voice. "Mom, can you hear me?"

Anne didn't stir or look up.

The telephone rang. It lay on a side table, within easy reach. Anne picked it up.

"Hello..."

Juliet watched her mother's face fall apart. "What? Juliet!? No! No, there must be some mistake. No! Oh, God, No!"

Juliet moved toward her mother, reaching for her. "I'm okay, Mom. Really, I'm okay. I'm right here. Can't you see me?"

Anne burst into tears, her trembling hand tightly gripping the receiver. "Where is she? What hospital!? Where?!"

In an instant, Juliet was gone. The silky blackness returned, blotting out the scene. Juliet felt herself floating upwards, higher and higher, past trees and clouds, up into a wide sky with a mass of infinite stars.

The sound of the wind chimes returned, merging with the sound of an intoxicating ethereal music. Music so lush and beautiful that Juliet seemed to melt into waves of bliss, as she rose higher and deeper into a gloss of stars and vivid, whirling planets.

In the distance she saw a tiny white light coming straight toward her. It was mesmerizing. She couldn't pull her eyes from it. As she watched, it expanded into dazzling colors of white, gold, and blue. It drew closer, a gorgeous bouquet of rainbow light and color.

She should have been frightened. All of this should have terrified her, but she felt only peace, wonder and a sense of well-being.

The light came before her and then opened up, like a gateway. It seemed to beckon. Within its glowing center, she saw vague shapes, heard celestial music. Without any fear, she glided ahead, crossing the threshold of what seemed to be the outer rim of a vast circle. She entered into a dazzling world of crystal light and color.

Floating higher, Juliet saw immense vistas of towering, snow-covered majestic mountains, sharp green meadows and forests flaming in colors of autumn. But then there were also the glittering pastel colors of blooming spring and rolling fields bursting with purple, red, yellow, pink and peach-colored flowers. They sparkled and rippled in ecstatic waves under a vibrant sun and a warm, intoxicating breeze.

There were sparkling clear streams and high waterfalls cascading down into soft emerald-colored pools, meandering across moss-covered stones, flowing inevitably into rivers that seemed to extend out into infinity. She saw toy-like villages stacked into the distant hills and people below inhabiting them. Their faces were joyful, their dress simple, their forms lithe and ethereal.

Above were songbirds, drifting and sailing among silky luminous clouds, their mellifluous melodies filling Juliet with a healing rapture.

Everywhere was a rich shining light that seemed to emanate from within every object; within every flower and blade of grass; within every cloud and bird; within her very being!

Overwhelmed by the sublime and enthralling scenes and feelings, Juliet couldn't help feel an unspeakable happiness in heart and mind and soul. It was as though she'd been a caterpillar that had pushed on the walls of its shell until it broke open. She'd wriggled free from her earthly skin and fluttered off as an enchanted butterfly into a world of blissful, eternal summer.

Then she saw him. In that paralyzing moment where reality and fantasy seemed fused and disorienting, Juliet felt herself gently descending toward an open green field, near a tranquil pond, just like the one near the house!

Waiting for her below was her father! It was him. He was standing there, waiting for her.

When she came to rest on a thick, plush carpet of grass, Rad rushed toward her, beaming, wide, welcoming arms outstretched. She did not think. She did not question. She ran to him at a gallop, and he caught her up into his arms, like he'd done when she was a little girl. He laughed ecstatically, and she cried out in joy and relief.

"What did I tell you, Juliet!? Life is a big ole' adventure!"

Juliet buried her face in his hair and neck, smelling his familiar Polo aftershave. The grateful tears wouldn't stop.

"I just can't believe it," she said. "I don't believe it and I don't care if I don't believe it!"

Rad bear-hugged his daughter, laughing and swinging her about in delight. Finally, after what seemed a timeless pleasure, he eased her down and released her. They stood staring, their eyes glistening with tears.

Juliet noticed that her father looked younger. His hair was the lustrous reddish brown it had been when she was a girl. His face was smooth and relaxed and boyishly handsome. He wore a light blue shirt and the brown khaki pants he often wore on weekends when he played golf. The horn-rimmed glasses and his perfectly contagious smile were the same; his warm, playful chocolate brown eyes were just the same.

Juliet looked about. "Where are we? What is this place?"

Rad looked down at his polished brown loafers and then up into the sky. "Well, I guess you could say we're in a kind of heaven."

Juliet stared hard and long. "Heaven?" she responded, vaguely.

He looked at his daughter. "A kind of heaven. I'm not really sure. I've heard the phrase 'many mansions' used here, but I'm not going to get into that, because I haven't been here all that long and I'm still going through a kind of adjustment period."

Juliet reached up and brushed her father's cheek. "Well, I don't care where we are, I'm just so happy to be with you again."

Rad took her hand and kissed it.

"It's so beautiful here," Juliet said. "It's strange, but in many ways this place seems more like reality than Earth does. I've never felt so good. So alive. So happy."

Juliet noticed someone approaching. The figure walked tentatively through the shade of a large spreading oak and then out into the brilliant sunshine. Juliet squinted a careful look at a young man of perhaps twenty-five. He was tall and thin, with shiny chestnut hair combed smoothly back from his forehead. He wore a white cotton shirt and jeans. He was barefoot, ambling toward them with the slightest hint of a smile. His brown eyes glistened with happiness and recognition. Rad turned and laid a gentle arm on his shoulder.

Juliet stared, straining to recall the face, the expression, the mischievous grin.

"You still don't know me, Juliet?" the young man asked.

Juliet's eyes widened in sudden recognition. "Jimmy! Jimmy, is that really you? But how could it be?"

He shoved his hands into his pockets and shrugged. "Yep, it's me... In the fles..." He stopped. "Okay, so maybe I'm not in the flesh, but I'm here. It's me."

She rushed to him and they embraced.

Juliet shut her eyes against ecstatic tears. "It's a dream. It's a crazy, wonderful dream!"

Juliet and Jimmy stood gazing at each other while Rad looked on, smiling.

"I wish Mom were here to see you, Jimmy," Juliet said. "I wish she could see you... and Dad."

Jimmy shrugged again. "Yeah, I wish she could too."

Juliet turned, looking, blinking, running her fingers through her hair. "What is all this? I mean, am I dreaming?"

Rad wrapped his arm around Jimmy. "It's hard to explain, Juliet. When I first got here, Jimmy and I went off fishing together. He's been here awhile, so he's been telling me all about this place."

"It takes some time getting used to," Jimmy said. "But, no, you're not dreaming."

Juliet shook her head a little. "Then I don't understand."

Rad smiled, lacing his fingers in hers. "Let's take a walk around the pond like we used to."

Jimmy leaned over and kissed his sister on the cheek. "I've got to go now, Juliet. I just came to say hello."

"Where are you going? Are you coming back? Will I see you again?" Juliet asked.

Jimmy shrugged. "Maybe. I don't know. See you."

Jimmy walked back into the shade of the trees. He turned, waved, and then faded from sight.

"I don't understand," Juliet said.

"Let's take the walk, Juliet," Rad said.

They started off, quietly, watching golden butterflies flutter, glide and weave an airy path over the pond, disappearing into cool green trees. Juliet and Rad strolled, listening to the gentle lap of the water, watching the orange shadow of fish wiggle near shore.

"Dad... Am I dead?"

He laughed a little. "Do you feel dead?"

"No. I feel very much alive. But if I'm not dead, then what am I doing here with you and Jimmy?"

"Ah, yes," Rad said, kicking at some pebbles. "Well, let's put it this way. You and I have been given a gift. A little Christmas gift, you might say."

Juliet looked up at him. She waited.

He stopped, released her hand, and met her eyes. "Juliet, I was briefly able to go back to Earth. I was with you and your mother after my death. I went back again recently. I saw what was happening to you. I felt your anger and disappointment. Like I said, all this..." Rad indicated with the sweep of his arm. "All this is new to me. There are beings here who are helping me to get acclimated. Jimmy is helping me. They all say it will take time, even though, as you see, there's no such thing as time here. Right now, you're here, but on Earth, only minutes have passed since your accident. You're still in the ambulance."

"How do you know that?" Juliet asked.

"It doesn't matter. I came here to meet you."

"Then I *am* dead?"

"Yes and no."

Juliet shook her head, massaging her forehead. "I don't understand, Dad."

Rad looked deeply into her eyes. "You have to go back, Juliet."

"Back?"

"Yes. It is not your time."

"I don't want to go back. Why should I go back?"

"Juliet, I asked for the opportunity to talk to you."

"Asked who? What?"

"It doesn't matter. Look, this is all very difficult, because things are very different here than on Earth."

"Dad, I'm not going back."

"Juliet..." Rad stopped, trying to find an explanation.

He took her hand and led her across the rocky beach to a narrow wooden jetty that extended fifteen feet out into the water. There was the occasional splash as a fish shot up, arched, and plunged back into the shadowy depths. Two overturned skiffs were high on the bank, nosing into tall grass. Dragonflies hovered and darted out over the water, making erratic patterns, as if confused.

Rad dragged one of the skiffs to the water's edge and he and Juliet flipped it over. Juliet climbed in while Rad grabbed the oars, gave the little skiff a shove, and hopped in, finding a seat opposite her. As they glided away, Rad pulled on the oars. Juliet leaned over, dropping her hand into the refreshing cool water. It sifted through her fingers as the wind played with her hair. She heard the creak of her wooden seat and watched the glip and liquid swirl of the oars.

"What a gorgeous day! I've never seen a day so beautiful."

Rad watched her lovingly. "Your mother needs you, Juliet."

Juliet stayed silent.

"And you have a lot of life to live," he continued. "You have many wonderful days ahead of you. Exciting times and good people to meet."

Juliet shot him a glance. "I don't want any of that. It's too painful."

"It's not *all* painful. There's joy and beauty as well. There is a sense of great adventure down there. There are many good people down there doing good things."

Juliet looked away. "So, you arranged all this? You arranged my accident?"

"No. Not that. I asked my advisors if I could see you and talk to you. They agreed. But the accident would have happened, anyway. You were tired, angry and distracted."

Juliet slapped at the water. "I had a good right to be."

"Did you?"

She avoided his eyes. "You know I did."

Her father rested the oars and the skiff drifted for a time, allowing the silky-scented breeze to wash over them.

"Juliet... judging others is poisonous to your body and mind. Anger is corrosive. It leads nowhere, except to nearly killing yourself and hurting other people."

"I don't want to talk about it," Juliet said. "Everything is fine here. I feel good here. I don't need to go back or even think about Earth. It's over."

"You've got to go back, Juliet," Rad said, firmly. "You must go back and face your life. You can't run from it. You can't hide from it. Face it and learn how to love and forgive. That's the best thing. That's the best way to live your life. It's not always so clear down there, because things can get complicated and confusing, but that's the whole point of it all. The whole point of living. That's why I asked for this meeting. So, I could tell you this. So, you can live happily—and not live in anger and bitterness."

Juliet flicked the water from her fingers. She remembered her mother's face when she'd learned of

Juliet's accident. She remembered how Anne had struggled with loss and depression. How grief-stricken she had been remembering Jimmy's death. How tired and sick she'd looked lying in her bed after Rad had died.

"Mom misses you, Dad," Juliet said. "She's very sad."

"And I miss her. I miss you both," Rad said.

Juliet sighed, looking out across the radiant surface of the pond. She imagined her mother sitting alone in that house, distraught and destroyed by grief, as yet another death had left her alone and beaten. How much loss is too much loss, and you finally break and shatter into a thousand pieces; into a thousand tears?

Juliet felt a sudden rush of love for her mother—felt an aching impulse to reach out and hold her and tell her that everything was okay. She wanted to tell her that her daughter was alive and well. She wanted to tell her how much she loved her.

"I wish I could stay," Juliet said. "It's so restful here. So peaceful."

"Try to remember this peace when you go back, Juliet. Try to hold on to it. You can, if you practice it."

Father and daughter exchanged loving glances.

"I'll go back," Juliet said, in a quiet voice of surrender. "I'll go back for Mom because I love her, and I know she needs me."

"Yes, Juliet. She does. She needs you very much. There are others who need you too; you just don't know it yet."

Rad dropped the oars into the water and resumed rowing. Juliet watched her father carefully, calculating her words.

"Dad... why did you do it?"

Rad stopped, leaning on the oars. He took off his glasses. As he took her in, his eyes were calm, but focused and waiting.

"Juliet...There are things I can't tell you. Things you must discover for yourself. I wish I could make everything easier for you, but I can't. You'll have to be strong and brave and help your mother as much as you can."

Juliet turned away from him.

"Don't be angry at me, Juliet. You have to find the truth your own way. That's the way it works. But know that, whenever I can, I'll be with you. Whenever I can, I'll help you."

Juliet looked at him with love. "I miss you, Dad."

He nodded. "And I miss you and love you. Always."

Juliet suddenly felt tired and weak. Her vision became blurred.

"I have to go now, Juliet, and so do you. I *can* tell you this: we will meet again. We will be together again."

Juliet felt a chill, despite the warm, nourishing sunlight that bathed her and the world around her. She shuddered. As she wrapped her arms about herself for warmth, she noticed that Rad was fading away into a kind of misty fog.

"Don't go yet, Dad. Just a few more minutes. Please don't go!"

"It's time, Juliet. It's time for you to go back. Remember this: I love you and will always love you. You'll always be my darling girl."

As Rad slowly dissolved, Juliet shot to her feet, forgetting where she was. "Dad! Wait!"

The skiff rocked carelessly. Juliet struggled for balance. In desperation, she reached out for her father, calling for him. And then she felt herself go. The skiff pitched left. She plunged into the pond and sank, her arms flailing, reaching, her legs kicking. Through dark, murky water, she descended, feeling a sudden and terrific shock of cold, as if she'd fallen into an icy pond. She gasped for breath, chest heaving. Down she went, deeper and deeper, freezing, coughing, and panting.

And then there was pain. A searing, hot pain that was so acute, she blacked out.

CHAPTER 13

Anne Sinclair paced the hospital lounge in an agony of despair, waiting for news. She'd called her sister before leaving for the hospital, and Carolyn had called Anne's good friends, Nora and Jon, who were on their way. It wouldn't be long before other friends and family members heard the news and called, but right now, Anne couldn't speak and couldn't listen except to simple sentences: Juliet is alive. Juliet will survive.

She stared at the floor, barely noticing the other people in the lounge who offered sympathy with their eyes. Earlier, one kind woman had held her hand for 15 minutes while she sobbed. But right now, Anne was oblivious to everything but the knifing pain that stabbed at her until she was numb. Her little girl had stopped breathing. She could still die. She lay in the ICU, close to death, with only IV lines, a feeding tube and a urinary catheter tethering her to the Earth. She had fractured ribs, a punctured lung, and a lacerated kidney. CT scans of her brain showed swollen tissue. That was bad.

Anne couldn't bear it. Her heart was kicking in her chest. A doctor had offered her medication, but she'd refused it. She had to be clear. She had to know what was going on. She had to pray with a focused mind. And, dear God, how she prayed. She begged and prayed. Prayed for help and relief. Prayed for her baby to be spared and prayed that, if someone had to die, she would be taken instead.

Anne was only vaguely aware of a man who sat close by, hands pushed deep into his pockets. He was staring down the hallway with tired, hopeful eyes. She'd met him when she'd entered the hospital. He'd saved Juliet, she was told. He'd saved her from certain death. It was a miracle that he saw the accident and had responded so rapidly and skillfully. Juliet had stopped breathing. Through CPR, he got her breathing again within four minutes. The doctors hoped that this early CPR had prevented permanent brain damage.

Anne sat in a paralyzed silence. At some timeless moment, Paul Lyons approached, staring down at her sympathetically.

"Excuse me, Mrs. Sinclair. I'm sorry to bother you. My name is Paul Lyons... I just wanted to say that I knew your husband and considered him a good friend. If there's anything I can do for you, please let me know."

Anne looked up at him with sick, suffering eyes. She worked at a smile.

"I'm... well, I'm so grateful. I'm truly grateful for what you did. I'm sorry I didn't thank you for saving her. I've just been..."

"There's no need to apologize, Mrs. Sinclair, and I don't want to intrude. I just want you to know that I'm here in case you need anything."

She nodded without responding.

The hours passed in an endless anguish of uncertainty as Anne received frequent updates and reports. Carolyn, Nora and Jon arrived; they took turns keeping around-the-clock vigils at the hospital. Paul visited every day, listening intently to the medical updates Anne or her friends provided.

After three days, Anne reluctantly spent a night at home, exhausted and sick with a cold that had worsened.

On the fourth day, Juliet improved. The swelling in her brain had gone down, her pulse strengthened, and her eyes fluttered open.

On the fifth day, Juliet was released from the ICU and taken to a private room, where her condition was listed as guarded. Her cold nearly gone now, Anne felt well enough to spend most of her time at Juliet's bedside, quietly speaking to her, encouraging her, whispering how much she loved her. Carolyn was always nearby, relieving her sister, standing vigil herself, or reading and offering bits of news or celebrity gossip to relieve the tension. Juliet, still under heavy sedation, said little, but looked at her mother lovingly with distant, searching eyes. Anne offered endless prayers of gratitude that Juliet had survived.

JULIET FELT LIKE A BROKEN RAFT tossed by swirling rapids. Her back burned with pain. She cried out. A nurse did something. Soon, she grew limp with relaxation, slipping deep down into calm water, into peaceful paradise, unconscious, not even dreaming. And then she'd swim up, just a little, fishing on a calm lake with her father and Jimmy, their knees touching in the small boat, their eyes glowing with sunshine and the simple pleasure of being together.

But she couldn't stay there—she had to go! So, she forced herself up through mucky clay, through dense matter, into the heat and prickly pain, through the tender torso, forcing a raw breath, and then she'd cough, whimpering, as pins pierced her insides.

She could hear herself cry out and feel her mother's light touch on her forehead. She'd squint, unable to pry her heavy lids open. Sometimes Aunt Carolyn was there, kind and careful Carolyn, shyly smiling and touching her cheek. She wanted to smile, but her mouth would only twitch. She was *trying* to come back.

But mostly Juliet slept, grateful to be hiding, not yet ready to take possession of the heavy bones and throbbing soft tissue that were her body.

AND THEN LATE ONE MORNING, she awoke. She took a deep breath, surprised she could inhale without sharp needles cutting through her chest. She opened her eyes slowly and looked around the room. Dr. Bowers was there, studying her chart at the foot of the bed.

"Doctor," she said, softly.

Dr. Bowers looked up, smiling. In her late forties, she was tall, fit and authoritative. There was kindness in her dark, steady eyes and strength in her prominent jaw and leonine face.

"Well, hello, Juliet. Welcome back. How are you feeling?"

"… Not sure." She swallowed. "Water?"

Dr. Bowers placed a cup to her lips. It was the best water she had ever tasted.

"How long…?"

"About a week."

Juliet's eyes swelled with tears.

Dr. Bowers remained standing, appraising Juliet's overall appearance for a moment, and then dragged a chair over to the bed and sat.

"What is it?"

"... Happy to be alive," Juliet said hoarsely. "I was dead. With my father. And my brother."

Dr. Bowers held Juliet's hand. She'd heard similar stories from other patients.

"Do you want to talk about it?"

Juliet nodded. Dr. Bowers listened intently as Juliet recounted her experiences in short phrases: floating above the trees, seeing her own lifeless body, watching a man give her CPR, going to some place like heaven, talking with her father and brother. Feeling such peace. Then coming back through muddy darkness.

"I miss the peace," Juliet said, as tears leaked from the corners of her eyes. The pain had returned.

Dr. Bowers understood; again, gently squeezing her hand. "You'll be better soon, Juliet. The pain will be gone soon."

Juliet struggled to compose herself, suddenly guilty for giving into pain, remembering why she was sent back. "Where is Mom?" she whispered.

"She and your aunt went for lunch. I'm sure they'll be back soon."

Dr. Bowers released her hand.

"Wait." Juliet's eyes searched Dr. Bowers' face. "Do you think... it really happened?" she asked.

Dr. Bowers patted her hand gently. "No one else can say. No one else can validate your experiences, Juliet. You obviously lived through something profound." She started to stand, but stopped, feeling Juliet wanted more.

"There's a lot of research out there on out-of-body and near-death experiences. You can read about them when you're better."

"But... was I really dead and floating above?"

Juliet seemed alert, so Dr. Bowers continued, not sure if Juliet wanted to hear what she was going to say, but feeling the need, as her doctor, to say it. "It's true you had stopped breathing, but I don't think you were clinically dead. The fact that you were observing yourself and the accident scene outside your body suggests that your consciousness was still intact. Most scientists think these kinds of experiences come from the right hemisphere of the brain."

"But when I was out of my body... was I away from my brain?" Juliet asked.

Dr. Bowers shifted in the chair, gathering her thoughts. "I can't answer that, Juliet. But I can tell you about some research that was conducted a few years ago. Doctors were treating a woman for epilepsy, and they implanted electrodes in certain regions of her brain where they suspected seizure activity. They used a weak current to stimulate them and as the current was applied to one particular spot, she experienced a sense of lightness, as if she were floating above herself."

Juliet frowned. Dr. Bowers did not want to distress her. "She had other sensations as well, of course... But the point is, Juliet, what you experienced could have been something that medical science doesn't yet understand, or it could have happened as a result of trauma."

Dr. Bowers' voice started to sound far away, like she was speaking from the back of a hollow cave. Juliet struggled to keep her focus on the doctor's face, but she failed, and her eyes closed. She wished she could be on that lake again with her father and brother. It was so peaceful there.

"We just don't know," Dr. Bowers said finally, aware of her patient's diminishing attention. "But in the final analysis, Juliet, it's your experience and you are the final authority."

Dr. Bowers stood, watching Juliet sleep. The doctor had learned years ago that there were many more mysteries in life and death than medical science could ever hope to explain. As she left Juliet's room, she had to wonder what had really happened to Juliet on that cold snowy night. Had she, in fact, left her body and gone to heaven? Had she really seen her father and brother in another realm?

Dr. Bowers turned back toward Juliet just before she opened the door to the hallway. It certainly was a comforting thought. Maybe she'd see her own daughter again someday, running and smiling in heaven, her 4-year-old little Chrissy, who'd died a slow painful death from Alper's disease ten years before.

"Juliet's recovery has been good so far," Dr. Bowers said later that day to Anne and Carolyn, who were sitting in the waiting room. "We're all surprised and impressed by the speed at which her body has healed itself. We might be able to send her home in a few days."

Anne's eyes flooded with tears. Carolyn placed a gentle arm around her sister's shoulders and held her close.

"That's such good news, Doctor," Anne said. "Thank you for everything you've done."

Dr. Bowers smiled. "Juliet's body did most of the work. She was very healthy, and being young helped.

Not that we're completely out of the woods yet. She'll need regular visits from a nurse for a few weeks so we can continue to monitor her progress."

Anne took her sister's hand. "Well, this is all such good news, Dr. Bowers."

"She was very alert this morning," Dr. Bowers said. "She said she was ready to see the man who saved her life. The man who gave her CPR."

Carolyn handed her sister a tissue and Anne blotted her eyes. "How did she know about him?"

Dr. Bowers blinked. "I thought you'd told her."

"No, I didn't."

"I didn't either," Carolyn added.

"Well," Dr. Bowers said. "Juliet told me she saw him… she claimed that when she was unconscious, she had an out-of-body experience and she saw him helping her. She said she watched the whole thing from above."

Anne's eyes narrowed with confusion. "I don't understand. What do you mean from above?"

Dr. Bowers adjusted her stance. "I'm sure she'll tell you all about it when the time comes. You should go see her now."

ANNE AND CAROLYN ENTERED the room, quietly excited, expecting to see Juliet sitting up and alert. But once again, her eyes were closed. Caroline motioned that she was going back to the lounge, and Anne eased into a chair, smiling down at her dozing daughter. She still had the IV drip, a black eye and a bandage on her forehead, but her color had improved.

She extended a hand to gently brush a strand of hair from Juliet's face, but as she did so, Juliet's eyes struggled opened.

Anne stood, beaming. "Hello, sweetheart."

Juliet blinked slowly, hearing her mother's sweet voice float down to her. She tried to open her mouth. "Hi," she said, at a whisper.

"Don't talk if you don't feel like it."

Juliet managed a little smile. "Good...to...see you."

"I've been here every day, but sometimes you didn't know me."

"Drugged," Juliet said. "So far away. I was so far away. So beautiful there."

"Yes, well you needed to sleep."

"I'm still tired. So tired. I feel strong... and then not so good."

"I'll just sit here, and you go back to sleep."

Anne sat as Juliet closed her eyes. A moment later, she opened them again.

"Mother... I want to see him."

"Who? Who do you want to see?"

"The... guy at the accident. The guy I saw...above..."

"Okay, darling. I'll talk to him. But you've got to rest now."

Juliet stared up into remoteness. "I was there, Mother."

"Where, honey? Where were you?"

"It was beautiful. Dad was there."

Anne watched her daughter with uncertainty. "You need to sleep, Juliet. Just go back to sleep."

Juliet slowly turned her face toward her mother. "I do want to see him. Do you know his name?"

"His name is Paul Lyons."

Juliet shut her eyes again. "Paul Lyons."

"I met him. He's been coming by every day to see how you are. He said he knew your father."

Juliet's face softened, her breathing deepened. She had to work to get the words out. "I want to see him... thank him..."

"Yes, Juliet. You will. But you need to sleep now. Just go to sleep. I'm here. I'll stay here."

CHAPTER 14

It was after 10 p.m. when Paul arrived home. His 5-year-old daughter, Amy, had been asleep for two hours and once again he had forgotten to call to wish her good night. He found his mother-in-law at her usual spot on the living room couch, drinking a glass of beer and watching TV.

Mrs. Donna Webber didn't look up when Paul entered the house. She sat in a dejected gloom, lights off, TV sound on low, so as not to wake Amy. Donna was fifty-eight but looked older. She did not dye her hair, and it was mostly gray. It lay short, spiky and careless, like an afterthought. Her once slim body had thickened; her lean face was now rounded out with sad eyes and an almost permanent frown. She dressed in the frumpiest of jeans and sweatshirts, and when she spoke, her voice was low, strained and flat, as if each word hurt her.

It was only when she was with her granddaughter that one saw any sparkle of life in her eyes or posture. Amy's wide, blue exploring eyes and animated face awakened Donna. Amy had her mother's pug nose and thick blond hair and, whenever she looked into her granddaughter's face, Donna saw her daughter, Tracy, as she had been at that age.

Paul lingered in the living room. "Everything okay?"

Donna's voice was barely audible. "Yeah."

"Did Amy fall asleep okay?"

"Okay. She kept asking when you were coming home."

"I'm sorry I didn't call her. It got so busy."

"All that publicity making you a lot of money? Making you a star?" Donna said, sourly. "I read on the internet about how you saved that girl. There's another article in the local paper, too. Must be making you a lot of money. That why you're so busy?"

Paul held his tongue. "Thanks for taking care of Amy."

"Of course, I take care of her," Donna said with force. "You think I'm gonna let that bubble-brained babysitter take care of my only granddaughter? She's always on her damn phone. She never even looks at Amy. I'd get rid of her. Fire her. She's no good. I keep telling you that."

"I'm trying to find another one. It's not easy."

Donna took a long sip of her beer. "I told you, you ought to let me find one for you."

"I'll do it," Paul said, fighting irritation.

"You go over and see that girl at the hospital again?" Donna asked, contentiously.

Paul took off his leather jacket and draped it over his arm. "No. I haven't been in a few days."

Donna began surfing channels. "You should have been here with your daughter instead of going to see that girl again. Amy hardly ever sees you. No mother and most of the time, no dad. It's not right. Sometimes I think you don't want to see her. Maybe that's the truth. Maybe you don't want to be with your daughter."

Experience told him that Donna had three or more beers. She was not a happy drinker, and she often went into attack mode when she'd had too much.

Paul breathed in his annoyance. "I'm going to hire some more help so I can be with Amy more."

Donna looked at him for the first time. Her doubting, accusing eyes narrowed on him in the dim flickering TV light. "You said that six months ago. And three months ago. And a month ago. You still have that same damned babysitter, and you're never home to put your daughter to bed at night."

Paul ignored her. "Do you want me to drive you home?"

She punched off the TV and got up. "No! I'm not drunk. I'm as sober as a preacher."

Donna marched over to the closet, mumbling under her breath. As she struggled into her coat, she turned to face Paul.

"I know you think I'm just a bitter old bitch, but I just want what's best for Amy, Paul. That's what Tracy would have wanted."

Paul gave her a long, focused look. "That's what I want too."

Donna stood still, her chin quivering. "Do you know what she told me, Paul? Do you know the last thing Tracy told me before she left? She asked me to make sure I took care of Amy. Her eyes filled up with tears when she told me that."

Donna pulled a tissue from her coat pocket. Paul knew Donna kept tissues stuffed in all her pockets, in her purse and in her car. Paul had heard this all before, of course, but he listened patiently.

Donna continued. "I had to be strong, Paul, so I didn't cry. I couldn't let my baby see me cry. But Tracy looked at me so strangely, like she knew something I'd never know. Like she knew somehow, she wouldn't be coming back home. Not ever. I'd never seen her look that way. It was almost as if she'd already left me."

Donna's eyes leaked tears, and she gently wiped them with the tissue. She stood staring at nothing for a few minutes, then turned and started for the front door. She opened it and was about to step out when Paul's voice stopped her.

"Thank you. Thank you for all you've done for Amy. I know how much you miss Tracy, Donna. I miss her too. Maybe I work so much so I don't have to think so much. Part of me wants to remember how it all was—how happy we all were—especially when Amy was born. But part of me just can't stand to remember any of it. None of it. You know?"

In the porch light, Paul saw Donna's defeated wet eyes look up at him. She seemed so small and frail to him, as if her life force was ebbing away a little every day.

She nodded absently, and then left. Paul didn't move when he heard Donna's car engine grind and turn over, growling. She needed a new muffler. He made a mental note of it, as the abused car made a noisy departure. His friend, Otis owned an auto repair shop, and he owed Paul a favor. Paul would call Donna and tell her to drive it over when it was convenient.

Paul's house was a classic A-frame with three bedrooms, featuring steeply angled sides that began near the foundation line, and met at the top in the shape of the letter. It was Rad, of course, who, at Paul's request, had examined the house when it had come up for sale. After Tracy's death, Paul wanted to move from his old house near town, having no desire to stay in the house he and Tracy had bought and lived in.

Rad had appraised the foundation, the plumbing, the boiler, the front and rear gables and the deep-set eaves. All were in good shape. Rad advised Paul of the advantages and disadvantages of the A-frame house, but Paul liked that it sat on a hill, nestled in trees, a good ninety yards from the nearest road.

After Donna's ragged car finally faded into the night, Paul turned back to the silent house, walking past his brown suede couch and climbing the oak staircase to the second floor, where Amy slept. He gently pushed open the door and peered in. She was surrounded by her usual stuffed friends: Mr. Teddy Bear, a dog, a pink elephant and a ballerina doll.

Paul crept silently over to the bed and stood lovingly watching his daughter sleep. He pocketed his hands and allowed himself to remember their joy the day Amy was born. Tracy had been in labor for nine hours. "Not too long and not too short," she'd said.

Paul had heard from other men that, after childbirth, their wives often had a glow about them. Paul saw that glow when he visited Tracy after Amy's birth. Though visibly tired, he'd never seen her prettier or happier.

"Have you seen her?" Tracy asked, her weary eyes filled with light. "Have you seen how beautiful she is?"

He had seen Amy, and she was, indeed, a little beauty. "Yes, I've seen her. She looks like you."

Tracy grinned—that little mischievous grin that always made him smile. "No, Paul, she has your eyes, your chin, and your nose. I studied her very carefully. She told me that she wanted to look like you because you are prettier than Mommy is."

"Yeah, right," Paul said, unconvinced. "I studied her too, you know, and we also had a long conversation about who she looks like. She has your forehead, your cheeks, your ears, in fact, all of your gorgeous face."

"Flattery, flattery, Paul. That's how you won me over. Always flattering me."

Tracy's eyes fluttered and then closed. She was drifting into sleep. "All I know is she's ours," Tracy continued, in a near whisper. "She's our little pretty baby and I'm so happy...so happy..."

And then Tracy fell into a deep sleep.

Paul stood in Amy's bedroom, hearing Tracy's words as if she were standing there beside him. And when he closed his eyes, he could almost feel her warm hand in his. It was so easy, wonderful and painful to remember those nights when they stood so close together, watching Amy sleep. In those deeply personal moments, peace, contentment, and love filled him with effortless gratitude. His life was blessed, and he knew it, and he thanked God for it.

Paul stood alone, lost, blinking about the room as if searching for Tracy, or for some new blessing that would help ease the pain of loss that never seemed to leave him.

He leaned over and gently kissed Amy on the forehead. She did not stir or make a sound. He left her room to begin his nightly pacing of the house, like a sentry keeping watch for old restless ghosts, who are also lost and ceaselessly pacing the night.

Paul paced, and once again, the same haunting thought lifted its persistent head. Why had Tracy been taken from him? And why did it have to be so sudden and violent? A bomb had targeted her camp in southern Baghdad, and she was in the wrong place at the right time. She and three others had been killed that night. Tracy was probably dead before she knew what had happened.

Why didn't he stop her from going? Why didn't he say, "You can't go to Iraq?" How many times since had he said it aloud to himself? How many times had he cursed himself for not stopping her?

But she wouldn't have listened, anyway. She'd joined the Army because she wanted to join. She wanted an education. She wanted the adventure. She wanted to serve her country. She'd joined because her father and uncle had both served in Vietnam. Her grandfather had fought in Korea.

After all, weren't these some of the same reasons he himself had joined the Marine Corps? Would he have refused to go if he'd been ordered? He had served one tour in Iraq and two in Afghanistan. He had gone. He had fought.

Tracy could have done no less, and so he loved and respected her for who she was and what she'd believed in. This is how he must remember and honor her. He could do no less.

But he was also aware that with each sunset and the coming of darkness, he'd be pacing again, asking the same old painful questions again. He'd done this for two years, and this would be the second year that Amy would celebrate Christmas without her mother. And she would ask him once again, "Will Mommy ever come back?"

"No, Amy, she's living with the angels now."

Paul and Tracy had met six years ago, when both were home on leave. He from his second deployment to Afghanistan and she from her first to Iraq. They'd met, of all the innocent places, in a Baskin Robbins. She was digging into a chocolate sundae, and he was working his fast tongue around two generous scoops of Rocky Road.

He saw her and thought, "Nice body, pretty face and a real good-looking sundae. I wish I'd gotten one."

He boldly walked over. She was alone, dressed in shorts, a bright green T-shirt and flip-flops.

"Nice lookin' sundae," he'd said.

She avoided his eyes. Her total focus was on the sundae. "Are you going to ask my chocolate sundae out?"

He laughed a little. "I don't know. Maybe."

She shined her bright eyes on him. He was wearing his dress blue Marine Corps uniform, complete with ribbons and medals, including the Armed Forces Expeditionary Medal and the Silver Star Medal he'd received for gallantry in action in Iraq. He'd just been to a military wedding, and he knew he looked handsome in it.

"Impressive chest," she said, squinting a look at him.

"Thank you, ma'am."

"Did you go to college?" she asked, throwing him a little off-balance.

"Well... Yes, ma'am."

"What was your major?"

"History."

She looked at his first lieutenant silver bars. "When will you make captain?"

Paul stepped back. "Well, aren't we a little aggressive?"

"I admire ambition," she said, winking.

Tracy scooped a mound of the ice cream, some chocolate syrup and the bright red cherry. She shoved it all into her mouth. Paul watched in awe as she chewed, savored, and swallowed.

"That's impressive," he said, arms folded in admiration.

"Thank you," Tracy said, licking both sides of her mouth with the tip of her tongue. "Let me warn you. If you ask my sundae out, I have to go along as chaperone."

Paul laughed, and he fell in love with her right then and there.

AT 2:30 IN THE MORNING, Paul was pacing the living room, remembering the past and feeling guilty because, for the first time since Tracy's death, he was attracted to another woman. Juliet Sinclair attracted him. What had impressed him most about her was her smile. As he'd passed her outside the diner, she'd smiled back at him. It was an open, honest smile. It was generous. It was alive. It had enlivened *him*.

When he'd witnessed the accident and watched in horror as her car slid over the embankment, something snapped in him. He could not—would not—let this woman die.

Though she had no pulse, he refused to concede defeat. "Not this time!" he'd said again and again. "Not this time," and then he'd prayed: to God, to Tracy, to Rad, to anyone who could hear, just as he'd prayed during his last firefight in Afghanistan, when his scouting team had been ambushed and two of his men had gotten hit. How he'd prayed for them. "Save them. Please God save them."

And so Paul decided to risk moving her. If he didn't, she would certainly die. If he took the chance, she might live. Holding her neck, he gently eased her from the car and slid her onto flat ground, unbuttoned her coat and quickly started chest compressions, thirty times, sixty times, his arms straight, the heels of his hands pressing on her sternum. He leaned down, hoping to feel some breath on his cheek. She gasped once. Good! But not normal breathing. Afraid to tilt her head too much, he gently lifted her chin and pressed on her forehead, opening her airway, and then he pinched her nose and breathed twice into her mouth. No response. He returned to chest compressions, the heels of his hands pushing faster and harder into her breastbone… one, two, three, four… thirty times. And when she finally shuddered and caught a breath, when she finally breathed on her own and returned to life, he started to cry. Tears streamed down his face, tears of relief, tears of joy, tears of redemption. He had saved a life. As he wiped his nose with his sleeve, he stared at her face and knew that something had returned to life in himself as well. His own pulse was drumming in his neck: he was alive, he was alive.

And then the ambulance arrived. EMS workers clambered down the hill. As they lifted her onto the stretcher and carried her into the ambulance, he felt the nudge of possibility. Maybe. Maybe he could open his heart again. Maybe he could trust again. Maybe he could fall in love and build a life with someone again. Maybe now that he had saved Rad's daughter, he could resurrect himself from the deepest pit of hopelessness and pain.

But then later, in the hospital, as he anxiously waited for word of Juliet's condition, the old fears and guilt returned like a charging army—the agony of confusion and doubt resurfaced. Inside, the war resumed, and he marched off to battle, fighting to survive another day of fear and remorse. He'd gone to the hospital every day, to confirm she was alive, to hear the news that she was recovering; that she would live.

Six days after the accident, Anne Sinclair called him. Juliet wanted to meet the person who'd saved her life. "Of course," he'd said. "I'll be there tomorrow." And he'd braced himself with a five-mile run in the frigid cold. He imagined standing beside her bed, his heart filled with relief and gratitude that she'd survived, just as he had in Iraq and Afghanistan, when his fellow Marines had survived bomb blasts or bullet wounds. He'd always whispered a simple prayer and felt a swelling gratitude. Life had triumphed over death. A heart was beating; a valuable life was saved; a wife, a mother, a father, a husband would be spared a visit from the Chaplin and the Casualty Notification Officer. No one would have to hear "I regret to inform you that your loved one was killed in action as a result of wounds received from hostile action."

He went to the hospital early, before going to The Coffee Mug. Juliet was sleeping when he arrived. Her mother greeted him with a whisper.

"Thank you so much for coming."

He nodded, quietly finding a chair near the foot of the bed. Her face was beautiful, though bruised and swollen. He watched her, trying to push away the warm, tender feelings which threatened to overcome him. They frightened him, even as he remembered the sensation of her lips against his, the feeling of her body under his hands, the force with which he'd willed her to live, the euphoria he'd felt when her chest lifted, and she took a breath.

Anne excused herself for a moment, and Paul was alone in the room, watching her chest rise and fall under the blanket. Though he sat quietly, Juliet must have felt the strength of his presence. She stirred and struggled to open her eyes. Paul was startled, seeing at first the glazed, faraway eyes of the nearly departed. But then she blinked and attempted to sit up.

He rushed to her side. "Don't sit up…"

But she persisted. "Paul?"

"Yes."

"You saved my life…" she said, smiling again weakly.

"Yes."

"Thank you." She readjusted her posture. "Thank you so much," she repeated, steadily meeting his eyes.

A fire passed between them; and then mutual embarrassment at the force of it. Paul felt as though she could see right into his soul.

He flushed and averted his eyes. Closeness meant risk. Closeness meant hurt and loss. It could cut your insides to pieces, just like a bomb rips into your skin and blows you apart.

"Why were you there?" Juliet whispered.

Paul struggled to look at her face. He remembered the rush of feeling when Rad had shown him her photo.

"I... I left the coffee shop right after you did. I just happened to be behind you," he lied. He wasn't ready to admit the truth. It might embarrass her.

"Incredible. My guardian angel..."

"Your father..." Paul stopped himself. "Must have been your father watching over you."

Juliet looked deeply into his eyes and smiled.

Anne came back into the room, and so Paul started to take his leave.

"Please, come again," Juliet said, extending her hand.

Paul took her hand, feeling the fragility and warmth of it. He longed to hold it, to look into her eyes and express the depth of his gratitude that she had been spared, but images of Tracy's maimed body suddenly shot through his consciousness. Love meant being blown apart. Love meant loss. He dropped her hand, not suddenly, but not gracefully. And he left.

His own inner pieces had never fully mended. Could they ever be? After Tracy was killed, he'd talked with Dr. Hollis, a Marine Corps psychologist. "I'm not going to lie to you, Captain," he'd said. "Combat will be easier to get over than the loss of your wife. It's going to be hard, it will take time, and it will take forgiveness. Mostly, it's going to take patience."

Paul respected Dr. Hollis. His personal awards included the Parachute Badge, Master Army Flight Surgeon Wings, and the Defense Superior Service Medal. He'd also lost a son in Afghanistan. Dr. Hollis knew and felt what Paul was going through.

Paul had wanted to see Juliet again in the hospital. The night after his visit, he'd driven to the hospital and sat in the parking lot, fully intending to enter the hospital gift shop, buy her some flowers and walk into her room with a smile, but when it came time to unbuckle his seat belt and open the door, he was incapable of lifting his heavy hands off the steering wheel to do so. Rad had asked him to take care of Juliet. He had. He had saved her life. But that was all he could do right now.

He shook his head and clenched his fists. Was he really that cowardly? Was he really so afraid of having another relationship? Could he ever let go of Tracy and the guilt he felt for letting her go off to be killed?

PAUL WANDERED THE HOUSE with his thoughts—then paced the kitchen with his thoughts—then cursed his thoughts—until exhaustion finally overtook him, and he dropped into the nearest chair. He shook awake again at 4:30 a.m. He rambled around outside in the yard, gazing up into a mass of stars and dark moving clouds that swam past the low crescent moon, and he prayed for help. He longed for just one good night's sleep.

At 6:30 in the morning, Amy found him asleep on the couch. And so, the cycle continued: his days ending in a loop of old memories and regrets, and his days beginning with new joy at seeing his daughter's sleepy face and brand new, ready eyes.

CHAPTER 15

On Saturday, December 10, Juliet was finally released from the hospital. She'd been dreaming about her freedom for several days, longing to be home, in her own clothes, away from hospital gowns, hospital noises and hospital routines. Dr. Bowers had insisted she stay an extra few days, even after x-rays revealed that the pneumothorax was resolved and that her ribs were stabilized.

The drive home was heaven. There was a light dusting of snow on the ground, the sky was clear blue, and sunlight sparkled on the snow and glinted off cars. Everything looked beautiful.

Juliet rolled down her window and offered her face to the cold wind. Her hair danced and scattered about her face as the world rushed by in a blur of trees, cars, and light. In that exceptional moment of exhilaration and freedom, Juliet smiled broadly. "It feels so good to be alive," she thought. And she did feel intensely alive, as if she were pushing up through deep ocean water to the bright sunlit surface, filling her lungs with clean, fresh air.

"Carolyn took all the flowers home and put them in the living-room," Anne said. "And I kept all the cards. I know you'll want to look at them again. You got so many. I didn't know people sent cards anymore."

Juliet turned to her mother, smiling lovingly. "Thanks, Mom. Thanks for everything you've done. I'm so sorry you had to go through all this, especially after what you've just been through with Dad."

"Oh, stop it. I'm just so thankful you're okay. I don't know what I would have done if... well, if anything had happened to you."

At Juliet's request, Anne had arranged the living room so Juliet could recover in the comfortable overstuffed brown leather rocker recliner near the fireplace. It was still sometimes painful for her to lie flat on her back. Anne stored Juliet's laptop, magazines, books and an e-Reader on the two-tiered side table. She could watch TV, have easy access to the bathroom, and look out through the large picture windows at the tall bare trees and open sky.

THE FIRST FEW HOURS JULIET was home, Anne behaved like a drill sergeant, ordering her sister around as if she didn't know what a cup and saucer were, had never fetched a blanket or a pillow, or had never prepared a peanut butter and jelly sandwich. Juliet caught Carolyn's eye, and they began to laugh. Juliet did a few impressions of Anne, and they finally convinced her she could relax. Friends and relatives came by for quick visits and Juliet received countless E-cards, emails, texts and phone calls. She'd even received a get-well card from Paul, but that was it. To her disappointment, he had not phoned or visited again. She recalled the strange look in his eyes when he was at her bedside. There was concern, of course, but many other emotions swirled there as well. Was it embarrassment? Guilt? Fear? Why hadn't he visited her again?

ON THE FOURTH DAY, Carolyn was convinced that things were going well enough for her to go home. She missed her cats and her own bed. Juliet hugged her long and hard, thanking her for her patience and kindness during the past several weeks.

"Mom could never have made it without you," she said. "Me either!"

"I'm just glad I'm retired so I could be here for you both."

"We'll miss you!" Juliet and Anne both said as she got into her car and set off for her home in Cincinnati.

By the fifth day home, Juliet was stronger. She'd gained a few pounds and felt strong enough to return to the privacy and comfort of her own bedroom. She even planned on cooking dinner to give her mother a much-needed break. She looked up a recipe for chicken Marsala and sent Anne to the store to buy chicken, mushrooms, and Marsala wine. While she was peeling potatoes, the phone rang. She answered it without checking the number.

"Juliet..." The sound of Evan's voice turned her stomach.

"Evan. Hi."

"Listen, I just heard about your accident. How are you, honey?"

She paused, deciding not to address the "honey."

"I'm just fine," she said with forced politeness. "I asked you not to call me again."

"Do you need me to come down there?"

"No, Evan. Mom's taking very good care of me."

"Do you need me to do anything for you up here?"

"No!" She rested her head on her hand. "I have friends who are doing all that."

"Oh, sweetheart, I miss you. I was sick when I heard about the accident. I couldn't believe my beautiful Juliet had come so close to dying."

Juliet recognized the sickening ploys and the neediness masquerading as affection. She didn't respond.

"Honey, I know I made some mistakes, but I'd like to see you. I think we were really good for each other."

"No, Evan, we were *not* good for each. I was good to *you*, but you were not good *for* me, or *with* me, or *to* me."

He met her anger. "You're like... so precious, you know that? Like you've never made a mistake. You won't cut me any slack because I made a few. You judge people, you know that, Juliet? You really judge people. You're like... so right and perfect all the time...so precious."

"Yeah, okay, Evan. Whatever. Goodbye."

She stormed around the kitchen. "Precious? No! Impulsive? Yes! And I'll never be that way again!" Deciding to marry a guy after just a few months of knowing him, and letting herself get caught up in some sort of romantic movie script, charmed by the handsome leading man she'd disliked at first but then quickly fell for when he wooed her with his extraordinary charm and swore, he couldn't live without her. It was just a typical romantic comedy, except that the leading man was empty underneath his great body and charming smile, and so, by the end, it was no longer a romantic comedy, but the sad story of a naïve woman who'd fallen for a vain, needy boy who wanted a stable, dependable mother who'd forgive him every time he was naughty.

Thank God that was over. Thankfully, over.

THE FOLLOWING EVENING, after the dinner dishes were in the dishwasher, Anne and Juliet were alone in a delicious peace. Anne closed her eyes while she was reading on the couch and began to snore gently. Juliet dozed off in the recliner for a few moments, tired from the day and still drowsy from medication.

As the fire settled into a soft orange glow and the silence of night descended, Juliet reflected again on the accident. She'd tried to explain her out-of-body and near-death experiences to Dr. Bowers and then to Carolyn and her mother, but she could tell they'd only indulged her, believing she had experienced some kind of hallucination, brought on by trauma. Finally, Juliet stopped talking about it. Struggling to explain it diminished it, anyway. How do you explain something that has no words to explain? How do you explain another reality that seemed more real than anything she'd ever experienced? She could not forget it, and she could also not forget Cindy Evans as much as she wanted to. As soon as she was fully recovered, she'd have to find Cindy and learn the truth.

When the doorbell rang, Juliet flinched, startled from her thoughts. Anne awoke, bug-eyed and whining.

"What is it? What's happened?"

"It's okay, Mom. Someone's at the door."

Anne sat up, disoriented, still wearing an apron. "What time is it?"

Juliet glanced at the clock on the mantel. "After eight."

The doorbell "dinged" again. Anne wiped her eyes, stood up, and went to the door. "Are you Juliet's mother?" the light tenor voice asked.

Juliet knew that voice!

"Well, yes, I am."

"I'm Max West, Mrs. Sinclair. I worked with Juliet in New York. Is she okay? Can I see her?"

Startled, Juliet sat up, tugging at the blanket that was spread across her legs. She hadn't washed her hair in two days and didn't have any makeup on. She was wearing a ratty old white sweatshirt from her college days that had BOGUS written across it in bold red letters. She grabbed a scrunchie from the side table and pulled her hair back into a careless ponytail.

"Oh..." Anne said, with some surprise. "Well, yes... come in."

Juliet waited in horror as Max entered, stamping his feet and wiping them on the rubber doormat. He unbuttoned his black parka and handed it to Anne as he glanced over at Juliet.

He brightened. "Hey, there, Juliet."

Juliet watched him with stunned apprehension. "What are you doing here?"

Max went over, rubbing his hands together. "Cold down here. Aren't we south of New York? Isn't the south supposed to be warmer than the north?"

"This isn't south, Max. It's the Midwest."

Anne hurried over and offered Max a seat on the couch. He declined and remained standing, studying Juliet.

"You look good. Carla said you looked good. I didn't know what to expect. I guess you had a wicked accident."

"I couldn't believe Carla came to see me at the hospital. She made me laugh so much the nurse almost asked her to leave."

"Well, she was our office representative, I guess you might say. We all chipped in for her airfare."

"That was really nice, especially since I'm not even working there anymore." She and Max both looked away. She softened her tone. "I really did appreciate the card and flowers, Max."

He shrugged. "Hey, we were all pretty freaked out, you know?"

"Can I get you something to drink or eat?" Anne asked.

"Oh no, no, thank you, Mrs. Sinclair. I'm not going to stay long. Hey, I'm sorry I didn't call or anything and let you know I was coming."

Juliet narrowed her eyes on him. "So why *are* you here, Max?"

Max nodded, uneasy. He sat on the edge of the couch. Anne sat down too, nervous and curious.

Max leaned forward and folded his hands. "I see you don't have your Christmas tree up yet. Are you going to get one?"

"In a day or so," Anne said.

"How long have you been home, Juliet?" Max asked.

"Since December tenth."

"Feeling good? Feeling strong again?" Max asked, visibly tense.

"I'm feeling good, Max. I'm feeling better than I've felt in years."

He lifted an eyebrow in surprise. "Really? Well, that's cool. I mean, that's really cool. I mean, how many of us can say that, huh? I mean, I feel like shit most of the time."

"So why are you here, Max?"

He sat up and then leaned back into the couch. "Well... I guess you could say I'm here for two reasons. First, I'm here as a kind of representative to let you know that everyone is happy that you're better and out of the hospital." He paused, his eyes sliding about, not finding any place to rest.

"And the second reason?" Juliet asked.

Max leaned forward again, folding his hands again. "Well, I had a meeting with Austen and Ellen a few days ago."

Juliet turned to Anne. "Austen and Ellen Price are the owners of DevelopIT Communications."

Max nodded and continued. "Yeah, and they said to be sure to tell you how glad they are that you're out of the hospital."

"The second reason?" Juliet persisted, enjoying her first-and-only-time power over him.

He looked at her, soberly. "Juliet, you remember about five months ago there was some talk about opening a European office in London?"

"Yes..."

"Well, it's going to happen next year."

Juliet processed it by scratching her cheek. "So business is good," Juliet said.

"Yes and no. I mean, well, there is a real potential to expand, first in London and then to Scandinavia. At least, that's the plan now."

"And you're going to London?" Juliet asked.

He grinned, but there was no mirth in it. "Yes. Actually, I guess I'm being banished. Our numbers are down in New York and they're bringing someone in to replace me. They told me I need a promotion."

Juliet was not surprised. Carla had kept her informed of all the gossip. "Need?"

"It was a nice way to say they're going to give me one more chance and, if I blow it, they're going to kick my ass out into the Hudson River."

Juliet twisted her body around to face him. "Okay, Max, just tell me why you're here."

Max cleared his throat. "I want you to go to London with me."

Carla had not told her this. "London?"

Anne shifted uncomfortably.

Max turned to her, saw her disagreeable expression, and then turned back to Juliet.

Juliet was still with no expression.

"The salary is negotiable, but it'll be generous. The Prices are ready to meet with you whenever you're able, to discuss everything. You won't even have to think about going until February or March of next year."

The room fell into silence. Max twisted his hands. "Juliet... we're a good team. I know we can make it work over there."

Juliet looked at him for a long time. "If I don't go, what happens to you?"

He took a breath. "Let me put it this way. They want us both to go."

"So, if I say no, you lose your job?" Juliet asked.

Max looked away. "I don't know. I was too afraid to ask that question. But let's face it. I'm not so easy to get along with."

"No, you're not, Max. You lost a lot of good people."

He held up a hand to stop her. "Okay, okay, let's not get into that. We both know that the more people get to know me, the more they either hate me or despise me. The point is, I respect you and I think you respect me. I'm good at what I do and you're good at what you do. In short, you and I can get along. The owners know that. I told them that."

"We didn't get along, Max. That's the main reason I quit, remember?"

"Okay, so I'll quit being an asshole and..." He stopped abruptly and looked over at Anne. "I'm sorry, Mrs. Sinclair. Excuse my bad language."

Anne frowned.

He stood. "I'll change, Juliet. And I *can* change, especially with you around to remind me. I already have changed. Look at me; I'm out of New York. When was the last time you saw me out of New York when I wasn't in the Caribbean or L.A.? And I'm not only out of town,

I'm out in the middle of nowhere. Somewhere near Columbus, Ohio! You have to admit, that is a big change. And I left the office early, before 5, to catch the flight down here. The thing is, Juliet, we did good things together."

Juliet stared at him. She could see the muscles of his jaw working as tension worked on his face. His dark eyes were fearful and hopeful.

Juliet was tempted. It would mean a clean break—a new start with new challenges in London, away from everything. Maybe this was just what she needed. Maybe this was her rebirth. The reason she'd come back to life.

Leaving her mother would be difficult, of course, but she'd fly Anne to London and show her the town. They could go on little trips to Paris, Italy and Spain. Anne would love that. She always loved to travel.

"What do you think, Juliet?" Max asked, expectantly.

Juliet noticed her mother was literally sitting on the edge of her seat, her lips pressed tightly together.

"I have to think about it, Max. How much time can you give me?"

Max shrank a little. Even his stiff punked-up hair seemed to wilt. "As much time as you need... well, I mean within reason. How about we say a couple of weeks? Before New Year's. That way, I can get over to London and start making plans."

"Okay, Max. I'll let you know in a couple of weeks."

Max sighed. "Well, that's cool, Juliet. Really cool."

Juliet eyed him carefully. "Max... couldn't you have just called?"

"No. The Prices and I both agreed I should come. It's easy to say no on the phone. We hoped that with my winning, persuasive and bubbly personality you'd like, well, rush to accept the offer."

Juliet looked at him doubtfully. "You are so full of it, Max."

Juliet saw her mother staring sadly down at the floor.

The doorbell rang.

Everyone jerked to attention.

"Now who is that?" Anne asked, getting up.

She went to the door and opened it.

"Paul…"

Juliet heard Paul's deep baritone voice. "I'm sorry to barge in like this. I was just passing by and thought I'd stop in and see how Juliet was feeling."

"Come in, Paul. Come in."

Paul stepped in and wiped his feet on the doormat. "I hope I'm not intruding. I just stopped by for a minute to see how Juliet is."

Juliet felt her face flush with heat. She felt a sudden rush of emotion, repressed disappointment and sudden irritation. Why was he coming now? Right after the accident, her mother said he'd been at the hospital every day to see how she was, and yet, after she got out of the ICU, he'd visited her only that one time. He'd sent a card but hadn't even called since she got home. So why now? A weird sense of obligation?

Juliet quickly rearranged herself on the chair, smoothed out the sweatshirt and struggled to put on a welcoming face.

Max lifted his hands as if to say, "Who's this?"

Juliet ignored him.

Anne and Paul entered the living room, Anne pleased and Paul awkward and uneasy.

Juliet's and Paul's eyes met. Max saw something pass between them. Something electric and thrilling. He could almost reach out and touch the surging current passing between them. Max felt threatened.

Paul saw that Max had a proprietary air toward Juliet, and it puzzled him.

"Oh, by the way, Juliet," Max blurted out. "I didn't tell you what your job title will be. You'll be Director of Sales and Marketing. You'll have a huge expense account and they're even talking about finding an apartment for you. Doesn't that sound cool?"

Juliet ignored him. Her eyes were fixed on Paul's.

CHAPTER 16

Paul and Max sat together on the couch, each looking uncomfortable, like two boys in school waiting for the principal to arrive. Anne was in the kitchen making coffee, while Juliet sat, as her father used to say, like a squirrel perched on the edge of a shaky limb. The conversation veered from the weather to Juliet's recovery, to Christmas shopping and finally to an inane discussion about whether real Christmas trees were better than artificial ones.

Everyone seemed grateful when Anne came in with coffee mugs and cookies.

Juliet wished Max would leave, but, although he despised most social gatherings and was noticeably ill at ease and conversationally annoying, he showed no signs of making an exit. And so, the conversation dribbled on again. Paul said business was booming. Everyone seemed to like the cookies. Max said New York had more tourists than ever before and he couldn't get into any of his favorite restaurants. They were filled with people who were fatter and more stupid than they used to be. Anne rolled her eyes and sighed.

Then there was a long coffee silence until Juliet couldn't take it any longer. She very pointedly asked Max when he was returning to New York.

"Early tomorrow morning," he said. "Six o'clock flight out of Columbus."

"You've had a long day," Juliet said, hoping he'd pick up on the hint.

"No worries, Juliet, I only need four hours' sleep a night." Then Max looked directly at Paul. Juliet was surprised to see a competitive expression.

Max continued. "But then you know that about me, don't you, Juliet? You know me better than almost anybody else does. All those late nights we worked together...well, you get to know a person."

Paul stared ahead into the fireplace.

Juliet bristled. "Max, whenever you and I worked late, we always had a team of at least two others with us."

"Yeah, that's cool, Juliet. I'm just saying that we're a good team. I'm just saying we're cool together."

Paul turned his full attention to Juliet. "You're looking well."

Juliet touched her face self-consciously. "Thank you. Bruises are almost all gone at least."

"Feeling stronger?"

"Yes, every day. Feeling better and stronger every day. And how have you been? I haven't seen you in... what is it? A week? Nine days?" Juliet said, suddenly embarrassed to realize she'd actually been counting the days.

"Well, yes... I..." Paul stammered. "Yes, well, I guess I've been just so busy. I should have come by sooner. But then I thought you probably needed to rest."

Juliet faced him sternly. "Well, a person can only rest so much! Some people think good company helps them recover much faster." She disliked the reprimanding tone in her voice. "So, thanks for coming tonight," she added, hoping to diminish its impact.

Paul nodded, feeling admonished anyway. "Yes... well, yes, that's true. I mean, I guess for some people that is definitely true. Of course, everybody is different."

Anne spoke up. "Paul, you should come to dinner some night."

Max spoke up. "Speaking of dinner. Do you have anything—left-overs or anything? I'm really hungry. I missed dinner. Just had a PowerBar."

Anne hesitated.

Juliet gave her a prodding stare.

Grudgingly, Anne stood. "I may have a little something."

Delighted, Max stood. "Good. I was wondering what people in Ohio eat."

Anne lowered her head, her eyes two irritated slits.

Paul stood. "I should go. I need to get home to my daughter."

Juliet sank a little. She threw off the blanket, released the recliner latch, and sat up.

"I'll walk you to the door."

Max stood. "Can I help you, Juliet?"

"No, Max. I can walk."

Max sulked. He watched Paul and Juliet start for the front door. He finally turned and followed Anne into the kitchen.

At the door, in the dim light, Paul faced Juliet. "I'm glad you're feeling better."

"I'm glad you came by."

He looked down. "I should have come sooner. I thought about it."

Juliet didn't want to reveal her disappointment again. "You already saved my life... you don't owe me anything."

Paul straightened, taking in a breath. "I'm not quite sure about that."

They let his words hang in the air.

"Do you have any plans for Christmas?" Paul asked.

"Not really. But I'm ready to get outside and have some fun. Maybe some of my high school friends will come home and they'll have a Christmas party."

"I'm always so busy, I never think about parties much."

"But at this time of year they can be so special, and fun."

"Yeah, maybe."

The moment lengthened. Juliet heard her mother ask Max something, but she couldn't make it out.

"Mom said your little girl is five years old," Juliet said.

"Yes. She's a real handful."

"I hope I can meet her someday."

"Yes. You two should meet. She's a lot of fun."

"What's her name?"

"Amy."

Juliet looked into Paul's handsome, timid face. It was a strong but kind face. In many ways, he looked like a soldier, muscular and fit. But there was also a quality of gentleness about him that was appealing and didn't quite fit the warrior type. She sensed a strongly loyal and sensitive man who didn't open up easily.

"Thank you again for being at the right place at the right time, and for having the training to get me breathing again."

Paul averted her eyes. "Oh, well, I think you would have probably been okay."

"No, Paul. We all know you saved my life. Dr. Bowers said if you hadn't been there, I would have died."

Juliet again noted a shy softness in Paul's eyes.

"I've had a lot of time to think about what happened to me that night," Juliet said. "Some time I'd like to share it with you. I want to tell you everything that happened."

Despite his attempts to stay aloof, Paul could feel himself become entranced by her. Exalted by her. "I'd like that," he said softly. "I'd like us to get to know each other."

Juliet's gaze slid warily over his tall, impressive frame. "I already know something very important about you."

"Oh... really?" Paul asked nervously.

"I know you make a great cappuccino."

He grinned and his shoulders relaxed. "Oh, well. Stop by anytime and I'll make you another, on the house."

Juliet shifted her weight from her left foot to her right. "I know you have to go, but I wanted to ask you something."

"Sure, anything."

"Did you know my father well?"

Paul paused a minute, thinking through the question. "Yes, I did. He was a good friend—a close friend. I know he loved you very much."

Juliet considered Paul's answer, but she didn't speak.

JULIET WAITED FOR PAUL'S car to disappear into the distance before she closed the door. She stood staring at nothing, hearing the distant murmur of her mother's and Max's voices coming from the kitchen.

Paul knew her father well. He said they were good friends. And she suspected that Paul had actually been following her the night of the accident. Sheriff Hansel had said as much when he visited her in the hospital, and she asked him what Paul had reported.

At first, Sheriff Hansel seemed evasive. "Well, somebody had to be behind you, Juliet."

Juliet had looked at him doubtfully.

"Okay, well, he told me he was worried about you. He said you'd been at The Coffee Mug, and you were crying. Paul said he just had the impulse to follow you to make sure you got home safe. That's all."

JULIET LOOKED DOWN AT HER unpolished nails. Did Paul know Cindy Evans? Did Paul know about Rad and Cindy?

Juliet shook her head as if to clear her brain. Why was she so suspicious and mistrustful of everyone?

Because of Evan's cheating? Because of her father's possible infidelity? She glanced toward the kitchen. London and the new job were sounding better all the time.

Max left a half an hour later, his nervous, eager eyes struggling to read Juliet's every word and expression. At the front door, he paused.

"Juliet... did I tell you that you'd be the boss? You'd be in charge of the whole rodeo over there. You'd hire the employees and deal with clients."

"What? What about you?"

"I'd be head of IT. And that's all. The Prices want you to be the front person."

"Are you sure about that? Why didn't they talk to me themselves?"

"They're in Australia. They said they'd call you in a few days, after I put the idea in your head. Give you time to think about it."

Juliet was stunned. "How does that make you feel, Max?"

He shrugged his right shoulder. "You've always been fair with me. Okay, maybe you're a little bitchy sometimes, but what woman isn't."

Juliet's mouth was open, and she was ready to attack, but he threw up a hand before she could respond. "I didn't mean it that way. Guys can be assholes, too."

"Oh, really?" Juliet said with a jerk of her head. "You think so?"

He softened his voice. "Juliet, every client we have likes and respects you. Our colleagues like you. What I mean is, I'm fine with you being the boss over there. In many ways, it will be a relief for me not to have to listen to everybody's bullshit all the time. I'm not good at that. That's not my strength. My strength is numbers, systems and IT. I think we can make the London thing work. I think it might even be fun."

Juliet folded her arms. "You are a real piece of work, Max West."

He grinned. "I won't deny it, fair Juliet. I'm a piece of work that most people would love to work-over or run over."

AFTER MAX FINALLY MADE HIS EXIT, Anne switched on the TV. Juliet studied her for a few minutes.

"Mom," Juliet said. "Let's talk." Anne turned off the TV, feeling the power of her daughter's gaze.

"What are you thinking?" Anne asked. "You look like you're trying to bore a hole in me."

Juliet remained silent.

"Are you thinking about London? The new job?"

"...Yes."

"It's a good opportunity," Anne said, but there was no life in her voice. It sounded flat and mechanical.

"...Yes."

Anne took off her sweater and placed it beside her. "Paul likes you, you know. It's easy to see that."

"...Yes," Juliet said absently, her eyes unfocused, her mind lost in thought.

"Do you like him?"

"...Yes."

"Rad always spoke highly of him."

"...Yes."

Anne grew annoyed. "Juliet, you're not listening to me. What on earth are you thinking about?"

Juliet blinked away her thoughts and took a breath to gather courage. "Mother... did you know if Dad was seeing other women?"

Anne grew defensively quiet. The two women stared eye to eye as the hall clock ticked and the fire crackled. "... *If* he was seeing other women?"

"Okay. Was he seeing other women?"

Anne seemed to contract into herself. "Juliet, some things parents don't discuss with their children."

"I'm not a kid, Mother."

"All right, some things a mother doesn't *want* to discuss with her daughter."

"Even if four-hundred thousand dollars are involved?"

Anne turned her head aside. "I don't know what was going on. Something changed Rad about a year ago. I told you that."

"Did you ever ask Dad? Confront him?"

Anne faced her. "I heard rumors of another woman. One day, I overheard a professor say something to another teacher, just as I entered the teacher's lounge. When they saw me, they dropped it and got quiet. The truth was, I didn't want to know. Call me an old, unliberated, silly, foolish woman, but that's the truth. If Rad was seeing someone else or more than someone else, then I didn't want to know about it, okay!? I knew he loved me. I loved him. We had thirty years of love and trust and memories so good and true that nothing—and I mean nothing—could ever take that away. If, for whatever reason, he found some other woman interesting..."

Anne's voice started to break. Tears formed in her eyes. "If that's what he had to do..." She stopped, lowering her head. She reached for a tissue and gently wiped her eyes. "Juliet, I know you're angry about your marriage to Evan."

Juliet jumped in. "It's not just..."

Anne cut her off. "Let me finish. Did the rumors hurt? Yes. Did I ask Rad about the rumors? Yes."

"What did he say?" Juliet said, gently.

Anne lifted her head, mustering some pride. "He said he loved me. He said he was going through a very difficult time in his life. He said he'd tell me all about it someday. Well, that someday never came because... well... So now he's out there scattered all over that pond. So, that's how life goes sometimes."

Silence gathered about them, leaving them in private, pulsing emotion. Neither could find any further words.

CHAPTER 17

Three days later, on December 18, Juliet was seated at the kitchen table, still in her blue cotton pajamas, eating a sandwich, reading about London on her laptop. The phone rang. She picked it up and mumbled hello, imagining herself talking on her cellphone while walking along the River Thames.

"Hi, Juliet. It's Paul. How are you today?"

Juliet sat up, alert. "Great! I'm feeling good. How are you?"

"Okay, okay... Listen, I know it's late, but I was wondering, do you feel up to going out for dinner tonight?" he asked.

The therapeutic effect of his deep voice surprised her. "Yes. I do feel up to it. Sounds like fun. What time?"

"I can come by at, say, seven o'clock. How's that?"

She glanced at the clock. It was 2:30. "Sure, good."

By three o'clock, Juliet was in a whirlwind of activity. She was wrapped in a peach robe, her hair turbaned in a towel. She was painting her nails red, trying to come up with an outfit, shoes, and earrings, all the while receiving and answering texts from her former colleagues about the London job.

"Are you going to do it?" one text asked.
"Can I go with you?" Carla wrote.
"New birth, new life," another wrote.

Juliet answered, *"Still thinking. Big move. Still need to finish some things here."*

At 6:30, Anne arrived home from an afternoon spent with friends. Juliet gave her a quick fashion show near their newly decorated Christmas tree, posing first in a pale green-gray dress, next in a zinfandel-colored long sleeve off-the-shoulder tunic top with leggings, and finally in a bronze satin top with a plunging neckline, black woolen slacks and black two-inch heels.

Anne placed a finger to her lip while she appraised each outfit. "You're going to be too cold in that satin top. It's thirty degrees out there."

"I feel good in it, though," Juliet said.

"I like the gold-hoop earrings. I'd go with the long-sleeved top," Anne said. "The color looks good on you. Keep the heels. Change the lipstick. Too red for that outfit, and you've got way too much eye shadow on."

Juliet mumbled something and headed off to the bathroom.

PAUL WAS ON TIME. When Juliet opened the door, her soft radiance, her long lustrous hair, her full mouth, her fetching smile gently startled him. She was regally tall in her heels and dreamy in her eyes. Perhaps he was projecting the dreaminess, feeling caught in a kind of vivid dreamy spell himself. Juliet was simply captivating.

Later, in the car, the spring scent of her was alluring and distracting. He searched for conversation, but nothing came. He realized he hadn't been out on a date, except with Tracy, in over six years. After her death, he'd felt dead inside and, even though women had made overtures, he'd never followed up. He wasn't interested. But Juliet was different. Once again, he felt as though he was waking from a long sleep.

They drove in a gathering anticipation, each stealing glances at the other, as if to gauge the mood or spot approval—searching for a foothold to begin the journey of the relationship. Paul scanned subjects he could communicate comfortably. Sports? No. How his business was going? No. American History? Definitely, no. He doubted very much if Juliet would be interested in hearing about his Marine Corps thesis on *The Schlieffen Plan,* an overall strategic plan for victory in a possible future war in which the German Empire might find itself fighting on two fronts. It was a good thesis, but...

"Stop it!" he thought. His emotions and feelings were so conflicted and tangled that he didn't feel like himself. In Juliet's company, he did not know himself.

"Where are we going for dinner?" Juliet finally asked.

Paul adjusted the rearview mirror. "I'm taking you to a place I'm sure you've never heard of."

"Okay. Sounds like an adventure. I like new adventures. What's the name?"

"I'm not sure it has a name yet. Well, I mean, it has several names but there's been no final decision yet. It's a kind of work in progress."

Juliet's eyes widened with interest. "Really? Well, this really does sound like an adventure. A restaurant with no name. That means no website. No Facebook. No Twitter. Hard to get the word out without a name. Tough for the PR guys. What's the menu like?"

"Very limited. Mostly comfort food."

"This is very mysterious, Paul. You've got my attention. This could be a great way to promote the restaurant. Keep it so mysterious and inaccessible that people can only hear about it through word-of-mouth. That could create buzz. They'll love it of course, and then they'll spread the word, all the time hoping that the word won't get out and spoil it for them. In short, the place will take off like a rocket. What a mysterious and wonderful idea! Who owns the restaurant?"

Paul glanced over. "I do."

Juliet studied him. "Well, now you really *do* have my attention."

Paul drove into the asphalt parking lot and stopped near the restaurant's front entrance. Juliet viewed the building. It was a square, red-bricked structure, with a large picture window and a peaked roof. The lights were on inside. A car was parked nearby. Paul pointed to the tan cloth awning over the entrance and the wooden panel above it. "We just had the wood-stained brown. We'll put the name on it once we've decided. Of course, your father helped me with the initial designs and then put me in touch with an architect who specializes in restaurants."

Juliet's eyes wandered, as if trying to understand something. "Was this my father's idea?"

"No, but I shared it with him. He looked the place over with me and thought it was a good idea."

"Looks like a little country schoolhouse. Very quaint and cozy."

They left the car, walking to the front entrance in a brisk, cold wind. Inside, Paul shut the door behind them, and Juliet took in an open room with glossy wood floors and soft track lighting. She noticed a stone double-sided fireplace, a bar under construction, a partially installed banquette, stacked tables and chairs, and a kitchen counter, with a milk paint finish and zinc top.

"It's very cozy with the fireplace," Juliet said. "And I like the little bar with the marble top and wicker stools. Very nice."

"Your father's idea," Paul said. "The fireplace is not functional yet, but it will be once everything is finished."

"When did you start all this?"

"The end of August, first of September."

"You've come a long way."

Paul placed his hands on his hips. "Yeah, not bad. Still a lot to do."

"How many diners will it seat?" Juliet asked.

Paul unzipped his brown leather jacket and stepped further into the room, gesturing nervously, anxious to see excitement on Juliet's face. "Well, it's about three thousand square feet, so we figure it will seat about ninety or a hundred people comfortably."

Juliet walked about exploring, feeling nostalgic, thinking of her father and how he loved to inspect a room, probing for possibility, letting his creativity run free.

"We were able to use some of the existing kitchen equipment, so that saved time and money. We already have our liquor license, and we passed the fire code inspections. The tables were built by a local carpenter. Oh, and the armoire I bought at an auction. I liked the look. We're going to use it to store things."

"When do you plan to open to the public?"

"Sometime in January. Obviously, we're behind."

Juliet lifted her nose, smelling a heavenly aroma. "What smells so good?"

"That's our dinner," Paul said, hoping she wouldn't frown.

She brightened. "Really! Are we having the first dinner at the No Name Restaurant?"

He smiled. "Yes."

"I'm honored. Are you the chef?"

"No. I'm afraid I'm not much of a cook, although I'm trying to learn, and I want to learn. But I did hire someone you know to be our chef tonight."

Juliet turned to see Karen Tiggs standing at the edge of the kitchen, clutching a bottle of champagne, her jeans and sweater covered with a big, white apron, her hair tied back.

"Cheers, girl! Welcome, Juliet."

Juliet lit up. "Karen!"

She hurried over and embraced her friend. "You're the chef?"

They stood at arm's length. Karen frowned. "No, I'm the cook, and right now, I'm behind. The mashed potatoes aren't ready, and the meatloaf and gravy need more time."

"Do you need help?" Juliet asked.

"Oh, no, no. This is a date. No way. You go drink champagne and have fun."

Juliet turned to Paul. "You don't mind if I help Karen, do you, Paul? Karen and I used to cook at the church when we had potluck suppers."

Paul crossed his arms, looking amused. "No, I don't mind. Maybe I can help too."

"No way," Karen said. "You hired me to cook this special dinner for you two and I'm going to finish it."

Juliet looked pleadingly at Karen. "Might be fun, Karen, if all three of us—too many cooks in the kitchen—jump in and mess everything up. It will be like in the old days when we burned the chicken, over-cooked the vegetables and put too much salt in the mashed potatoes."

Karen laughed. "Yeah, and then everybody always said how good the food was, even though they pulled the skin off the chicken and pushed the mashed potatoes off to the corner of their plate."

"So let me help, Karen. We can screw this dinner up too, just like we did in the old days."

"Oh, why not. Come on."

Paul's voice stopped them. "Wait. First let's have a toast."

Paul took the champagne. He peeled back the foil, released the wire mesh and twisted. The ladies grimaced and turned away as the cork popped. The gals applauded, and Paul found three flutes and poured.

"Let's toast to the No Name Restaurant," Juliet said. "May it feed thousands of hungry people, may they be happy and come back for more, and may the No Name be profitable and fun!"

They clinked glasses, sipped, and went to work. Karen poked and prodded the meatloaf and stirred the thick brown gravy, while Juliet drained the cooked potatoes. She added cream, melted butter, and salt and pepper and then reached for the new stainless-steel masher. As she worked, the heels pinched her right big toe, and her left little toe. She took turns lifting first her right foot and then her left, shaking them while taking sips of champagne.

Paul drained the peas and pearl onions, found a brown ceramic bowl, and poured them in. He watched Juliet as she worked, noticing her foot action and her assiduous application of the potato masher. He smiled down and away from her, greatly amused.

"Add butter to the peas and onions, Paul," Karen said. "Lots of butter. Oh, and salt, too. I forgot."

Paul obeyed. Next, he took a loaf of freshly baked bread he'd brought from The Coffee Mug and sliced it.

Twenty minutes later, the three were seated around a deep and padded booth that Paul had kept from the previous restaurant owners. They toasted once more in candlelight, as Nat King Cole sang *The Christmas Song* from Paul's docked iPod.

"In case you haven't noticed by now," Paul said to Juliet, "this restaurant is going to be all about families and comfort food. Mac and cheese, burgers, fried chicken, meat loaf and spaghetti and meatballs."

Juliet tasted and swallowed. "I love this meatloaf. Whose recipe is it?"

Karen stabbed at the mashed potatoes, bringing a mound of it up to her anxious mouth. "My grandmother Pike. She worked in a restaurant in Chicago during the

1950s and said she got it from some famous chef who had a thing for her."

"I love it," Juliet said. "And the gravy. Paul, where are you getting the other recipes from?"

Paul took a sip of champagne. "We're still working on that. I've been asking some friends and, of course, searching on the internet."

Juliet stopped eating and grew quiet, seized by an idea.

Paul looked at Karen quizzically, who looked back at him.

"Everything okay?" Paul asked.

Juliet reached for her glass of champagne and held it close to her lips. She stared into it, as if it held some deep secret.

"Paul... what if you asked your customers at The Coffee Mug to bring in their favorite comfort food recipes? They're going to be your first and best contact list. They already know and like you, and believe in you."

Paul watched her with interest, waiting for more. Karen, too, straightened with curiosity.

Juliet continued. "You could gather up all the entries and use *them* as your recipes."

"All of them?" Paul asked.

"Well, most of them. You don't want to hurt anyone's feelings, but you may have to use some discretion if they're really bad. Anyway, you could feature a recipe for, let's say, a month at a time, and then feature a different recipe the next month. You could send out an email when a person's recipe is going to be featured on the menu. You could even print their name on the menu under the item—or call the entrée something like *Mary Smith's Mac and Cheese* or *Tony Coppola's Spaghetti and Meatballs*."

Paul canted his head, considering the possibilities.

"I like it," Karen said. "I really like it. They'd bring their families and friends. They'd contact their friends on email and *Facebook*!"

Juliet sipped and thought. "It's a great way to get free marketing. You could do a whole Facebook thing with pictures and links and maybe even do a blog. Call it *Paul and the Family,* something like that. You have to come up with a name for the restaurant soon, so we can spin the blog off. Do you have a Facebook page for The Coffee Mug?"

"Yes," Paul said. "I hired a high school kid to keep it up for me."

"Good. We can start getting the word out there and on Twitter. The rest we can do by word of mouth at The Coffee Mug."

Paul leaned back, wiping his lips with his napkin. "You don't waste any time, do you?"

Juliet continued on. "I do this kind of thing for a living. At least, I used to. Anyway, you have to contact your attorney to draw up some kind of release form, just in case somebody decides they want a cut of the profits from their recipe. But that's easy. Most people would sign the release and really get into it. Have you started your publicity yet?"

"Some," Paul said. "Still trying to hammer in the restaurant's name."

Juliet snapped her fingers. "Ask your customers," Juliet said. "Put it out on Facebook. Hold a contest. The person whose restaurant name you choose gets a free dinner for the whole family. Something like that."

Paul pursed his lips in thought. "That might work."

"Yes. It would definitely work. No doubt."

Juliet placed the champagne flute down, her brain working, her eyes shifting from side to side. "You have to take advantage of Christmas. Got to. Speaking of potluck suppers. Send out an email to friends and family and invite them to a potluck dinner at your restaurant on Christmas Eve."

"Christmas Eve?" Paul asked.

"People want to be with family on Christmas Eve," Karen said.

"Some yes. But others would love to do something different. They'd love to bring their families and join in. Some could come before church. Some after. It's all in how you present it. During the event, you get somebody to take a bunch of photos so you can post them on Facebook and your blog. Use *them* when you're ready to open to the public in January. It's free advertising and it gets the entire neighborhood involved. It's another fantastic way to get the word out that the restaurant is about to open."

Paul stared at her attentively. "That's another good idea."

Karen drained her glass of champagne. "Juliet, you're a genius."

AFTER DINNER, KAREN presented a chocolate layer cake with fudge icing. Juliet poured coffee. They pounced on the cake, eating, laughing, and falling into an easy playful mood.

Paul surreptitiously studied Juliet any chance he had—her slender fingers, her lively eyes, and her shining auburn hair. Even her slightest glance at him revived the desire he'd thought was dead and buried. Her face was lovely in the flare of candlelight. This was Rad's daughter, all right. She had the same impulse of creative ideas; the same contagious enthusiasm. She was wonderful.

Paul suddenly liked himself more, just being in her company. It was an odd thought, he knew, but that's what he felt. His mind, nearly always spinning and muddled, was settled and relaxed. He felt a natural impulse to smile and laugh. He felt thankful for the moment, just as it was. He didn't want to check his phone for messages or think about the restaurant opening or The Coffee Mug, and whether Linda and her brother, Biff, were handling the customers and the closing. He didn't want to examine the past, the guilt, the uncertainty of life. Not tonight. Tonight, he wanted to be happy in Juliet's company, and he was.

At one point, he thought of Tracy, and he missed her—but he missed her in a new way, an unfamiliar way. He would explore all that unresolved feeling later, but not tonight. Tonight, he would simply enjoy being in the presence of this lively, beautiful woman, whose aura and fresh magic might force him to take a fresh look at his life. He might have to reinvent himself, and maybe it *was* time for a radical change.

As he watched Juliet, so alive with ideas, he felt high and silly. He felt again that when he'd saved her from death, he had somehow saved himself too. Of course, he would never share these feelings with anyone. They were too deeply held and private.

What would his old Marine buddies think of him and his thoughts? Maybe they'd laugh and mock him. On the other hand, maybe they'd understand. Some would, anyway. Hadn't combat changed them all? Didn't fear, death and loss confuse things and break things down to the bare essentials? Didn't they rattle around in the gut, causing constant pain and disorder? Weren't most of his buddies looking for ways to cope and heal? To put themselves right again? To find peace?

Juliet was opening doors to inner, undiscovered rooms. Was he courageous enough to walk into them and explore? Would Tracy be in those rooms, too, waiting to judge him? To blame him? To hate him?

CHAPTER 18

Cindy Evans was only twenty miles from Fairpoint, Ohio, when she began to have second thoughts. Could she face Rad's wife and daughter? She'd wrestled with herself for days, swinging back and forth like a pendulum, first wanting to get the truth out and then, conversely, wanting to keep it to herself, forever. Was it really anybody's business? If Rad didn't talk about it, why should she?

But Cindy knew why Rad had been silent. He had his reasons. Rad always had good reason for his actions.

The sun was setting, and to Cindy it looked tragic: blood red, orange and violet. Stringy purple clouds gathered on the edge of the horizon and a flock of ducks drifted across her field of vision. She wondered where they were going, and how fortunate they were to be together, working as a team. But then, she didn't want to think about her workplace and all those issues, both past and present.

As the ducks disappeared over a bank of trees, Cindy grew lonely. It had already been a cold, snowy winter, and she longed for warmth and blue skies. She'd been born and raised in central Florida and during these Ohio winters, she could never manage to shake the chill from her bones, even if she dressed in layers and had a cup of hot coffee in her hand. She was a sunshine girl. That's one of the names Rad had called her.

"You are a sunshine girl. That's what you are and what you'll always be, Cindy Cinderella."

That was the other name he'd called her. God, how she loved it when he called her Cindy Cinderella. The memory of it brought sudden, unwanted tears. She'd never known a man so playful, smart and supportive as Conrad Sinclair had been. That's why he had so many friends. That's why every woman who ever met him fell in love with him, in one way or the other. Rad also had the inspirational gift of creating lasting friendships with boyfriends, fathers and husbands, so that no one hated him or was jealous of him. Rad Sinclair was simply a magnetic marvel.

Cindy had never known a man so filled with a burning love for life, with all its tragedies and comedies. She'd never known a man whose laughter inspired, healed and brought such a contagious desire to celebrate.

"You think too much, Cindy Cinderella," he once told her. "A good laugh is much better than a brilliant thought."

WHEN CINDY SAW THE SIGN, Fairpoint, Ohio 10 Miles, she edged into the left lane and slowed down. She felt the rise of anxiety. Could she go through with it?

Cindy Cinderella. The memory of Rad's voice and intonation pricked her heart yet again.

Rad knew her story—her entire life story. When she'd talked to him that first night, it had spilled out of her like a gushing fountain at one of those extravagant Las Vegas hotels. Rad the father confessor. Rad who didn't judge. It had been so easy to talk to him. He listened—didn't say a word—just listened.

She'd been born into a poor family. Her father, "Big Donny," was an abusive alcoholic and her mother a weepy victim, who never passed up the opportunity to tell her two children how awful life was and how God just loved to punish her. But then, in all fairness to the woman, her life had been a living hell.

"Men are such selfish bastards!" her mother raged, after Big Donny had once again beat her and once again taken all the money she'd earned working as a chamber maid and a waitress. Before he stormed out of the house, he'd threaten Cindy and her brother with a belt-beating, driving them cowering into a corner. He towered over them, like some mad monster, showing broken, dirty teeth. And then he was gone, and they never knew when he'd reappear, drunk, angry and demanding her mother's money.

Finally, her mother had had enough. On one hot summer day, they all packed their things and fled to their grandmother's home in Jacksonville.

It only took two months for Big Donny to find them. When he tried to get into the house, Granny Fields lowered her shotgun on him. "You get your big ugly carcass off my porch. Now!"

Big Donny backed away, descending the porch steps, his wary eyes moving, his expression dark. He watched

Granny Fields exit the house to the porch, shotgun raised and pointed at him.

"Now what's a little ole woman like you gonna do with that big old gun, Granny Fields? You know, you ain't gonna shoot me."

Granny had been a small woman with poor eyesight. She fired both barrels. The recoil slammed her back against the front door. She bounced off, recovered, and reached for more shells.

It was not a perfect shot, but it was effective. The impact blew Big Donny backwards. He slammed down hard onto the coarse grass, the wind bursting from his lungs. Stunned and wounded, he stared bug-eyed up into the spinning sky, trying to recover reality. He squirmed and sat up, face slick with dirt, sweat and blood. He refocused his blurry eyes. To his horror, he saw Granny reloading, shoving the shells into the chamber with a grim determination. Now firmly convinced of Granny Field's murderous intent, he pushed to his feet and hobbled off on all fours, like a whipped dog looking for a hideout.

"I'll blow your damn head off, you no-good son of a bitch!" Granny yelled.

With a straining effort, Big Donny managed an unsteady trot, glancing back over his shoulder to see Granny's double barrels staring back at him like death itself. He hurried on, whining and mumbling.

Granny Fields stood resolute, like an old soldier, until Big Donny limped off around the corner and was gone.

Cindy never saw her father again.

When she was eighteen, she met an older man. He was thirty. He told her she was beautiful, and he loved her. He was wealthy. He said he'd take care of her for the rest of her life. Cindy's mother was old and beaten beyond her years. She spent most of her days drinking whiskey and watching television.

"Go with him, Cindy. He's got money. It don't matter whether you love him or not. He's got money and with money you'll be Cinderella."

Cindy laughed, harshly. "You'll be Cinderella," she repeated sarcastically.

Fairpoint, Ohio was just ahead. From the GPS on her dashboard, Cindy knew that Rad's house was about seven miles away. She turned left onto Pine Ridge Road, switched on her headlights, and meandered along a quiet two-lane road, past a DEER CROSSING sign, tall birch trees and a distant A-frame house.

CINDY WENT WITH THE WEALTHY Hal Lansky to live in a palatial beach house in Tampa, Florida. For three years she bought anything she wanted, ate at the best restaurants and drank herself to sleep with champagne or vodka martinis. They traveled to Europe and the Far East. They spent summers in Maine and winters in Florida. She sent money to her mother and brother and did whatever she pleased, as long as she was there for Hal when he returned from wherever he'd been.

"Business calls, Cindy," was all he'd say as he jetted away to the next somewhere.

Hal did not want children, so she didn't get pregnant.

"Life's too short to have those dirty little aliens running around the house screaming and breaking things," he said. "They're cute for about three minutes and then they're nothing but a pain in the ass for the rest of your life."

The relationship ended one day in June. Hal was away, and when he returned, Cindy planned to ask him if they could get married.

Instead, Hal sent her a fax.

I'm gone to Paris. Won't be back for months. There's $50,000 in your bank account. Had a great time, Cindy, but let's move on now. Gonna level, because you know I always level, baby. I've got another cute baby gonna move in with me when I get back. What a ball it's been!
Love, Hal

When she was twenty-two, she met another man. They were together for two years. Then there was another and another, until she woke up one day and she was thirty years old, finding gray hair and wrinkles around her mouth and crow's feet forming around her now sad eyes. Sad eyes that reminded her of her mother's sad eyes. How she hated that! She'd vowed never to live, think or look like her mother, who'd died in a nursing home, alone, babbling on about some damn TV show.

Cindy knew many men, mostly rich and powerful men. She changed her make-up and dyed her hair and let everyone know she was still attractive. She met Carl T. Hazard, who took her into his south Florida real estate company and patiently taught her all aspects of the business. She received her license, obtained some good leads, and was on her way.

A few months later, she was pregnant. She and Carl T had become lovers, even though she didn't love him, and he knew it.

"You will grow to love me, Cindy, I guarantee it," he'd said, slapping his knee and grinning. "Everybody loves Carl T after they get to know me. They just can't help themselves."

They were married two months later. Cindy was thirty-three years old.

When her son, Kevin, was born, Cindy loved for the first time. Kevin opened her heart. He captivated her, warmed her, exalted her. She and Carl T were blissfully happy, lavishing gifts and love and dreams onto Kevin.

"Thank God he looks like you, Cindy," Carl T said. "He's a damn good-looking kid. He's gonna be a woman killer. Just a heart-breakin' woman killer."

Carl T drank heavily. Cindy ignored it for a while. But when Carl T's business fell off, he was drunk nearly all the time. After an auto accident, she confronted him.

"You've got to stop drinking, Carl T. You're going to kill yourself or somebody else."

Carl T thought about it for a minute and said, "It's all I've got left, Cindy. I can't get up in the morning and face it anymore. I've got to have help. I have to have the booze."

Cindy remembered her father. She grew to hate Carl T and his weakness.

One morning, she took Kevin and left Carl T. She walked out on him. Three weeks later, he shot himself in the head. He was dead by the time they got him to the hospital.

WHEN SHE WAS THIRTY-FIVE, a former Florida colleague offered her a job in Ohio. Cindy, confused, grieving, and scared, jumped at the offer.

Now, at fifty-two years old, she was still living in Ohio. She'd wanted to remarry for Kevin, but she'd never found the right man. The truth was, she was just too weary of it all. She loved her independence and was sick of men.

And then she woke up one morning and Kevin was about to attend Princeton University. He was smart and committed. He wanted to major in political science and go to law school and do some good in the world. She thought, "God, where did he get that from? Certainly not from me."

The tuition was fifty-five thousand dollars a year.

Rad Sinclair had listened to her entire story without once speaking or commenting.

His calm presence gave her the courage to continue. She told him her secret—a secret she'd held inside for months. A secret that had been discovered and was threatening to destroy her and Kevin's life.

As she revealed the entire awful story, Cindy recalled every detail of Rad's strong face. She recalled his tender, understanding eyes. She remembered when he'd reached out and touched her hand. She'd trembled.

"Don't worry, Cindy, everything is going to be just fine."

She believed him. She fell in love with him. It was a love that washed over her in waves of trust, joy, and liberation. It was a love she'd prayed for and never believed was possible. It was a perfect love. Her love for Kevin had opened her heart and allowed her to love a man for the first time. Her love for Rad stunned and astounded her.

Cindy approached the Sinclair house. Trees extended down both sides of the road and then ended near the sprawling ranch style home that loomed just ahead. She felt the steady drum of her heart in her ears. Her throat tightened. Her chest constricted. Could she do this? She'd promised herself to come before Christmas. She wanted to begin the New Year fresh, without regret and persistent heartache. Christmas was the time for forgiveness. It was time to tell the truth and then move on.

But the house was dark. There were no lights, no cars, no signs of life. Cindy felt disappointment and relief. She pulled off to the side of the road, waiting, thinking, calculating. Reaching over to open the glove compartment, she noticed the tall fir tree Rad had talked about.

"We decorate it every Christmas. The thing is over twenty feet high. I almost broke my neck once putting the angel on top."

Cindy smiled at the thought as she opened the glove compartment and took out the white envelope.

She took a deep breath and shut her eyes. She'd wait. She'd wait for a while. She'd wait and remember that once in her troubled and disappointing life, she'd been in love. Truly in love. And this is where Rad had lived.

CHAPTER 19

Anne Sinclair roamed the mall, making a Herculean effort to Christmas shop, but she was just walking in circles. Nothing interested or excited her. Her mind wandered along with her tired feet. She heard Christmas carols from ubiquitous unseen speakers above, noticed Christmas lights and decorations, and pushed herself on, like a weary pilgrim seeking some remote holy relic.

The truth was, she didn't like shopping alone. Juliet was on her first date with Paul, and she was happy about that, but Anne didn't want to be alone in that big empty, echoing house, staring into the smoldering fireplace, as memory and mystery haunted her.

The greater truth was, Anne felt lonely and misplaced. Though she'd spent the afternoon with friends and was grateful to have their companionship, they could never fill the void. Rad was gone. He'd just disappeared—there one minute and vanished the next. What an odd thing, she thought. What a strange and odd thing to find herself so utterly alone. And she'd be even more alone when Juliet left for London. That thought nearly paralyzed her. So, Anne trudged on, hoping to fatigue herself sufficiently so she could return home and fall asleep without taking another sleeping pill.

Unlike most men, Rad loved Christmas shopping. He bounced around all over the mall, pointing, shouting and buying. He was enthusiastic to the point of annoyance, and he spent way too much money. He was carelessly extravagant and always had been. It was this thought that inevitably altered the trajectory of Anne's thinking. As much as she'd tried to muscle the damn thoughts away, they boomeranged out and then came predictably back. What had Rad done with those four hundred thousand dollars? Why had he not discussed it with her? Why had he done it?

Anne walked aimlessly, trapped by her bullying thoughts and volatile emotions. She was angry at him—furious at him! He'd died and left her alone, confused and lost. Everybody loved him. Everybody talked about how great he was. Rad was this. Rad was that. How nice he was. How good he was. How kind he was. Did they know how much money he'd spent on stupid, frivolous things? How much he'd spent on that damn house? Money she now needed for her retirement?! Did they know how much he'd spent on cars and the latest phones and laptops and tablets and things she didn't even understand? Did people know how many nights he'd spent away from home, often forgetting to call to let her know where he was?

Did people know how distracted he could be? Did they know that because of his distracted preoccupation with fishing on that awful Sunday morning so many years ago, he'd let their only son, Jimmy, drown? Did they know that? Could she ever forgive him for that? Had she forgiven him for that? Isn't that what nearly drove her mad and nearly led to their divorce?

Anne sagged under the weight of memory, guilt and anger. She drooped under the burden of love. Yes love. She loved Rad more than she loved her own life. She loved him and she missed his great big loudmouth and good heart. She ached for him.

Anne felt faint, so she searched for some place to sit. Her feet hurt; her legs were stiff and sore. A fast-food restaurant was close by and she wandered in, ordered a coffee and a hamburger and sat in the back, in a yellow plastic chair. She unwrapped the burger and ate absently. She chewed, staring down into the table, feeling loneliness seep into her body like a malevolent virus.

Shoppers came and went with bloated shopping bags and dancing children. A mall Santa wandered by, ringing a bell, seeking donations for the needy. Couples roamed, arm in arm, poised in love. One young couple sat hovering in a corner, kissing and whispering. Abruptly, they separated to stare intently into the glow of their cellphones, as if *real* love lay panting for them there.

Anne decided, what the hell, she'd check her phone too. Maybe Carolyn had texted or emailed her. Maybe Juliet had texted, letting her know how her date with Paul was going. Anne connected and was notified of a new text message. An unknown sender. She stopped chewing and tapped the link. It opened and she read.

Dear Anne:
It's a voice from the past. I found your phone number from your husband's obituary. I hope you're not upset that I'm contacting you. It's been a long time.

Flabbergasted, she read on. It was from Marshall Gray.

OUTSIDE, IN THE SHOPPING center walkway, Cindy Evans strolled by, passing the fast-food restaurant where Anne sat, rapt, reading the text she'd just received. Cindy had left the Sinclair house fifteen minutes before dropping the envelope under the front door. Her courage had failed her after thirty minutes of fretful waiting, when neither Anne nor Juliet had appeared.

The car had grown cold, and she was taunted by doubt and fear. In the final analysis, although tired of her secrets, Cindy still wasn't ready to bare her soul to people she didn't know, to rise up to face truth and honesty. Not yet. So, she crept to the front porch like a petty thief and slid the envelope under the door. She hurried away with a pounding heart and piled back into her car. She drove away, feeling blunted and bitterly disappointed in herself.

Now Cindy ambled about the mall, window shopping, lingering over gowns and shoes and jewelry, with no real intention of buying anything. She'd only stopped in the first place because she was hungry and feeling low. She thought the mall might distract or even uplift her. After all, shopping almost always gave her a lift; just looking at good quality sweaters and jewelry and accessories gave her pleasure. Buying anything for Kevin inevitably brought joy.

Kevin hated shopping, of course, just as most men did, but she'd drag him along anyway to buy the slacks and jackets and ties and sweaters and belts he never bought for himself. She wanted him to learn about quality. But what could she buy him this Christmas? She'd have to cut back. Money was tight and her prospects weak. She hated feeling poor. Hadn't she taken a vow when she was eighteen years old and living in that broken down Florida shack that she'd never be poor again? No matter what it took?

Christmas was everywhere in the mall, blinking, singing, promoting—banners shouting out discounts. Crowds streamed by, children screamed, and wide-eyed teenagers wandered, pre-occupied with their phones and endless banter.

Cindy felt lousy, out of focus and sinking, like a leaky boat on a journey to nowhere. The truth would have probably set her free, but she couldn't face it, and so she shouldered on, distracting herself, picking through racks of sweaters and winter coats.

She caught a glimpse of her reflection in the window. She wasn't the young foxy girl anymore—nor the elegant, sexy woman men used to chase after. Her figure was still good, yes, but she had to work at it now. She'd had some face work done, but somehow, it didn't seem to hide the guilt, the loss, or the years of selfish living. Men didn't give her a second glance now, at least none under sixty, and those were the only men she was interested in; preferably men under forty, if she had her choice. Under forty and with lots of money.

She stood staring, listless. Rad was over fifty. Why had she fallen for him? Because he was an irresistible original? She didn't care why. She *had* fallen in love with him. That's why she went after him.

JULIET AND PAUL CAME to the mall, thinking to catch a movie, but the one they wanted to see had already started. They decided to browse through the stores instead. They walked close, but didn't touch. Juliet wanted to touch. The possibility of touch aroused her, but there was a remoteness in Paul that kept her at a distance. Did he just want to be friends? She was moved by his smooth, assured masculinity, but he seemed oddly unmovable, and this both frustrated and fascinated her.

They walked in silence, passing the designer shop where Cindy Evans searched the racks, skimming the details of design and color. Minutes later, they sauntered across the emerald marble tile, passing the restaurant where Anne had sat and was now in the women's room, washing her hands, recovering from the text she had just read.

"I want to buy something for Amy," Juliet said.

"She loves surprises," Paul said.

They walked into a toy store and browsed the aisles. Juliet stopped and pointed. "Does she have a Princess Play Makeup set?"

Paul scratched his head. "No, I don't think so."

Juliet grabbed it up. "Okay, she'll love it. All little girls love to play with makeup."

After Juliet had paid, they left the store, Juliet carrying the shopping bag. "Now I want some flowers for my mother," she said.

"There's a shop down that way," Paul said, pointing.

They strolled into a small flower boutique. Paul looked on as Juliet created an extravagant bouquet of red roses, white lilies, white chrysanthemums, red carnations, holiday greens, red glass balls, three candy canes and a red and green festive ribbon. The flowers were wrapped into a cone of white tissue and then surrounded by white and red paper.

"She'll love it," Juliet said, beaming.

As they left the shop, Juliet took Paul's arm. He stiffened at her touch, caught off guard. Although Juliet felt his tension, she held on and, a few minutes later, he began to relax.

"More shopping?" he asked.

"Oh yes. Now I'm going to buy something for you."

"Me? No, you don't need to do that. Really."

"I already have the perfect gift in mind."

"I can't imagine."

"No good restaurateur should ever be without one."

Juliet handed Paul the shopping bags and flowers and then marched into Hally's Hardware Store. She found Hally behind the counter, sucking on a *Tootsie Roll Pop*. Hally was a short woman, about forty-five, with short dyed blond hair, broad shoulders and big front teeth. Juliet knew of Hally because Rad loved her store and always talked about it.

"Hi, Hally, I'm Rad Sinclair's daughter, Juliet. We met at Dad's funeral."

Hally lit up, jerking the sucker from her mouth. "Rad's girl? Hot damn! He said you'd never come in here."

"Well, I'm here to see if you have that 180-Piece Maintenance Tool Set Dad loved so much. I want to buy one for a friend of mine."

Hally snatched up her black-rimmed glasses, slid out from around the counter and worked her stocky body through the narrow aisle, nosing up and down until she found the tool kit. She tugged it down and brought it to the front counter.

"Is that it?"

"Perfect," Juliet said.

Juliet handed off her credit card. "I suppose you don't gift wrap, Hally?"

Hally looked at her, frostily, over the top of her glasses. "Are you shittin' me?"

"Okay, fine. I didn't think so."

As Juliet exited the store, Hally called to her. "I loved your old man. He was the best."

Juliet turned back and smiled. "Thanks, Hally."

Juliet toted the bag outside, and Paul looked on warily. With both arms raised, she presented the bag.

"What have you done?"

"Take it."

They exchanged packages. Paul took the bag and peeked inside. "A tool set?"

"You'll need it. You don't already have one, do you?"

Paul laughed, shaking his head. "No. Bits and pieces, but not one like this. Thank you." He stared at her admiringly. "You're a lot like your father, Juliet."

She grinned happily at the comment, and they started off to the parking lot.

They didn't notice that Cindy Evans crossed their path only twenty feet ahead. Juliet asked Paul if she could go to The Coffee Mug to start working on the social media contest for the restaurant. She wanted to compose the letter to announce the Christmas Eve potluck dinner.

Paul was about to answer when his phone rang. It was Donna Edwards.

"Where are you?!" she barked.

Paul turned and walked away from Juliet. "I told you I was going to be a little late tonight."

"Well, you'd better get home. Amy's sick and she's crying for you. I can't do anything with her. She has a fever and her tummy hurts."

"Okay, okay," Paul said. "I'll be right there."

Paul hung up and went back to Juliet. "I have to go home. Amy's sick."

As they approached Juliet's house, Paul turned to her. "I had a great time."

"Me, too," Juliet said. "I hope Amy is okay."

"Yeah. Hope so. Your present will help cheer her up."

"Thanks for letting me be the first to try out your new restaurant. I think I may have gained back a few pounds tonight."

Paul glanced over. "I'll pay you for the work you do."

"Don't worry about it. It will give me something interesting to think about. I'm getting antsy, anyway."

"I insist on paying you," Paul said. "My father used to say that no one should ever work for nothing."

The headlights swept the driveway, and Paul drove up to the garage and stopped. Juliet saw the house was dark.

"I wonder where Mom is."

Paul looked around. "Maybe she's out Christmas shopping."

They sat, staring and waiting.

"When will you leave for London?" Paul asked.

"Oh, I don't know. Mid-January, I guess."

"Sounds like a good opportunity."

"Yeah...but it's a long way from home."

The quiet deepened. Finally, Juliet turned, said goodnight and gathered up the flowers.

She pushed the door open. "Thanks for a wonderful dinner, Paul."

"Thanks again for the tool set."

Juliet hoped he'd say more, but he didn't.

She watched as Paul's car backed up and drove away.

She approached the front door, feeling introspective and confused. The night air was crisp and cold. Suddenly feeling tired, she inhaled a breath. The date had gone well, but she sensed something was wrong. Paul seemed to enjoy himself, but he was holding back, unable, or unwilling to express himself fully or enjoy the experience of being together.

Juliet inserted the key into the front door and pushed. She reached right and switched on the foyer light. She saw something on the floor. It was a white envelope with her name written on it in an artful script.

She shut the door, lay the flowers down, gently opened the envelope and drew out a piece of folded typing paper.

CHAPTER 20

Juliet slept fitfully, her dreams weird and erratic. By eight o'clock, she was up brushing her teeth, checking her messages and texts. There was nothing from Paul. There were three texts from Max.

"Talk to me. What's going on down there?"

"Things are moving along on the London thing. Exciting."

"Wassup, girl? Waiting for your answer."

There was also a text from Karen.

"Great time last night. You and Paul are a perfect couple."

Juliet tapped out a text to Paul. *"How's Amy? Feeling better?"*

She tossed her phone down on the bed, folding her arms, fighting indecision and anger. She turned toward the nightstand, where the envelope and letter lay. The same letter she'd found last night in the foyer. During the night, the words kept looping around in her head, along with faces of her father, old clients and bizarre shapes and images. Juliet had memorized Cindy's note.

Juliet:

It's Cindy Evans. I came to talk to you, but you weren't home. I'm leaving it up to you now, whether we should meet and talk. Whether we meet or not, I want to put this whole thing behind me and move on with my life. I'm leaving town for a few days. Please call or email. Tell me when and where you want to meet.

Best—
Cindy

Juliet paced her room, the smoke of irritation all around her. Cindy wanted to put the whole thing behind her? Really? Cindy wants to move on with her life? Really? What about Anne? Last night, Juliet was slipping into her pajamas when her mother arrived home. By the time Juliet went to check on her, Anne was already in her bedroom, the door shut. Juliet knocked. She heard her mother crying. She said she didn't want to talk.

And what about the money? Did Cindy know anything about the four hundred thousand dollars? If she did, why didn't she say so? Why be so vague and mysterious? If she wanted to talk, why didn't she call first, or wait until she and Anne arrived home?

It took all Juliet's strength not to shoot off an angry email as soon as she'd read the letter. But she'd learned, after years in PR, never to respond to anyone when you're angry—especially by way of email or text. So, Juliet had waited, trusting she'd be calmer and more composed after a good night's sleep. The good sleep didn't come and neither did her composure. She felt tired, pissed off and hungry.

She stalked back and forth, as the acid of anger continued its climb into her head. And why hadn't Paul texted or called? What was that all about? She snatched up her phone. It was almost 8:30. Why was he so withholding? The more she thought, the closer to righteous rage she came. Why was everybody so withholding?

Finally, still in her pajamas and wrapped in a terry robe, she left her room and headed off to the kitchen. Anne was seated at the kitchen table fully dressed for work, hovering over a cup of green tea and the local paper. The flowers Juliet had bought for her were beautifully arranged in a glass vase, in the center of the table. The card lay open beside it.

To Mom: with gratitude and love. Juliet.

Anne lifted her head as Juliet marched in.

"Good morning."

"No, it isn't," she said, curtly.

Juliet went to work making coffee, using a green Melitta coffee pod and #2 natural brown filter. She anchored the pod on her mug, scooped the coffee from the canister and poured it in the filter.

"Anything you want to talk about?" Anne asked, not looking around.

"Have you ever known me not to want to talk about anything?"

"Nope. You got that from your father."

"And that's a bad thing!?" Juliet snapped.

Anne lowered her voice. "No, my dear. It's not bad. It's just a fact."

"Well, I'd rather talk about things instead of holding things in and exploding later on, although I guess I've been known to do that too."

Anne laid her glasses and the paper aside. "Oh, so you're saying you're not Saint Juliet?" she said, playfully.

"Funny."

"By the way, thanks for the flowers. They're beautiful. Just what I needed to cheer me up last night and this morning. And look, the sun is shining. It's a beautiful day. It's supposed to go up to forty degrees."

Juliet placed the kettle on the coil, turned it on high and turned around, leaning back against the stove.

"They couldn't have cheered you up all that much. You were crying last night."

"I was tired."

Juliet wondered if Cindy had contacted her in some way. "Anything happen I should know about?"

Anne slipped her glasses on and glanced down at the paper. "No. How did it go with Paul last night?"

"A clever change of subject, Mother."

"You were home early."

"Amy, his daughter, got sick. We cut it a little short."

"And... before you cut it short?"

Juliet gave her mother the highlights of dinner and shopping, and then she pushed away from the stove and joined her mother at the table, sitting to her right.

"In the hospital, a nurse who's known Paul since high school told me about his first wife. How she was killed. It was awful. She told me how he'd never gotten over it and how he's struggled to move on with his life. She also told me he'd lost a couple of his Marine buddies when he was in Afghanistan."

"Yes, Rad told me about him. He really liked Paul. I think I met him once, so I was really embarrassed I didn't recognize him at the hospital."

Juliet raked her fingers through her hair, staring out the window. "How do you get over something like that?"

"You don't," Anne said. "But time helps, so they say."

Juliet looked at her mother. "I see such sadness in his eyes, even when he laughs. And there's always this part of him that doesn't or, I don't know, just can't seem to get out. And you know me, I feel like I have to try and bring everybody out. I'm just like Dad in that way. I guess I just look into his beautiful sad eyes and..." Juliet stopped, making a resigned face.

"And what?" Anne asked.

"I want to help him. I want to heal him. I want to get lost in those beautiful sad eyes."

Anne removed her glasses again, astonished. "After one date, you want to do all that?"

The kettle whistled. Juliet stood up and switched off the burner, feeling embarrassed she'd revealed so much of her feelings, even to her mother. She hadn't even admitted that much to herself. She poured the steaming water into the cone and watched the mountain of coffee bubble and collapse.

"He's very attractive, Mom. And I sense he's a very good man. In case you haven't noticed, I haven't been with many good men—certainly not with men who seem honest and solid, despite having gone through hell."

"You just said he's holding part of himself back. Is that honesty?"

"That's not fair. It's not dishonest when you try, but you don't know how to climb over the pain and loss. Some people never figure it out."

Anne stared down at the paper, but she wasn't reading it. "Have you had any more dreams about your father and brother?"

Juliet took a careful drink of her coffee. She lowered the intensity of her voice. "It wasn't a dream, Mom. I can't really say what it was, but I do know—without a doubt—that it wasn't a dream."

Anne stood. "Well, I've got to get to campus. I'm already running late."

FIFTEEN MINUTES AFTER ANNE left the house, Juliet received a text from Paul.

"At the doctor with Amy. Her temperature's down and her tummy is better. Pipe burst at the Mug. Plumbers on the way. Can't open. Crazy morning."

Juliet had just showered. She finished drying off and wrapped herself in the towel. She texted back.

"Can I help? Should I meet you?"

As she waited for Paul's response, she pulled on jeans, a white turtleneck, and a red sweatshirt. His response came only minutes later.

"I must stay with Amy, until mother-in-law comes. Can you meet the plumbers?"

Juliet texted him she was on her way.

As she drove through pouring sunlight, Juliet was startled by an instant sensation. She felt cheerful. She felt high, despite Cindy's letter. She was going to see

Paul today and the thought thrilled her. Could she be falling in love with him? God help her.

CHAPTER 21

Paul arrived at the Coffee Mug to find Juliet swinging a mop and wringing it out in a yellow plastic mop bucket. The plumber, Howie Kroft, was on his knees beside the stainless-steel sink, inspecting a jagged hole of broken concrete and an exposed piece of pipe. He was dressed in a faded royal blue uniform with the name HOWIE stitched on the right breast pocket.

Juliet saw Paul and brightened. "Hi, Paul. Howie's a real artist. He found the problem in just a few minutes."

Howie, a heavy-set man of forty-two, glanced up with big liquid, hound-dog-brown eyes. "Hey, Paul," he said, in a slow, lugubrious voice. "You had a broken pipe under the concrete slab. Had to drill some relief holes with a masonry bit, then use the hammer and chisel to break it up."

Howie pointed to his left, to the old rusty pipe. "Just rusted out on you, Paul. Then the cold weather just finished it off."

Paul looked at Juliet. "You don't have to do that. Where's Ramon? I called him. He should be here. He should have opened the place."

"He did," Juliet said. "But his mother called. She had a flat tire out on the interstate. I told him to go and help her."

Paul scratched his head and sighed. "Ah, the joys of owning your own business." He stepped over and peered down at the hole. "Is it fixed, Howie?"

"Yeah," Howie said with some pride. "I cut a new pipe and glued one side of it into place and then tightened the elbow connection."

Howie always explained his work in great detail. It was part of the package—a guilty overcompensation—preparing the customer for his bill.

"Well, as long as it works. Can I open?" Paul asked. "I've been getting a slew of texts and calls from people asking me what's going on and when I'm going to be open."

Howie pointed at the pipe. "I want you to see this. After I glued that one side of it into place, I used a sleeve on the other end. I slid that into place and tightened the connection."

"Yeah, yeah, that's great, Howie," Paul said, trying to rush him along. "Thanks. Can you cover the hole with fresh concrete any time soon?"

"Oh sure, Paul. It might take me a couple of hours. You can open up, though. Juliet's got the floor and the place looking real good."

Paul looked at Juliet. He lifted a hand and dropped it, his expression apologetic. "I didn't mean for you to do all this."

"I didn't mind. It's fine."

"Well... thank you. You're not getting overtired, are you?"

She smiled at him. "No. But thanks for asking. How's Amy?"

"Much better. She finally went to sleep about the time my mother-in-law arrived. Oh, and Amy loved the Princess set. It was all she could talk about this morning."

Howie made little gasps of effort as he tightened the pipe. Paul glanced over and grimaced. Howie was making it obvious how hard he was working for the exorbitant price he would charge.

IT WAS AFTER ELEVEN WHEN PAUL finally opened The Coffee Mug. By then, Ramon had returned, the coffee was made, the pastries were in the display cases, and the soup was in the soup pots. The lines began forming by 11:30 and Paul and Ramon spent the next two hours in hectic motion, arms, hands, legs and bodies engaged in a choreographed dance.

Juliet helped, pouring soup, restocking paper cups and napkins, refilling the cream and sugar containers and wiping down the marble table tops.

Paul watched her with wonder and appreciation. Why was she doing this? He began to worry about her, believing she was working too hard. He asked her to slow down, to rest, to return home if she wished, but she brushed him off, keeping to her work. Paul noticed many of his customers watched her with admiration and speculation, passing him a wink of approval at his pretty new employee. Many knew she was Rad's daughter. Paul just shrugged.

By 1:30, Paul insisted Juliet rest, and so he installed her in his back office at the computer. She leaned back in his desk chair and studied the gold-framed photograph of Tracy and Amy that sat next to the printer. At first glance, it saddened her to see the joy and pride emanating from the photo. Tracy had been a smiling, attractive woman, and Amy was a little blond beauty.

Juliet refocused on the task at hand, spending the next hour scanning The Coffee Mug's email lists and discussing the ad campaign and potluck email with Paul's high school student graphics designer, Tilly Wayne. She ate a turkey sandwich and a cup of mushroom barley soup, while the noise and clamor from the café rose and fell into the afternoon lull.

Paul stepped in, leaning against the door frame. "Can I afford you?"

Juliet looked up. "Probably not," she said, with a little grin.

"I have to go over to the restaurant to deal with a few things. I'm interviewing a couple of cooks who might work out, a waitress who has waitress friends and a vegetable vendor who promised me a deal. Then I have to interview a new babysitter and swing by and check on Amy. She still doesn't feel well, and she wants me to come home."

"You're a busy man."

"Yeah... some days it gets pretty hectic."

Juliet fixed her eyes on him. "Maybe you need a partner?"

As soon as the words left her mouth, she wished she could retrieve them. She heard the flirtation in them. She heard a warm invitation, and her boldness surprised and embarrassed her.

Paul was still. Her words both confused and stirred him.

"The restaurant was Tracy's idea. We were going to buy it and she was going to run it... when she got back from..." His voice trailed away. Immediately, he wished he'd stayed silent.

Juliet lowered her eyes.

Paul lowered his eyes.

They heard the rattle of dishes and the low murmur of voices in the café. They heard a siren pass outside on the highway.

Juliet returned to the computer screen. When she spoke, her voice was low and flat. "I talked to Howie about the restaurant and came up with a name: Paul's Place."

Paul kept his eyes down. "Not very original... and it was never supposed to be mine. It was always Tracy's thing."

There was another long silence. Juliet was hurt, but it was her own fault. Paul obviously wasn't ready for a relationship yet. She managed a placid dignity.

"I'll be leaving soon," Juliet said, coolly. "The banner ad for the restaurant name contest will go out in a couple of days. Tilly can handle it. Your customers will be able to email back their entries."

Paul lingered for a moment and, for the life of him, he couldn't think of anything else to say. Finally, he pocketed his hands, staring at nothing.

"Thanks, Juliet, for all your help."

She didn't respond. She'd turned insular and private.

As Juliet was driving home, she decided Paul was still in too much pain, too remote and too withholding to be able to begin and sustain a relationship. Maybe he never would. She'd known people who couldn't. They'd loved too much; their loss was too great, and they just couldn't move on. It was better to find out now, instead of two or three months from now.

THAT NIGHT AT DINNER, Juliet tried to engage Anne in conversation. Every topic fell flat. Anne was being vague and elusive. They ate their roast chicken, potatoes and broccoli in silence, each sipping a glass of California Chardonnay. Finally, Juliet slapped her hand on the table.

"This silence is killing me, Mom. What happened? Something must have happened that you're trying to keep from me."

Anne ate quietly, chewing thoughtfully. As she laid her folk down, she sighed wearily.

"I'm not a loner, Juliet, and I never have been."

Juliet waited for more.

"You're going to be leaving for Europe. I'll sell the house and try to find a condo. I'll visit Carolyn in Cincinnati. Jon and Nora will stop by now and then. Maybe we'll take in a movie once in a while. Maybe we'll have dinner. I have a couple of girlfriends at the college. One is divorced, the other never married. I suppose we'll trudge off to Columbus to discover a new restaurant or designer shop; maybe we'll stop at a trendy wine bar, packed with kids in their twenties and thirties.

The music will be loud and awful, and I'll feel so awful and lonely that I'll drink three glasses of wine instead of two."

Juliet had stopped eating. She looked at her mother with concern.

Anne's eyes held tears. "I know I'm just feeling sorry for myself," she said, blotting her eyes with her white paper napkin. "I'm just so damned emotional lately. I can't seem to crawl out of this dark depression."

"You will, Mom. It just takes time."

"I'm everything I never wanted to be: old, weepy, afraid I'm not going to have enough money for retirement and, worst of all, alone."

Juliet reached for her mother's hand. "Mom... You'll never be alone. I'm here. You'll come to London and stay with me. We can travel. Paris isn't that far. We can go for long weekends. We can go to Spain and the south of France."

Anne sat back. "You'll be busy, Juliet. It's a new job, with stress and problems. You're not going to be on vacation over there, you know, especially if you're working with that Max guy, who, by the way, seems a little nuts to me."

"He's very smart. Extremely bright."

"Well, he may be, but whenever I look into his eyes or hear him talk, I remember something Oscar Levant once said."

"Who's Oscar Levant?" Juliet asked.

"He was a pianist in the fifties. Had his own TV show. He's been dead for years. Anyway, he was also nuts. He once said, 'There's a fine line between genius and insanity. I have erased that line.'" Anne gave a firm nod. "I think Max has erased that line, too."

"So come to London for a few weeks and explore the city, maybe in February after I'm settled."

"My life is here, Juliet, I'd have to come back to it at some point and face it."

"So after a few weeks over there, you'll be ready to face it. You'll be rested. You'll have experienced new things. It'll change your outlook."

"I can't go on vacation at this time of year. I have to work. It's the only thing that keeps *me* sane."

Anne grew quiet. Her forehead knotted into a frown. She gave a little shake of her head. "But I do *not* want to be alone. I'm not built for it. I hate it. I'll just wither up and die."

Juliet leaned in close. "Mom, you're still young and attractive. There are plenty of men out there who would love to be with you."

Anne swallowed. She turned and looked at her daughter, pointedly. "Well, my dear, there's at least one man who wants to be with me, and I'm going to see him in a few days."

Juliet batted her eyes, her mind working to understand. "Now I don't know if you're joking or..."

"I am not joking."

Juliet sat back in her chair, narrowing her eyes, assessing her mother's sudden and startling disclosure.

Anne went back to eating.

"I guess you're going to tell me the whole story?" Juliet asked.

Anne chewed, swallowed, and drank her wine. "I know how it seems. Rad's just died and..." Anne's face twisted up into self-righteous anger. "But for all I know, he was with some other woman. Maybe more than one. Oh hell, I'm just so confused and sometimes I get so angry at him."

Juliet pushed her plate aside. "Who is this guy you were going to tell me about?"

Anne cupped the wine glass as if for security. "His name is Marshall Gray. I met him long before I met your father. He lives in San Diego. He said he'd been looking for me for a long time. He found my name on the internet, from Rad's obituary."

"Did he call you?" Juliet asked.

"He texted me. I guess he was too afraid to just call. Anyway, we met in college and dated a couple times before he graduated and went off to law school, and then we met again, just after he finished law school and I was getting my Master's Degree in Music Education. Well, we fell in love. It was my first time. I fell like crazy. Marshall said he loved me, too, and I knew he meant it. A woman knows when she's loved—I mean really loved by a man."

"Where was this?"

"In Chicago. I was student teaching, and he was sending out resumes and interviewing for jobs. We went to museums, Cubs games, the theatre. We had so much in common. We loved so many of the same things. He was crazy about jazz and classical music, so we went to all the jazz clubs and to the symphony."

Anne grew more circumspect. "He said he was madly in love with me, and he'd never really been in love before. We were going to move in together. Then he got a job. A big firm out in L.A. His father was in politics, a congressman or something, and I guess he pulled some strings. Anyway, Marshall packed up and said he'd find a place for us and get in touch with me."

Anne set her wine glass down. She placed her hands in her lap, barely breathing.

"He wrote me long, loving letters. I kept them for a long time and read them over and over. I finally threw them out about ten years ago. He sent me boxes of candy and flowers too. He knew I loved cherry chocolates, so he sent me boxes of them."

Anne laughed at the memory. "Of course, I gained weight and joined a gym. Anyway, he called five times a week. I kept asking him when I should move out there. He said as soon as he made enough money, he'd send me a ticket."

Anne smiled sadly. "Well... I waited." And then as an afterthought, Anne said, "I should have thrown those letters away long before I did. I wonder if your father ever found them and read them?"

Anne made a little dismissive gesture. "Well, it doesn't matter. The ticket never came, and Marshall's letters stopped coming—and that was before all this email and online business we have today. That was more than thirty years ago. It's hard to believe..."

Juliet spoke up. "Mother, what happened? Did you find him?"

"I nearly went out of my mind, of course. I was frantic, thinking something must have happened to him. I wrote to him. No response. I called him. I even called his parents, but they were, well, let's just say challenging personalities, and they wouldn't tell me anything about him or where he'd disappeared to. So, I piled into my little—oh what was the make of that car?" She tapped her forehead, and then lit up. "Duster! That's what it was. Anyway, I drove like a mad woman to Moline, Illinois to see his parents and find out what had happened to him."

Anne stopped and grew quiet, as though the thought injured her. "He'd married someone else."

Juliet sat motionless, feeling the pain of her mother's memory. "Why? Why did he do it?"

Anne sighed, lifting her wine glass by the stem. She drank and swallowed. "He did it because his father told him to do it. Marshall was always a little scared of his father. He was a very powerful and stern man. Finally, one beautiful autumn day, when things were withering up and dying, Marshall called me and told me everything. He told me his new wife was from a political family. It was a wealthy family; a prominent American family; you've probably heard of them. I didn't know them then. Years later, their name would appear in the papers. Nothing big or anything, just little social and political events."

Juliet laid her napkin on the table. "What did you do?"

Anne shook her head a little. "I hurt for a very long time. I cried until I seemed to dry up inside. I got sick, physically sick—pneumonia—and wound up in the hospital. God, it was a bad time."

Juliet laid a gentle hand on her mother's arm. "Is that when you moved back to Ohio?"

Anne nodded. "About a year later, I met your father. He shook the sadness out of me, like he did with everybody. I fought him, too. I'd grown happy to be sad, as all the country songs say. But little by little, I fell in love with him and when he asked me for the fourth time, I said, 'Are you sure you want to do this?'"

Anne laughed out loud at the memory. "Rad said, 'Anne of a thousand moods, you are the prettiest, greatest and fun-est of them all. I do want to marry you, I do.'"

Anne looked at Juliet wistfully. "How could I not say yes to that?"

CHAPTER 22

On December 20, Juliet and Anne spent most of the morning cleaning house and opening the final boxes of Christmas ornaments, many of which were Rad's favorites. With every Victorian caroler or hand-crafted gingerbread boy, they shared a memory, sometimes of Rad, sometimes of the entire family. There was a small oval ornament they especially treasured: a red leather picture frame containing a small photo of 3-year-old Jimmy, holding a new robot toy. Because they knew Rad would want them to, they hung a Christmas ribbon wreath on the front door.

After lunch, Juliet planned to sit by the fire, write a few Christmas cards and finally send off that email to Cindy Evans. It was time they met, preferably before Christmas. She'd composed the email in her head many times, reworking it until she achieved the right tone and pitch. She would keep it short and succinct, but make it clear she wanted to know the entire, unvarnished truth.

If truth be told, Juliet was weary of thinking about it. Meeting Cindy was not something she was looking forward to. In fact, the thought of it nauseated her. But if she was moving to London to begin an entirely new life, she wanted closure on the old one. She had to learn what had happened to the money to see if she could recover any of it for her mother.

The other tough decision was whether she should tell her mother about Cindy. But that decision could wait until after the meeting.

Juliet carried a mug of coffee into the living room and arranged herself on the floor before the fire, sitting in a cross-legged position. She opened her laptop, checked and responded to a few emails, and then began composing the one to Cindy. Just as she'd proofed it for the third time and clicked the SEND button, Anne entered, wearing old sweatshirt and sweatpants. She'd just washed her hair and was towel-drying it. Her expression was tense.

"Am I wrong for doing this? Am I just being selfish and silly for meeting Marshall? I mean, what will people think? Rad's only been dead for..."

Juliet cut her off. "Don't think about it so much, Mom. You've already arranged to meet him. So, meet him. You're just getting together with an old friend after thirty-five years. It's no big deal."

"Oh, I suppose you're right. We're just going to have dinner and talk. We'll probably talk about our families. He'll tell me about his kids and his wife, who died a year ago, and I'll blabber on like I always do about who knows what. The truth is, I probably won't know what to say or I'll bore him and that will be the end of that."

"Mother, stop being so negative."

Anne's voice dropped an octave. "Oh God, I just keep thinking about how old I look. I saw so many wrinkles in the bathroom mirror just now. I'm not the young girl he remembers. I was seven years younger than you are now when we were dating. I was only twenty-three years old. I can't even remember who or what I was at twenty-three years old."

"So, he's not a kid anymore either. He's over sixty."

Juliet's phone rang. She saw it was Paul. She glanced up at her mother and whispered, "It's Paul." And then she whispered again. "Why am I whispering?"

Anne lifted an eyebrow, turned, and retreated to her bedroom.

Juliet answered coolly. "Hi, Paul."

"Hey! How are you feeling?"

"I'm feeling great. Thanks. How about you?"

"Good... real good. I'm glad to hear you're feeling good. You've been resting a lot today, I guess."

"Yes," Juliet said, clipping off the "s."

His voice sounded strained and nervous. "Juliet... I was just thinking, wondering... I mean, I know it's short notice and everything, but I was just wondering if you'd like to join Amy and me tonight for hamburgers or pizza or something like that?"

Juliet waited.

Paul continued, stumbling over his words. "If you can't, I understand. I know it's short notice. It's just that I'm closing The Mug early tonight and...and, well, I thought it would be nice if you met Amy. She loves that Princess makeup thing, and I thought maybe we could just talk about things."

Juliet beat back resentment, even though she knew it wasn't warranted or even what she wanted to feel. What things did he want to talk about? Every time she thought they'd connected, he shut her out. He was struggling with too much stuff—old demons. Did she really want to get involved with him, especially since she'd be leaving for London in a few weeks? What could come of it?

"We haven't really had the time to talk about things," Paul repeated.

"Paul... Maybe the timing isn't so good."

"You mean that you've decided to take the London job?"

"Yeah... Well, I haven't definitely decided, but I probably will. And you have so much going on in your life right now, with the new restaurant and your other business and Amy. And Paul, I know it's been difficult for you these last couple of years."

There was an uneasy silence.

"Juliet, I want to get to know you, even if it's only for a short time—even if it's only for tonight. Even if you leave and I never see you again. I'm not good at saying certain things. I've always been a doer; an action person. It takes me awhile to figure things out inside. I don't know, maybe I never figure anything out because life is too confusing or something. Anyway, right now, I know I'd like to see you. I want to be with you."

Juliet raked a strand of hair that had fallen across one eye. She smiled, unlocked her folded legs, and stretched them out toward the warm fire. "Then tell me what time you want me and give me the directions to get there."

THERE WAS A LIGHT PINK GLOW in the west as Juliet started off down the serpentine two-lane highway toward Paul's home, about four miles away. Light snow flurries fell, causing her to remember the night of the accident, when she'd swerved to miss the deer and had gone spinning off into that other world. It seemed now to have happened in some misty dream. She slowed down, taking the turns with caution, recalling the beauty and the peace of that distant shore, while puzzling about the encounter with her father and feeling again the sting of his words.

"Anger is corrosive and leads nowhere, except to nearly killing yourself and hurting other people."

She couldn't help it, but she was still fighting anger. Anger at Cindy Evans and, if she admitted it, anger at her father. It's all well and good to espouse words of wisdom when you're in paradise, far away from the battle of this world. It's quite another to be lost in a storm searching for peace and a way out.

As snow blew around her like a mass of white insects, she felt a pang of anxiety. Why was she going to see Paul? There was definitely an attraction there, but did she really want to fall in love with him? Could she trust him? He was emotionally damaged. Did she really want to put herself through that? Did she want to pass up the fantastic opportunity to live in London and work at a job she loved, had been educated for and had mastered after years of hard work and sacrifice? The fact that she even considered not taking the job caused her even greater anxiety.

As she turned into Paul's driveway, his porch light blinked on. A second later he appeared, dressed in a blue flannel shirt, gray quilted down vest, jeans and boots. Her face felt flush as her entire body responded to his sturdy masculinity and handsome face. She paused to steady herself, then killed the engine, climbed out into swirling snowflakes and hurried up the front stairs into the house.

"Thanks for coming," Paul said.

"You're welcome!" Juliet answered crisply, avoiding his eyes.

She swung out of her coat and handed it to him, watching as he hung it on a walnut coat rack. Then she appraised the place in a slow wonder. She saw a two-story house with exposed ceiling beams, just a few vertical walls and a twelve-foot Fraser fir Christmas tree, blinking red and white lights. Its heavenly sweet evergreen scent filled the house. The décor was mostly country.

Most of the first floor was a combination living room and dining room, with ladder-back chairs, rocking chairs, a dark green recliner and a comfortable-looking brown corduroy couch near the fireplace. There were baskets of stored wood for the masonry fireplace that blazed comfortably behind glass fireplace doors. Brass candle holders held flickering candles that softened the atmosphere and made the space cozy and welcoming.

"It's beautiful," Juliet said.

"Well, it's a mishmosh of things right now," Paul said. "Some things are from the old house. I'm still adding new things. It's a work in progress."

Amy appeared on the upper balcony, with her round dumpling face and springy blond curls. She was shy, twisting, and frowning. Juliet recognized her immediately as the little girl she'd seen on the playground a few weeks before. She'd helped her to swing.

"Hi, Amy!" Juliet exclaimed, waving. "Remember me? We met at the playground awhile back?"

Paul looked over, surprised.

Amy kept twisting, her hands stuffed in her pink dress pockets. "I swing good. I like to swing."

"I gave you a little push. Remember? At the playground?"

"...No."

Paul said, "Juliet gave you the Princess make-up. Do you want to say thank you?"

"Yeah..."

"Can you say thank you?" Paul said.

"Yeah," Amy said.

Paul shrugged and Juliet laughed.

"Want to see my earrings?" Amy asked. "I got earrings and stick."

"She means lipstick," Paul whispered.

"Yes. Can I come up?"

"Yeah."

"Are you hungry?" Paul asked.

Juliet nodded.

"Okay, I'll start the hamburgers."

UPSTAIRS IN HER ROOM, Amy came alive. She was a scrambler, reaching, grabbing, showing and telling. She introduced Juliet to all her stuffed animals, her dolls and her black stuffed cat named Coots.

"Why did you name him Coots?" Juliet asked.

"Because that's his name."

"Oh, okay."

Amy barked at the cat a couple of times before dashing off to snatch up the next item. Juliet watched and participated, touching the toy ukulele, the pink purse, complete with toy cellphone, keys and wallet. Amy bounced and danced, making a girlish grimace of despair when something fell from her clumsy grasp.

When Amy was finally settled, Juliet found the make-up kit. She applied sparkling lip gloss on Amy's button mouth and helped her snap on a set of Princess earrings. Juliet held up the mirror and Amy stared at herself in a confused wonder.

"I like these." Amy smacked her lips. "I like this lipstick."

"You are so pretty."

Amy turned, looking directly into Juliet's eyes. "Are you staying here?"

"Yes, for dinner. We're going to have hamburgers."

Amy turned back to her image in the mirror. "You can stay here. You can stay if you want to. You can stay in my room with me."

TEN MINUTES LATER, Juliet and Amy joined Paul in the kitchen. The hamburgers sizzled in a cast-iron skillet, smothered by melting cheddar. Bermuda onion lay sliced, round and potent.

Juliet took in the hutch, cupboards and open shelves, filled with stoneware pots, plain glazed earthenware and glass jars. She wondered if these had all been Tracy's, but she didn't ask.

Paul put them to work. Juliet and Amy made a salad and set the table as they all nibbled on potato chips and cheddar cheese. Paul toasted the hamburger buns, found a country music station on the radio, and turned the volume down low.

When the burgers were ready, they ate spiritedly at a refinished mahogany table, talking about Christmas and Christmas presents, and about Amy's upcoming date to see Santa Claus. During a lull in the Christmas conversation, Paul mentioned that the response to the restaurant name contest was overwhelming. They'd received over two-hundred suggestions. Excited, Juliet asked what some of them were.

"Paul's Home Cookin' Café. The Comfort and Joy Café. The Good Eatin' Restaurant." Paul paused to think. "Oh, and Paul's Stop and Eat Café. My favorite so far is "The Eat, Meet and Greet Café."

Juliet paused, thinking. "None of them are grabbing me. Can I look through them sometime?"

"Be my guest. I have a feeling some of my friends are going to be mad at me when I don't pick their entry."

"So, you'll give them a free beer or glass of wine," Juliet said. "How is the response to the Christmas Eve potluck supper?"

"It's amazing," Paul said. "Tilly said more than fifty people have confirmed so far and more have responded as 'maybes.'"

"I want to go," Amy said.

"Of course, you'll go," Paul said.

After dinner and the clean-up, the three sprawled onto the couch and watched Amy's favorite movie of the season, *The Polar Express*. She was riveted to the TV screen, her eyes widening, her expression changing with each action sequence. When Santa appeared, she sat up, bolt erect, pointing at him, as if he'd just magically materialized before them.

"There's Santa!"

By the end, Amy grew drowsy. She leaned over and rested her head on her father's leg and drifted off to sleep.

"Does she do that often?" Juliet asked.

"I don't get home early enough. I've got to change that. It's tough, you know, when so many things are going on. So many calls and problems and decisions to make all the time."

Juliet lowered her voice. "Do you like it that way? Living that way?"

Paul stroked his daughter's hair. She didn't stir. "Good question. I don't know. After Tracy's death, all I knew was I had to keep busy. I had to keep moving. I had to tire myself out so I could sleep at night."

Juliet stared down at Amy. "When I was a little girl and I didn't see my father because he was working, I'd say, Daddy, why are you so busy? He made up this poem. *'I'm busy once, I'm busy twice, I'm busy like a herd of mice. I want the cheese so I can please, go off and... not work anymore.'*"

Paul gently laughed. "Yeah, that sounds like Rad. He was a great guy. A good friend. I miss him."

"Me too."

Juliet gathered her courage, trying to sound casual. "Paul, did my father ever mention a woman named Cindy Evans to you?"

Paul thought about it. Amy made a sleepy groan and went back to sleep. "Maybe..."

"Maybe?"

"Let me think. Yes, he was working on a house in some small town..."

"Holland Grove?" Juliet asked.

Paul looked at her. "Yes, it could have been Holland Grove. I'm not real sure. He said he met a woman."

"And?"

Paul paused. "Look, Juliet. I don't know what you're trying to get at here. Whenever Rad and I talked, I always understood that it was between the two of us. He trusted me and I trusted him."

Juliet folded her arms. "Paul, something happened to Dad about a year ago, and I've been trying to put all the pieces together. There was a lot of money involved and a woman named Cindy Evans. The night I had the accident, I had learned something that really upset me. Well, anyway, I'm just trying to find the truth. I've got to find out what happened."

Paul averted his eyes.

CHAPTER 23

Paul spoke softly, carefully considering his words. "Rad never told me what happened. He and I were at The Mug one night and we were talking about personal things. I was talking about Tracy and he... well, he said he'd met this woman. I'm pretty sure her name was Cindy. He said he'd done something that really troubled him, because he hadn't told his wife about it."

Juliet waited, her breath slow, her body still.

"He said he didn't know if he'd done the right thing. He said he kept remembering his son and how he died. It was really bothering him. He said he didn't know how he could ever forgive himself for what he'd done. And then he looked at me, and he asked if I understood myself, like why I did certain things, but I wasn't sure why I did them."

"Did he tell you what he was referring to?" Juliet asked, anxiety building in her chest.

"No, Juliet, he didn't, and I didn't ask. I suppose I didn't really want to know. And then Rad just looked away. He thought for a long time and finally said, 'Paul... I did it because I had to do it. Maybe I'll pay for it later, but I just had to do it.' Then he changed the subject."

They were silent as Juliet absorbed Paul's information.

Amy awoke, rubbing her tired eyes. Paul gathered her up in his arms, studied Juliet's troubled expression, and took Amy upstairs to bed.

Juliet wandered the house, looking at old family photographs, touching the Christmas tree branches and staring out the window to see that the snow had blanketed the ground. The forecast was for just a couple of inches.

When Paul returned, he poured them both a glass of Merlot and found Juliet warming her hands by the fireplace. He handed her a glass.

"Cold?"

"A little."

He looked at her tenderly. "I'm glad you came."

They touched glasses.

"I am too. Here's to life, with all its surprises," Juliet said.

They drank. When Juliet looked into Paul's face, she suddenly felt as though she were facing a kind of sunrise. She saw beauty there. She saw possibility and hope. She saw desire and longing. They stood in a wary intimacy, studying hair, face and eyes.

"There are so many things I want to say," Paul said. "So many things I've been thinking about and want to share with you."

"Yes," Juliet answered, suddenly realizing how much *she'd* longed to talk to *him*. "I wanted to tell you about that night... the night of the accident."

"Yes, please tell me."

Juliet blushed, suddenly nervous, hoping to lighten the mood. She pointed a finger at him, smiling. "First of all, Mr. Lyons, I want you to know that I saw your hands all over me, all over my chest."

Paul stepped back, gently startled. "What do you mean?"

Juliet grew more serious. "I watched you give me CPR."

Paul was confused. "You saw me? What do you mean, you saw me? How did you see me?"

Juliet hesitated. "Please don't think I'm crazy... but I was floating outside my body, looking down at us. I could see everything as clearly as if I was watching a movie."

Paul stroked the bridge of his nose with his forefinger.

"You do think I'm crazy, don't you?"

"No, Juliet. No. I don't think you're crazy at all."

"I saw you pull me out of the car and do chest compressions, and breathe into my mouth..." Juliet looked down. "And I saw you start to cry when I started breathing."

Paul stared into the wine glass. "Yes... that's what happened."

He lifted his eyes, and they narrowed on her.

"I didn't go back in my body right away," Juliet whispered. "I went off someplace...to a kind of heaven."

Paul remained silent. Juliet placed her wine glass on the mantel and tentatively began the story of how she saw Rad and Jimmy. At first, she presented a condensed version, but as she struggled to find the right words to describe the scenes and emotions, her descriptions grew more elaborate. She remembered details she had forgotten. She found herself searching for elusive phrases to convey the ineffable sensation of peace and joy.

At times she paused, searching Paul's face for his reaction. He was focused and still and, once or twice, Juliet thought she saw a kind of recognition play across his face. Slowly and methodically, Juliet allowed the events to unravel until finally, her voice softened into a near hush, and she was finished.

They stood in throbbing silence, caught in a kind of wonder, savoring the words and the feelings. They let the power of the story dissipate.

Juliet waited for his response. Paul wandered back to the couch, but he didn't sit. He placed his glass down and pocketed his hands, deep in thought.

"I was in a firefight in Afghanistan. A guy next to me got hit. I got to him fast, but he was already going into shock. A couple of us went to work on him. We stopped the bleeding, got him stabilized as best we could. The bad guys were still shooting at us from our right flank, and I really thought we weren't going to get out of there. But we did, and we managed to get the wounded soldier out too.

"We got him back to the forward operating base and then he was taken to another base that had a medical facility. I went to visit him. He was okay. He made it.

They were going to ship him to Germany and then back to the States."

Paul paced to a window and looked out. "We talked. He told me, almost apologetically, that when he'd gotten shot, he flew out of his body. He just popped right out, and there he was, watching everything that was going on from above it all. He said he didn't feel any pain. No pain at all. He was just hovering, kind of floating, above the whole scene."

Paul turned toward Juliet. "He told me he saw me go to work on him. He saw the bad guys advancing and shooting at us, all from above his own wounded physical body. And then he saw his grandfather and his grandmother in this white light smiling at him, but telling him to go back, gesturing with their hands, saying it wasn't his time yet. He was really spooked. He asked me if I thought he was crazy. I said, no. I believe you. Why shouldn't I believe you? He said he was afraid to tell his doctors because they'd think he was nuts or something. He said it was nothing like any dream he'd ever had. He said it was as real as real could be."

Paul smiled.

"Did you think he was crazy?" Juliet asked.

"No... I saw something in his eyes. I've seen fear in soldiers' eyes. I've seen raw fear and terror. It's an experience you never forget. It's real. It's authentic. You don't have to think about it or analyze it or anything like that. You just *know* it. You experience it. That's what I saw in that soldier's eyes. Not fear. I saw that he'd had a life-changing experience."

Paul's active eyes finally settled on Juliet's face.

"When you told me your story, Juliet, I saw the same thing in your eyes. The very same thing. You *had* an experience."

Juliet felt as though a door had opened and she was safe to walk through it. A rush of warm passion swept through her body, stirring the air around them. She knew Paul felt it. He saw the passion in her eyes.

Paul moved toward her. Her face was turned at an angle, lit golden by light, her lips moist. He studied her burnished hair, the shape of her cheek, her elegant neck. He saw a soft invitation in her eyes that moved him.

They stood close, meeting each other's gaze, barely breathing. Waiting. Juliet smelled the clean, masculine scent of his skin and saw a tender strength in his eyes. She wanted his lips.

He slipped his hand into hers. Juliet smiled, feeling heat flush her cheeks. Paul brushed a kiss across her lips, and she shuddered, lifting her chin, wanting more. He pulled her close and kissed her deeply, his tongue exploring her mouth. Juliet responded, surrendering into his chest, yielding to his embrace.

"You are so beautiful," he whispered into her ear.

"I want to be beautiful for you."

Paul felt his body awaken to love. He found her lips, her cheek, her neck. Juliet swayed, allowing her fingers to explore the hard muscles on his back and arms. She wanted to fall into him, to feel the weight of him, to feel the masculine power of his body.

Paul suddenly looked at her, his eyes bright with passion.

Without a word, they turned toward the couch, but their hands didn't stop reaching and touching. Paul slid his hands up her arms, onto her shoulders, kissing and touching, her breasts pressing into his chest, his hands rubbing her lower back, massaging, cradling. Finally, they settled onto the couch, releasing themselves into passion.

Paul stopped, startled by a thought. Juliet followed his gaze up toward Amy's room.

He stood, conflicted. "She wakes up sometimes."

Juliet blinked fast, caught between desire and caution. They each considered the moment and then, slowly, their faces changed, and the mood changed, and they became resigned to the situation.

As if on cue, Amy's door opened, and she shuffled out, rubbing her eyes, squinting into the light.

"Daddy... I had a bad dream."

Juliet smiled when Paul glanced over at her, apologetically.

"Okay, Amy, I'll come up and put you back to bed," he said, with a little shrug.

FIFTEEN MINUTES LATER, Juliet and Paul sat close on the couch, not quite touching, sipping wine and staring into the fire. Paul had apologized again, and Juliet told him there was no need. They returned to safe conversation, feeling uneasy and awkward, somewhere between strangers and intimate friends who had shared a secret.

They talked about their families and their childhoods and, little by little, they relaxed and grew drowsy. Their nerves untangled; silence softened their thoughts and emotions. Neither felt compelled to talk. It was as if they'd each found a space to rest in; a safe place where nothing had to be explained, nothing had to be recounted, and no one had to be impressed. At some point, Juliet closed her eyes and listened to the crackling fire; soon, she drifted off into a peaceful sleep.

Paul watched her for a while, feeling an immense pleasure. As he watched the gentle rise and fall of her chest, just as he had at the hospital, he again felt as if something was shifting and flowing inside, like a fresh clear spring was bringing a new source of energy that could wash away his fears and hurts.

And then he, too, fell asleep. As the silent night lengthened, Juliet's head found his comfortable shoulder, and she nestled into it. He leaned into her, feeling her warmth. His sleep became rich, his breathing easy.

Deeper into the night, Paul's head fell back, and then to the side, and then to the other side. He awoke to see Juliet's body spread out on the couch, her head now resting on his leg. He wanted to awaken fully to enjoy the intimate moment, but long-welcomed sleep overtook him. It was the deepest sleep he'd had in months. So he slept, and Juliet pulled her knees up to her chest and reached for his hand. Then, like an old married couple, they just slept.

AT 5 A.M., PAUL'S MOTHER-IN-LAW, Donna, was looking down at them, scowling, her arms folded. They awakened sharply, blinking about with sleepy eyes, looking like two guilty teenagers who'd been caught necking.

CHAPTER 24

As soon as Juliet entered the house, Anne scooted out of her bedroom in a white robe and house sippers and marched down the hallway toward her.

"Where have you been? Why didn't you call or text me?"

Juliet stopped, and they met in the kitchen.

"I did text you at ten o'clock and told you I'd probably be late."

"Late, yes, but all night is not late. It's early."

"Okay, I'm sorry. I just... just," Juliet searched for the right words. "The truth is, I fell asleep."

Anne narrowed her eyes on her. "Truth?"

"Truth."

Anne paused a minute to process it. "Well, I don't care what you did, but you should have called me. I was ready to call the police. I called Paul's phone. Why didn't he answer?"

"I don't know. I guess he was asleep, too. I mean, he *was* asleep. Mother, we both just fell asleep and didn't wake up until his mother-in-law found us. Wow, is she a piece of work. She let us both have it. She called me a... oh never mind."

"She found you where?"

"On the couch. Asleep!" Juliet said, strongly.

Anne tilted her head, lifting an eyebrow. "That's all you did? Sleep?"

"Yes."

"Really?" she asked, looking slightly disappointed.

"Yes."

"You fell asleep? On your second official date, you both just fell asleep?"

"Yes, Mother. I know that's hard to believe because it's hard for me to believe too, but that's what happened. I played with Amy, we ate dinner, we watched a movie, we drank some wine and talked... and then we both just went sound asleep."

Anne turned to leave and then glanced back. "Did you sleep well?"

Juliet exhaled audibly, and then laughed. "Yes, Mother. I slept great. When Paul walked me out to the car, he said he slept great, too. He said he hadn't slept that good in months."

"What did you say?" Anne said.

"We *are* really nosey, *aren't* we?"

"Yes, *we* am. What did you say? I know you well enough to know that you had the last word."

Juliet made a face and lowered her voice, as if sharing a secret. "I said, 'I like the way you kiss.'"

Anne perked up. "Really? What did he say?"

"He said, 'Yeah.'"

Anne narrowed her eyes again. "Yeah? Just yeah?"

"Yeah."

"Wow... You must have taken his breath away. When are you seeing him again?"

"I don't know. Mother-in-law got all crazy on us. I had to flee. We were so close last night... I mean, we really connected. We weren't thinking, analyzing or caught up in our pasts. We just connected, and it was so nice."

"And?"

"And then this morning it was different. We were both kind of distant and weird."

Juliet slid out of her coat.

"I made some coffee. Want some?"

"Thanks."

Juliet sat at the table. "I really like Paul. He's a good man."

Anne poured a mug of coffee, turned, and brought it to Juliet. "But?"

"But it scares me to think of getting into another relationship, and one with a ready-made daughter."

Anne sat down and tightened the belt around her robe. "So you give it more time. And next time, call me so I'm not pacing around like some bear in a cage worrying about you."

After breakfast, Anne dressed for work, grabbed her bag and slipped her coat on as Juliet walked her to the door.

"So you're meeting Marshall Gray tonight," Juliet said, pointedly.

Anne shouldered her purse and reached for the doorknob. "I dread it. I wish I'd never agreed to this. It just makes me feel so uncomfortable, so soon after Rad's death."

"Mom, like I said, Dad would want you to move on with your life. He was never the type to sit around and get depressed about things. He's probably looking down on us right now and laughing."

Anne blew out a sigh. "Oh, God, the thought of it just gives me chills. I'm going," she said, reaching for the doorknob.

"Marshall's coming at 6:30?" Juliet asked.

"Yes."

"I'll be here."

"I hope I am," Anne said.

"I hope you'll call or text me when you both fall asleep together tonight," Juliet said jokingly.

Anne glared at her. "Not funny."

"Mother, I saw a great quote a few months ago. It was something like, 'Women are not like wine. They do not age better if left unnoticed and undisturbed.'"

Anne pondered. "Well, I'm certainly *dis*turbed."

She pulled open the door and left.

AFTER ANNE LEFT, Juliet sat before the fire, stroking a purring and yawning Eaton, and then opened her tablet to check emails. Surprisingly, there was one from Austen Price, one of the owners of DevelopIT Communications. A quick scan of other unopened emails revealed one from Cindy Evans, responding to Juliet's email sent the day before.

Juliet felt the start of nerves. Her mood darkened. She ignored it, clicking first on Mr. Price's email, recalling that he'd been born and raised in London and still carried the British accent.

Dear Juliet:

First, my wife, Ellen, and I wish to stress to you our delight at hearing you have recovered from all your injuries and are growing stronger daily. We trust that you are taking a much-needed rest, as well as an extended period of enjoyable time with your mother, after undergoing so many unfortunate trials and difficulties. It would be our pleasure to offer you any practical help, should you require it.

Ellen and I also want to extend to you an invitation to travel to New York at your earliest convenience, so that we can personally meet with you to discuss the opportunity of your accepting the position of Director of PR and Management in our new London office.

Please list some open dates when this meeting would be agreeable to you, and we will arrange all travel and any additional expenses in this regard.

As an aside, we are currently exploring the possibility of taking DevelopIT Communications public in the near future. Obviously, you would be included in any and all the company's prosperity, with stock options, etc., when the goal is achieved.

We look forward to this meeting and to having you as part of our growing family company once more.

Again, our best wishes to you and your family.

Yours truly,
Austen M. Price
President and CEO

DevelopIT Communications

Juliet closed her eyes, allowing the words to sink in and settle. Obviously, the owners were ready to move to the next stage, and they wanted her decision. The trip to New York was a polite way of saying, we're ready to deal and now it's your turn to make a decision. It was a kind and generous letter and she'd be a fool not to accept the job offer.

Cindy's email awaited, like some Wild West gunslinger under a big, hot, high noon sun.

Juliet opened her eyes. Was she having a change of mind? Did she really want to pursue this? Did it really matter what her father had or hadn't done? He was gone, and the past was the past. Dream, hallucination or reality, he was happy, and her knowledge of what had occurred certainly meant nothing to him anymore.

Surely, Cindy didn't know anything about the four hundred thousand dollars. Why would she? Dan Marcus' investigation would probably turn up some very reasonable explanation in the next few weeks. He'd find the paper trail.

In London, she'd be immersed in her work, meeting new friends, expanding her knowledge and developing her full career potential. The entire odious incident would dissolve into a half-forgotten dream. Life was like that. Like footprints dissolving in sand. Meet Cindy? Why? To hear about some sordid affair and to have her heart broken again, just when she was recovering? Just when she felt new hope, new life and new love pumping in her veins?

To her right, her cellphone beeped a text message. She picked up the phone to see it was from Paul. She brightened, touched and read.

I cancelled my day. Can we meet? I'd like to take u some place special. I'll come by if ok with you? Time?

Juliet smiled and responded. *Yes. 10:30?*

She ignored Cindy's email. She pushed up, showered, washed her hair, and wondered where Paul was taking her. She loved surprises. She loved the thought of being alone with him. Last night felt like a burning secret. Kissing him was wonderful. Sleeping next to him was sweet and exciting. Even though she was asleep, her body was awakened by his hand, his smell, and his muscular leg. She'd slept in comfort and fantasy. She'd dreamed of his touch, and he did touch her in one of her dreams, a firm, gentle, cunning movement of hand and fingers across her stomach, her neck, her burning lips. She saw the enjoyment in his dark eyes, and she had reached for him, eager and wanting.

As Juliet blow-dried her hair, she thought, "How did I sleep at all?"

PAUL ARRIVED a few minutes early, dressed casually in jeans, a blue turtleneck, cowboy boots, and a brown leather jacket. The wind had tousled his long hair, and his eyes were clear and expectant. Juliet was glad she'd worn jeans and boots, too. When Paul leaned over and kissed her, she was surprised. Paul straightened, looking awkward.

"So where are you taking me?" she asked, pulling on a yellow ski sweater and white down jacket.

"Someplace where we can be completely alone, and no one can bother us."

They drove for fifteen minutes along Highway 54, past snow-covered fields, under bare quivering trees and a gray rolling sky.

"Did you know," Paul said, "that Ohio is known as the Birthplace of Aviation, because it's where Orville and Wilbur Wright were born?"

"I may have learned that in school," Juliet said. "If I did learn it, I'd forgotten it. Are you taking me to a museum?"

Paul glanced over and grinned. "No."

He pointed ahead. "See just beyond those trees?"

Juliet probed with her eyes. She noticed a tower and some airplane hangars. As they turned left down an asphalt road, she saw single engine airplanes lined up and tethered on the tarmac. A blue and white single-engine plane took off and drifted up over some trees.

She turned to Paul, uncertainly. "An airport?"

"Yep."

"And?"

"You and I are going to fly away."

CHAPTER 25

Juliet settled back into her seat, with a lift of an astonished eyebrow.

Paul parked in the lot, and they walked up to a chain-link security gate. Within a little wooden hut sat a skinny guard on duty, who was sipping coffee and staring out sleepily. Paul flashed him his security card. In a chilly wind, the couple passed through the swinging gate, down a walkway and onto the tarmac. Paul looked skyward, appraising the conditions.

"A bit of wind. Not bad. Visibility could be better."

"Do you know how to fly?" Juliet asked.

"I certainly hope so. Otherwise, it's going to be a bumpy ride."

At the edge of the grass Juliet saw the single prop plane, a Cirrus SR22. It was snow white with two-tone blue and silver accent stripes.

"What do you think?" Paul asked.

"Is it yours?"

"No. It belongs to a friend of mine, a banker. He helps me with my business loans and lets me use his airplane whenever I want to, assuming it's available. I give him free coffee and pastry anytime he wants it. I think it's a pretty good deal. I called him earlier, and he had them roll it out of the hanger for us."

Paul helped her up into the front passenger seat. After she settled in, she fastened her seatbelt snuggly and looked about. The interior was gray leather with contrasting dark gray center seat inserts. The primary flight instruments were directly in front of the pilot, with large-screen multi-function displays for a moving map, engine details and checklists.

The entire cabin was incredibly luxurious, with leather trim and fold down cup holders complete with Poland Spring water bottles.

Paul climbed in, fastened his seatbelt, and put on his headset. He turned to her. "Ready to go?'

Juliet lifted an open hand. "Yeah... sure. Why not? Drive on, Captain."

"Are you scared of flying?"

"Not until now. I've never been in a plane this small."

"Don't worry. It's a good plane and I'm a good pilot."

Paul started the engine and took hold of the side-mounted control stick. He preflighted and began his taxi. With tower clearance, he turned onto Runway twenty-five and advanced. He stopped, waiting for an incoming plane, did a run-up check and programmed the avionics, entering in his flight plan.

He'd have clearance to four thousand feet. He'd climb at seven hundred feet per minute. Paul checked to make sure both radios were working and put the flaps at fifty.

He called the tower again for clearance.

He looked at Juliet. "There are a couple more airplanes in the pattern, so Departure is going to try to find a hole for us in the opened arrivals. Sometimes it takes a minute… or five. Seatbelt fastened? Comfortable?"

"I'm ready for launch," Juliet said, saluting.

When they were cleared for takeoff, Paul looked left to make sure no other plane was on a final approach. He lined the Cirrus up on the runway and went to full power. The plane rolled and gathered speed as Paul applied a lot of right rudder to keep the plane straight, and studied the panel, waiting for seventy knots. Juliet's eyes shifted curiously and nervously.

At seventy knots, Paul eased back on the side-mounted control stick and the plane left the ground. At four-hundred feet, Paul pulled up the flaps and switched the computer screen to check area traffic.

"Looking good," he said, checking all his instruments.

Juliet watched the ground fall away into a white, unraveling quilt. She kept turning her head, looking in every direction, because there was so much to see. So much to marvel at! She saw a dull flat charcoal lake ahead, and a long expanse of trees meandering around a newly built housing project. She saw yellow bulldozers and little men crawling across roofs. She saw ducks sliding away to their right, skimming over ponds and roads, their wings beating toward the distant milky horizon. She saw the nebulous shadow of another plane descend from the clouds on its way to the airport for a final approach.

She tilted her head back and stared up into a surging gray sky as it lowered to meet them. A sharp feeling of freedom lifted her up, like the plane, and she unrolled her tight fingers from their fists. And then suddenly they were engulfed in a boiling mass of gray and white clouds.

Paul saw Juliet tense up.

"It's okay," Paul said reassuringly. "We'll be out of this soup in a minute."

At twelve thousand feet, as the plane continued its ascent, Paul banked left. He contacted the tower and was told to continue his climb and then maintain an altitude of five thousand feet.

Minutes later, the cloud cover shredded, and they were drifting over the laundered white countryside, a silent witness to the toy-like, miniature, moving world below. The drone of the engine was comforting, and Juliet began to relax.

"It's beautiful," she whispered with a touch of reverence.

"I can always think better up here," Paul said, taking off the headset and wrapping it around his neck.

"When did you learn to fly?"

"About seven years ago, in the Marine Corps. I took to it right away. Loved it ever since. I feel like I can look at things clearly up here, without all the noise and the phones and the talk. I make most of my big decisions when I'm in the sky."

Juliet opened the bottle of water and took a drink. "Did you ever take my father flying?"

"Once. He loved it." Paul eyed the control panel. "Rad was like a father to me. He got me through some hard times. He was always so easy to talk to. Always laughed at things and helped me laugh."

Juliet stared out the window, as ragged clouds rushed by. "Yes, he was like that. He was special," Juliet said. "Of course, he was my dad."

Paul stared into the blurring propeller and eased back on the power. "Juliet, I've been thinking. You're obviously great at what you do. So, I was thinking, well, have you ever considered starting your own business? Starting your own PR and marketing business?"

Juliet looked at him with an expression of inquiry. "A few times. Not lately."

"I know people. People who own businesses. People who manage businesses. People who could use your skills and experience. Your father had such a vast network of businesspeople who respected and loved him. They could use your expertise and help you find other opportunities."

Juliet stared ahead, tranquil and thoughtful.

Paul waited for her response. When there was none, he continued. "After you left this morning, I kind of got confused. Last night felt so good. So natural. It felt right and easy, and it's been a long time since I've felt that comfortable with anyone." He screwed up his face, searching for words. "That's not what I mean, exactly."

Juliet looked at him. She waited patiently, her anxiety indicator rising.

"If I don't tell you now how I feel, then you'll go, and... well, you won't know how I feel."

When Juliet stayed silent, Paul slumped a little. He gazed out into the low-hanging clouds, feeling suspended, like the airplane dangling in thin air, unsure of what to say or where to go.

"Juliet, I think that you and I would be good together. I think we could build a good life together. I know that Fairpoint, Ohio is not London, England, and building your own business will take time and hard work, but if we work together, I think we can build something that will last."

Juliet studied him for a slow five-count, and then she looked away. Below, she saw patterns of farmland and a scattering of houses. She saw a river snaking its way through shadowy hills and meadows, and watched the fields roll away and disappear into a scrim of low clouds.

She moistened her dry lips. "It's been a very stressful couple of months, Paul, a very strange holiday season. So many things have happened, and I have so many decisions to make."

Paul listened silently, his eyes sliding over the instruments.

Juliet continued. "I just got divorced, and, frankly, I still feel awful about it. Not that I did it, but because I made such a bad mistake. Then my father died—the rock of my life. Then I quit my job, and then I find out about some woman named Cindy and four hundred thousand dollars are missing, and then the accident. And then I meet you..." Her voice trailed off.

She continued. "You were obviously very much in love with Tracy. I see it everywhere: in the café, in the restaurant. I see her in your office and in your house, and in your sad eyes. That's okay. What happened was awful. Terrible. I don't know how anyone ever gets over something like that. And to be honest, I'm a little envious of Tracy—of what the two of you had together. You had a love I've never had, and may never have."

"I want to move on, Juliet," Paul said, abruptly. "I think I'm ready to move on."

"I just don't know, Paul. I care for you, yes, I can't deny that, but to give up my career for the possibility that you *might* be ready to move on and begin a new relationship... I don't know if I can do that. And then, I don't know if *I'm* ready to move on. I got burned pretty badly." She shook her head. "Sometimes I feel like my head is filled with so much stuff that I just can't think straight."

"We were very close last night, Juliet. I know you felt it too."

"Yes, I did, but..." She stopped, sighing audibly. "I just don't know. There's no guarantee it will work."

She twisted her body to face him. "Paul, everywhere you look, you see a past that reminds you of Tracy: your memories, your beautiful daughter and your mother-in-law, who's obviously still in a lot of pain over her daughter's death."

The sun broke through the clouds and Paul squinted and slipped on a pair of sunglasses. When he spoke, his voice took on strength and conviction.

"Are you telling me how *I* feel, or are you really saying that *you're* afraid to take a chance on our relationship?"

Juliet pursed her lips in thought. "Okay, fair enough. I don't know."

"Look, Juliet, everything you just said is right. There are no guarantees in life about anything. But I don't care about that. I don't care that things might be difficult or confusing. I don't care if life gets all messy and crazy. That's just the way it is. Okay, I accept that. All I know is, the night I found you unconscious in that car—the night you finally came back to life—something changed in me. It was a slow thing at first and I barely recognized it. I think it scared me a little bit, and I tried to run away. But when I did slowly begin to see it and feel it, I had the incredible feeling that I was finally waking up. I felt like I was coming up for air and coming back to life. A new life. A better life. Last night, as we kissed and as I watched you sleep, it hit me so strongly and gently, if that makes any sense."

Juliet felt a swell of unwanted emotion. She pushed back against it. It frightened her. She had flashbacks of Evan, their early dates, their marriage. She recalled him saying how much she meant to him; how much he loved her and only her. How he'd make her happy for the rest of her life. Fantasy? Lies?

Paul continued. "Maybe I did save your life, Juliet, I don't know, but on that night, when you finally breathed and moved and your eyes briefly opened, I breathed too. I woke up too. I breathed new breaths and came back to life. If I saved your life, then you definitely saved mine."

Paul took off his sunglasses and looked at her earnestly. "I didn't know it then, but that was the night I fell in love with you."

Juliet was on the edge of tears.

"I love you, Juliet, and I want you to stay. I want us to build a life together."

CHAPTER 26

Anne sat, stood, paced and moaned. It was 6:25 and Marshall Gray was due to arrive at any moment. Juliet sat on the couch, her chin on her fist, staring blankly into the fire, her mind a mass of tangled thoughts, emotions and sensations. The afternoon with Paul had completely thrown her off what little sense of balance she'd managed to maintain during the past few weeks.

"Why did you let me do this, Juliet?"

Juliet frowned. "Mother, you really need to relax."

Anne wore a black satin, boat neck, A-line evening dress, with one-inch heels. She'd agonized for days, searching online at the mall and then at a few Columbus boutiques, conferring with Juliet and Nora, who had advised and encouraged her. All totaled, Anne had tried on thirty-five dresses, finally choosing the one she was wearing because Nora and Juliet had agreed she looked beautiful in it. Anne strongly disagreed but bought it anyway.

Anne's hairdresser, "feisty Debbie", had colored, cut, and gelled. Since Anne had medium length hair, Debbie created a perked-up style with flipped ends. Anne asked what that was.

Debbie spoke in her usual raspy, impatient tone. "Don't worry about it! I know what I'm doing."

"Yes, I know *you* know what you're doing," Anne said, nervously, "but *I* want to know what you're doing too."

"So I'm going to part your hair. With this style, you can part it any way you like. Then I'm going to give your hair an uneven or jagged part to make the flipped effect more flattering. Then I'll put a bit of gel to the ends of your hair and you'll look awesome. That's it. Simple. Loosen up some! You're tense as hell!"

Anne went to the hall mirror and checked her mouth, her eyes, and her new hairstyle. She patted, picked and grimaced. "I don't know why I keep going to Debbie," she said, sourly. "I look like somebody's pet dog, with all this flip and gel."

Juliet turned. "Mother, you look great. Debbie did a great job."

The sound of a car approached. Anne froze. "Oh, God. Here he is."

Juliet stood. "Mom, take it easy. You're acting like some high school girl on prom night."

"Well, that's what I feel like."

Juliet joined her mother at the front door and peeked out.

"What kind of car is he driving?"

"I don't know," Anne said, all fidgety.

"It's a Lexus."

"It's a rental. He drove down from Columbus. He had a conference or something there."

They waited, hearing the car door open and then chunk shut. As his footsteps approached, Anne swallowed, and Juliet nodded encouragement.

When the doorbell rang, Anne flinched. She pulled a breath, opened the door, and forced a quivering smile. Marshall Gray stepped into the room, smelling of aftershave, dressed in a black cashmere overcoat. He was about 5'11", of medium build, with a statesman face and thick senatorial silver gray hair. When he flashed a friendly, confident smile, Juliet saw a lot of white teeth.

"Hello, Anne. It's been a long time," Marshall said casually.

"Marshall, how nice to see you," Anne said, extending a hand, but Marshall drew her near to him in a loose hug.

"This is my daughter, Juliet," Anne added nervously.

Marshall eyed Juliet. "A beautiful girl. Nice to meet you! You're almost as beautiful as your mother." He grabbed Juliet's forearm with one hand and pumped her hand with his other.

"Thank you," Juliet said with a smile, looking into his sparkling blue eyes. And then they moved into the living room. They sat on the edges of their seats around the fireplace, managing to mold the awkward situation and conversation into a work of comfortable apprehension. Juliet's impression was that Marshall Gray was a smooth, practiced communicator, with a charming worldliness. She liked him. Nonetheless, she was relieved when they finally left. She just hoped her mother would enjoy herself and not feel guilty for having a night out, or for imagining a new, long-term relationship, if that's what she wanted.

In the quiet room, now, she had to acknowledge what she'd felt the moment Marshall had walked into the room. He'd felt like an intruder. "He shouldn't be here!"

the little girl in her had screamed out. "This is my father's house!" Juliet stared at the stone fireplace, Rad's pride and joy. This truly *is* Rad's house, she thought. His spirit still inhabits it. His life force dwells in the foundation, in each beam and stone and pane of glass. His radical love, his energy and boisterous laughter live in the ether of the house and wander the woods and circle the pond. He's as alive as ever, and Juliet could feel it. She could almost reach out and touch him. And how she wished she could touch him. She needed his advice and his humor.

She'd left Paul, troubled, bewildered, and deeply moved by his declaration of love. After his declaration, she'd become elaborately conversational.

"Paul...did I tell you I talked to Tilly? It sounds like the Christmas Eve potluck supper will be a big success. So many people have responded." And... "I've never flown so low. The world looks so different up here." And... "Amy is delightful. Look at the clouds over there."

Paul grew progressively quieter. She kept right on blabbering away until she annoyed herself and then she shut up.

After they'd landed and were driving back to town, she'd turned to Paul in the bright afternoon light. "Paul... I just don't know. I need time to think. Things are just moving way too fast right now."

The velocity of her changing life was dizzying and disturbing. It was as if her near-death had finished killing off the girl she'd been last summer, the confident businesswoman with a handsome husband and a supportive, trustworthy father, and the new Juliet was still some indistinct, amorphous thing not fully formed or fleshed out. She was an amateur artist's first sketch, and she didn't recognize herself.

Should she meet Cindy or just forget about it? Should she take the London job? Should she stay in Fairpoint, start her own business and try to build a life with Paul?

With her hands locked behind her back, she gazed out the back window into the early darkness, as a light snow began to fall. The night seemed to call to her. The quiet seemed to beckon. She looked right toward the lake, and an impulse sent her grabbing coat, hat, gloves and scarf, rolling back the glass patio doors, and stepping out onto the wide, broad-bricked veranda.

She rambled down toward the pond, looking skyward, feeling the random surprise of stinging snowflakes on her face. The reverent silence stilled her thoughts and opened her to sensation, and to a kind of fairy tale awareness. There she was, wandering alone, threading her way through the dark, past black shaking trees, in a magical haze of snow. She was so far away from the real and restless world where life demands initiation, cadence and, that insistent word, DECISION.

She lingered at the pond, and old memories crowded in, flickering across her eyes like home movies: startling spring days, fishing summer days, blazing autumn days, and freezing winter days, with ice skates and cross-country skis.

Juliet circled the pond, hands pushed deep into her jacket pockets. The wind whipped at her face, but she welcomed it, recalling hot chocolate nights with her parents and friends, and campfires and plenty of laughter.

Through the frosty night she continued on, completing a second circumnavigation of the pond. Finally, she stopped and looked up into the fractured night of scattering snow, silently calling out to her father. She whispered his name. "Conrad Sinclair. Dad. Any advice? Any words? Any help at all?"

She waited as the snow slanted in against her. She bent into it—heard the rattle of tree branches, heard an animal's lonely howl.

But she heard nothing from her father. No words. No guidance. She would always feel his love and support, but the comfort of his advice was gone. Really gone. She turned, fighting loneliness, and ambled away on a meandering journey back toward the house.

WHEN ANNE RETURNED home at 11:30, she found Juliet asleep in the recliner, covered by a green afghan blanket, Eaton stretched out beside her. Her laptop was open near the hearth, and an empty cup sat beside it. Anne gently closed the laptop. Eaton stirred, looked up, yawned, blinked, and decided to stay put.

Anne was grateful not to have to describe the night's events. She was weary and drained of emotion. She watched her daughter lovingly, switched off the lights and went to bed.

CHAPTER 27

The next morning, Juliet left the house at 7:30 and drove out into a gray, cold, unfriendly looking morning. Anne was still sleeping. It was Friday, December 23, and Juliet was off to meet Cindy Evans in Decker's Park, Ohio. The meeting place had been Cindy's choice; it was halfway between Fairpoint and Holland Grove.

Juliet and Cindy had exchanged several email messages the previous day. With the last, Juliet had printed Cindy's directions and slipped the page into the side pocket of her purse.

Forty minutes out of Fairpoint, Juliet left the interstate and was traveling on Highway 57. The road wandered aimlessly for miles, past desolate white fields, old houses and cattle farms with silver grain silos. Crows blotted the sky, soaring over far trees, merging into the gray haze of early morning.

Following Cindy's directions, Juliet saw a wide-open field, an old leaning brown barn on the right, and a sign that read:

NO HUNTING, HIKING OR TRESPASSING

Cindy's instructions were to ignore the sign.

Juliet turned right onto a lumpy asphalt road and crept ahead. The car ramped and pitched over deep ruts and holes. "A tank would struggle across this road," Juliet thought. Her head nearly slammed into the ceiling several times. A rabbit darted a path across the road and fled into a hedgerow, just as a flock of honking geese sailed over, gliding off across snowy fields.

Juliet drove past a dense set of trees. Just beyond them was an open field. She craned her neck to get a better look. Several hundred yards away, she saw a low line of tattered white fences and a crumbling field stone wall. Not far from there, sat a rusty, battered house trailer and a black car. Juliet swallowed. Why did Cindy want to meet out here? It was unnerving. Maybe the woman was a little crazy. Laughing to herself, Juliet even imagined that maybe Cindy and Rad had been spying for the government, and they had to meet out here to avoid wiretapping and surveillance.

Juliet approached the late model gray Prius that was parked near the trailer. She saw a figure emerge from the car and stand facing her. Cindy was wearing an elegantly long, black cashmere coat, a red scarf and a white, fox fur Russian hat. Juliet was intrigued. She stopped the car and killed the engine. In a bleak, windy silence, she reached for her coat, hat and gloves. She climbed out, her heart racing, hands damp despite the cold. She had been waiting for this meeting, and dreading this meeting, for a long time.

The morning wind came in bursts, like little punches. Juliet turned her back against it as she slipped into her coat. Cindy waited, motionless. About twenty feet separated them. They stood firmly, each carefully studying the other. Juliet slowly closed the distance, giving Cindy a dubious look. Cindy's eyes were blank and cold. Juliet stopped and they waited.

"Hello, Juliet," Cindy said. It was a cool and careful voice.

Juliet nodded, feeling a knot in her throat. She tried swallowing it away. Cindy was an attractive woman with very convincing elegance. There was an alluring energy about her, a sturdy confidence in her sherry eyes, and a natural sophistication in her bearing. Juliet thought of royalty as she studied Cindy's slim figure and stylish, expensive clothes.

"Forgive the location," Cindy said, her deep, probing eyes focused and still. "There's a reason."

Juliet remained silent. The two women stared, eye to eye.

"You're pretty, Juliet. Just like the pictures your father showed me."

Juliet tried not to smirk, but she felt it all over her face. She pulled herself taller.

Cindy pocketed her hands; even that movement looked graceful and stylish. Juliet speculated that most men found her beguiling. As a young woman, she must have been irresistible.

"I wanted you to see all this... all this land, because this is where I first met Rad, your father. As you know, I'm a real estate agent. A few years back, just before the real estate market crashed, our company was engaged to sell parcels of land for a new housing project. I was the lead agent on the deal. Back then, Ohio cropland averaged $4,000 per acre for top land, $3,370 for average land, and $2,750 for poor land. This was considered poor land. Well, anyway, Rad Sinclair knew some people who knew other people, because Rad knew a lot of people, and he was brought into the project as one of several architects."

Cindy turned and indicated toward the trailer. "That was the first construction trailer."

Cindy's voice grew a little sad and dark. "Well, you can see what happened. The market crashed and everything went to hell."

Juliet listened intently, feeling the cold seep into her bones.

"Rad and I grew to be friends. Close friends."

Cindy turned her full gaze on Juliet. "I fell in love with him."

Juliet stared, soberly.

"We spent a lot of time together: lunches, dinners, parties. It wasn't difficult to fall in love with Rad. He seemed to draw strength from being with people, and they certainly responded to him. People loved him. Women loved him. He was filled with life, with enthusiasm. He expanded life. He expanded peoples' strengths and overlooked their selfish natures, their pettiness and their weaknesses."

Cindy lowered her eyes. The light went out of her face, replaced by the sorrow of memory. "So... I fell deeply in love with Rad, and I can say with all my heart that I'd never loved a man before... never truly loved. Affairs? Many. Marriage? Yes. But not love. I didn't even know what love between a man and a woman could be like until I met Rad."

Cindy toed at the ground. "Like I said, when the market crashed, everything just fell apart. I had real estate investments. They evaporated. The real estate company I worked for nearly went bankrupt and, because I'd lived way beyond my means for many years, I was heavily in debt."

Cindy walked away, toward an open field, staring out at the flat, expansive snowy barren land. Juliet followed, coming up beside her.

"I have a son," Cindy said. "He's home for Christmas. He's just finishing his first semester at Princeton. He's the love of my life. He's the only good thing that's come from my life. The only worthwhile thing I've got to show for living on this crazy earth."

Cindy reached into her pocket and drew out a lace embroidered handkerchief. She clutched at it, lost in thought, and then she gently dabbed at her nose.

"I had to sell our house for much less than it was worth. Sales dried up. People weren't buying houses or condos. They were trying to sell, like me. People were scared and panicked. I kept going deeper into debt. My son is smart, and he was about to start college. He wanted to go to Princeton. How could I manage that? I was desperate. Rad knew people. He knew I had some bookkeeping experience. I'd kept the books for one of my husbands, and I'd told Rad this. So, he found me a job at a boutique company as a kind of treasurer/bookkeeper. Very exclusive. Very expensive boutique with wealthy clients from all over. The people that can afford to buy exclusive designer clothes don't worry about losing a little money in the stock market now and then. So business was not great, but not bad either."

The wind kept rushing at them, punishing their faces. Juliet was noticeably cold. Her teeth began to chatter. Cindy looked over.

"Let's get out of here. I know a little place where we can have breakfast and warm up."

Juliet paused, wanting the painful explanation to conclude, but feeling like she was freezing to death. They returned to their cars and Juliet followed Cindy down the unfortunate asphalt road to the main highway. Juliet stared flatly out at the cold world, thinking of her mother, trying not to think about what she'd have to tell her someday, when the right moment came.

CHAPTER 28

Juliet and Cindy drove into a small town, turned into a restaurant parking lot and parked side by side. It was a yellow and red semi-circular restaurant that overlooked Sunset Pond. The restaurant was connected to a newly renovated inn that, according to the conspicuous broad green sign, featured comfortable modern waterfront suites.

Inside, the dining room was spacious, with plenty of windows, natural light, and an empty expanse of mahogany bar. They were escorted to a booth next to a window, with a clear view of the lake, and were told by the lively young hostess that the restaurant had breathtaking sunset views. Christmas music drifted from overhead speakers, and poinsettias skirted the windows.

The two ladies studied their menus in silence and ordered in low voices. There were only two other booths occupied by business types, lost in a fog of numbers, problems and little whispers.

Juliet sat in stoic silence, her eyes trying to avoid Cindy's. Cindy was wandering in and out of memory and regret, reviewing episodes of the glowing panorama of her life. Juliet kept waiting for the continuation of Cindy's saga, but Cindy seemed in no particular hurry.

Coffee was poured, and they drank absently, although Juliet was grateful to be thawing out, grateful for the warmth on her face and hands.

Finally, Cindy spoke. "I'm good with numbers. Always have been. If I'd had a college education, I probably would have gone into finance or investment banking. Anyway, I kept my job in real estate, but made most of my money from my job at the boutique. The company I worked for had other boutiques as well; in Columbus, Cincinnati, Chicago; and I crunched the numbers for them. I was cheaper than the other guy. They'd let him go because he was demanding a raise and a promotion. Imagine that? He'd only been with the company for ten years." She made a little flick of her hand. "Well, anyway..."

Juliet stared into her coffee.

"I needed money, Juliet. I'd always had money, and I'd made a vow years ago that I'd never—and I mean never—be poor again."

After the food was delivered, the ladies took a few uninterested bites. Juliet picked at her scrambled eggs, and Cindy pushed around her eggs benedict.

"I began siphoning off money. I knew how. It was easy for me. I'd learned the tricks from one of my more resourceful boyfriends. Anyway, I took a little here and a little there until finally, I'd taken over two hundred thousand dollars. I paid off some bills, bought myself and Kevin a new car and lived, as I always have, beyond my means. Life was improving."

Cindy's face was set and pallid, as if the reality of finally confessing sickened her. "I was able to have the money to send Kevin to Princeton. Big money was coming in and no one suspected me. I was good. Real good, or so I thought. Thieves are never as clever as they think they are. They always slip up somewhere; you get confident, and you get a little lazy."

Cindy took a bite and chewed slowly. "One morning, I was called into the president's office. I sat down before her large oak desk and flashed her my practiced innocent expression. She stared back at me coldly. She said she knew I was stealing money. I tried to deny it, but she had all the documentation. The books had been scrutinized by professionals."

The waitress returned and refreshed the coffee. Juliet leaned back, rapt.

Cindy continued. "I was given an ultimatum: either I pay the money back or they would turn me over to the police."

Cindy poured milk into her coffee and stirred. "I called old friends, but they weren't really friends, and those who were didn't have that kind of money. I called an ex-boyfriend millionaire. He hung up on me. I don't blame him. I left him in Rome without saying goodbye. So, I was staring at prison time. Needless to say, I was scared to death."

Cindy drank some coffee and stared out at the tranquil pond. "Rad found me at a bar. I'd called him. True to form, he'd come. Dropped what he was doing and drove for over an hour to meet me. He sat down next to me and ordered a beer. I couldn't face him. I'd betrayed him. He'd gotten me the job. He'd trusted me, and I'd betrayed him. I just told him I was sorry. That's all I said. I'm sorry. We sat there for... oh, I don't know how long. Maybe we sat there for five minutes before he finally turned to me and said, 'How much do you need, Cindy?'"

Cindy shut her eyes, briefly, as if to hide from memory. "I broke down right there and cried like I'd never cried before. I couldn't stop the tears. So, I left the place. I went out into the parking lot and cried until I was exhausted. Rad followed me out and stayed with me. He waited for all the tears to just drain out of me."

Cindy took in a breath and let it out slowly. "Well, you know the rest, Juliet. He loaned me four hundred thousand dollars."

Juliet sat motionless.

"You know the worst part, Juliet? I knew Rad would never trust me again. I knew after what I'd done, he'd never love me the way I wanted him to love me. I believed he'd write me off as a stupid greedy bitch, which is just what I was, and that hurt more than anything else."

Cindy wiped her misty eyes. "He took me home that night but didn't come in. We stood outside at the front door. I said, 'Please don't judge me, Rad. I don't think I could take it if you hate me and judge me.' You know what he said? He said, 'If I judged you, Cindy, I'd have to judge myself, and I've been trying to forgive myself for a long time.'"

Cindy paused. She lay her fork down and eased back in her chair.

"Then he told me how he'd let his five-year-old son drown. He told me the whole, dreadful story, and he had tears in his eyes. He said he lived with his guilt and self-hate constantly. It never left him. Then he looked at me with those beautiful warm eyes of his and said he was loaning me the money so that Kevin would never find out what I'd done. He said he didn't want my son to lose respect for me. Rad also said he wouldn't let me go to prison. He said he was doing it as a kind of redemption for the mistake he'd made so many years ago. He said he owed that to the world. He said he owed it to his son, Jimmy."

The two women sat staring at each other with wounded eyes. The moment expanded into a moving timelessness.

They were still lost in thought when the waitress presented the check. Cindy took it and handed the waitress her credit card. After she'd gone, Cindy reached into her purse, drew out a letter-sized white envelope and placed it on the table.

"Before you read this, I want you to know that I have all the money Rad loaned me; every dollar of it. It was a loan and now I'm ready to pay it back. I've had a good year and, weirdly enough, I received some money from an old lover, who died a few months ago. It seems he still had some feelings for me, and so he left me a good chunk of change. I don't deserve the money. I wasn't faithful to him, but, what the hell, I took the money."

Cindy laid her hand on the envelope. "Inside is a letter from Rad to me. It will explain all the other stuff. The stuff you want to know about him and me. Let me just say this. One night, months before Rad had loaned me the money, I asked him to my place for dinner. Kevin was away, and I decided that this was the night I was going to get Rad in my bed and in my life for good."

Juliet looked away in sudden aversion.

"I wore a sexy red dress—very expensive. Two-inch black satin heels, nails and toenails done to perfection. I wore diamond stud earrings and a dazzling diamond necklace. I had my hair done by a professional and I looked pretty damned sexy for a then fifties something broad. I cooked one of the best meals of my life: New York veal chop with pea greens and morel sauce. When Rad came through the door, he whistled and laughed, and then twirled me around like I was a ballerina. Cindy Cinderella, he called me. He said, 'I thought this was supposed to be a work dinner.'"

Cindy smiled reflectively. "He knew what I was up to. So, I poured the champagne, and I flirted and waited on him; I batted my eyes and lowered my husky voice and I turned on all the sexy charm I could muster."

She crossed her arms, shaking her head. "I got pretty high on the champagne. Rad told funny stories, and we laughed and ate and danced a little. And then I looked at him and said, 'Rad, I love you and I want you more than I've ever wanted anything or anybody. Stay with me tonight. Stay with me forever.'"

Cindy let out a sad little laugh. "He stared at me for the longest time, and I tried to read his eyes. Finally, he stood back a little, keeping his hands on my bare shoulders. He looked deeply into my eyes and said, 'Cindy Cinderella, you are every man's dream girl. You are a wonder. But you know what the problem is? I already have two dream girls: my wife, Anne, and my darling girl, Juliet. Now, let us *not* be the best of fools. Let us be the best of good friends.'"

Cindy wilted a little, as if the burden of finally unloading the story had exhausted her. Juliet, too, slumped, weighed down by truth and emotion. Cindy slid the letter over to Juliet.

"I'm going now, Juliet. It's time for me to get out of your life forever. Let me know how you want me to send the money. It's there for you and your mother."

She slid out of the booth and stood. Juliet looked up at her, her emotions muddled.

"Cindy... what will you do?"

"I'm leaving Ohio and moving back to Florida. I'm not much welcomed around here anymore. Word has gotten around; a lot of whispering. I don't blame them. I'll start again in Florida, where I can roam the beaches and find some man who may love me as much as your father loved you and your mother. It can still happen. I've always been a crazy optimist."

"Thanks, Cindy. Thank you for everything," Juliet said. "I hope everything works out for you."

Cindy winked. "I always land on my feet, Juliet. I'm a tough old girl."

Cindy started off, then stopped, turned and came back. "Have you met a guy recently?"

Juliet was taken back. "...Yes."

"Your father said he had some great guy all lined up for you. He was so charged up about it. We talked about it during one of our last conversations. He said there was a guy who owned some coffee place. I forget his name, but he thought the two of you would be perfect together. He said he was going to introduce you to him. Did he?"

Juliet smiled. "Yeah... I think he did."

Cindy smiled, warmly. "Good. That's good. He was so proud of you, Juliet. He lit up like the Fourth of July whenever he spoke of you."

Juliet watched Cindy's retreating figure disappear. She had an easy, graceful and majestic walk, like a queen. It was the walk of a real lady.

After Cindy was gone, Juliet reached for the envelope. She opened it and drew out the handwritten page.

Dear Cindy Cinderella:

Last night was delightful and fun! What a great chef you are. What a perfect hostess. What a sexy dress. How many more 'Whats" can I get in here?

*You and I are close friends. I will always be there for you, and I'm sure you'll be there for me. We know that about each other. That's a fixed thing. A good thing. So, don't be mad at me or hurt that I can't be **that** guy—and you know what I mean. I ain't that guy. I have to be the Rad guy. The guy who is boring and loyal. The happily married guy.*

Anne has been my best friend and lover for many years. We have weathered many a storm together, and she's always been there for me. She's supported me when I didn't deserve to be supported. She's loved me when I hated myself. I will always be there for her. Enough said.

Let's keep our good friendship, and savor all the good things life gives us, because we never know when the big dark guy with the hood and scythe will come knocking on the door to take us away, over the rainbow.

How morose! How glum! How depressing! That's the end of the 'Hows', and the end of this badly written note. (I never could write worth a damn.)

—*Rad*

P.S. Wear that sexy dress to our next client's meeting. That'll keep us all awake!

Juliet folded the letter and replaced it in the envelope. She sat quietly until sunlight broke through the clouds and a shaft of gold bathed her in a kind of glory. It warmed her. She squinted into it, gazing up into a patch of deep blue sky.

CHAPTER 29

Christmas Eve morning was cold. A gentle snow fell, sugar-coating the trees, silently adding another two inches to the three inches already on the ground. Juliet and Anne padded around in the kitchen, still in their housecoats and slippers, preparing food for the Christmas Eve party at The Coffee Mug. Cranberries were bubbling on the stove and Anne was cutting out Christmas tree and star cookies to bake in the oven. Juliet was rinsing out a twelve-pound turkey, which would go in the oven after the cookies came out. They frequently bumped into each other, crossing from sink to stove to oven.

"Did you finish all your Christmas shopping yesterday?" Anne asked.

"Yeah, pretty much,"

They worked, shuffled, and sniffed. Juliet reached for more coffee. Anne reached for a sweet roll.

"Are you ready to talk about your date with Marshall Gray?" Juliet asked. "You keep saying you'll tell me later. Isn't this later?"

Anne turned away, keeping her hands busy, keeping her body in motion, while nerves and doubt nibbled at her. Finally, she stopped, not facing her daughter.

"It was so much fun, Juliet. I feel so guilty because I had such a good time. We talked and talked, and I felt like no time had passed. We talked about the past and about our families, and I felt like I was twenty-eight again. I felt young and pretty."

Juliet leaned back against the kitchen sink. "Then why feel guilty?"

"You know why."

"Dad wouldn't want you to feel guilty. He'd want you to be happy. You know that."

"Let's not talk about it. I'm just all mixed up right now."

"Are you going to see him again?"

Anne turned around. "We're going to take it slow. We're giving it time. Maybe he'll come for a visit in a month or so. In the meantime, we'll email and talk on the phone."

Juliet took her mother's hand. "Mom, I'm happy for you. I want you to be happy." She gave her a hug. "I'm glad you reconnected with him."

Anne sighed deeply and went back to the cookie dough. "Now that I've told you about Marshall, are you going to tell me where you went yesterday and why you didn't get home until late?"

"I told you, I went Christmas shopping, and then I met Karen for dinner. We had a few glasses of wine, and we just kept talking, and I totally lost track of time."

"Did you see Paul?"

"No," Juliet said, softly. "But I called him."

"He knows we're going to the potluck tonight, doesn't he?"

"Yes. I texted him. Said we'd be there by 7:30."

"Has he come up with a name for the restaurant yet?" Anne asked.

"He's supposed to announce it tonight."

"Have you contacted New York about the job?"

"Mother... so many questions so early."

"I heard you up and roaming around three different times last night. Couldn't you sleep?"

"If you heard me, you must have been awake, too."

"I was."

"Because?"

"Now it's *you* with the questions."

They ate breakfast in segments, while listening to Christmas music, checking the oven and surfing the internet. Juliet spent the rest of the morning and early afternoon answering emails and wrapping presents.

Cindy's letter was inside a big square box, beautifully wrapped in red paper and topped with a rich velvety green, red and white bow. It was under the Christmas tree with a label that read:

To: Mom
From Santa. A Big Surprise!

Anne shook it a couple of times, holding it close to her ear. "I don't hear anything."

Juliet stood by, grinning. "You'll never guess, Mom, so you might as well give up and put it down."

By late afternoon, Anne and Juliet were both napping, Anne curled up on the couch and Juliet in the recliner. When evening descended and stars began to appear, Juliet suddenly shook awake, aroused. An image of Paul clung to her eyes; his name reverberated in her ears. She'd dreamed of him. What was it? She strained to pull the dream back from the fading depths of her mind. It was gone, but the power of it lingered, and she was left in longing and imagination.

As she lay there in an odd kind of fever, she suddenly remembered his touch. In the dream, he had touched her, ever so gently, in the hollow below her neck, and then his fingers had traveled down her chest, resting in the place between her breasts. He had caressed her there, with a circular motion, causing desire to be released, the alarm of passion awakened.

Juliet sat up, abruptly. Why had she shut him off during the airplane ride, when he'd been so open with his feelings? That couldn't have been easy for him. What was wrong with her? Why hadn't she responded?

Juliet placed her hand on her chest and took a deep breath, suddenly frightened and elated at the same time. Her relationship with Paul had awakened something inside her. "I love you, Juliet. I want you to stay. I want us to build a life together." She repeated his words, feeling them penetrate to the core of her being.

And then something shifted. It was subtle, but it was there. She felt lighter. Free. She turned her gaze to her mother's Christmas present, the one that held Cindy's letter. Was that what she needed to know, to be released?

Paul had said he loved her. *Paul had said he loved her!* Juliet stood up, staring at the blinking Christmas tree. Did she love him? *Could* she love him? She pictured him at the No Name restaurant, in the plane, at The Coffee Mug. She remembered their kisses in front of the fireplace, the comfortable feeling of his body as they lay on the couch. Why had she denied what her body had been feeling ever since she floated above the accident scene and saw him scramble down the hill to her car? Or when she'd awakened in the hospital and seen him sitting next to her bed, as if he belonged there, as if he had always been beside her?

What had she felt? She'd felt safe and protected. She'd felt the strength of him, the truth of him. Every time she saw him, she knew: he was someone she could trust. So why was she holding back? What was she afraid of?

There was definitely a physical connection. His touch and his lips had opened her to love that night. She could sense that their bodies were good together, that when they made love, she would slide in and out of her skin, living and dying at the same time.

While dressing for the potluck supper, she felt the rise of heat. She combed her hair, feeling heat. She dressed, feeling uncharacteristically warm and agitated. She wore black woolen slacks, carefully tailored to her slenderness. She slipped into a gold silk blouse, open to reveal her elegant neck and a bit of cleavage. She wore gold hoop earrings. She wore ruby red lipstick. She pulled on heels and stood before her full-length mirror, trying on expressions: first sexy, then playful, then coy, then bored and finally, a bold and frank "come hither" stare. She repeated them, fine-tuning each one until she felt practiced and confident with her repertoire.

She'd use them all on Paul. She'd tempt him. Play with him. Taunt him. Which would he respond to? After the airplane ride, she had him off-balance. He was confused, waiting, perhaps calculating.

But if he was off balance, she was absolutely reeling. It was his words that kept repeating in her head, like a mantra that destabilized and moved her. It was his words that brought heat and desire. It was his words that finally touched her heart and reawakened her to a new and vibrant love. "I love you, Juliet. I want you to stay. I want us to build a life together."

They were wonderful words. They were words that healed. They were absolutely lovely.

ANNE DROVE HER CAR to the restaurant with Juliet sitting quietly beside her, lost in imagination and speculation. The lot was already over half full. A high school kid, tugging up his baggy pants, shoveled newly fallen snow, as another directed traffic with a flashlight. The restaurant was illumined by soft yellow flood lights, as well as Christmas lights strung from the eves and threaded through shrubs. A large wreath hung on the front door.

Anne toted a shopping bag containing the cranberry sauce and the Christmas cookies. Juliet carried the turkey.

Inside, the room was alive with holiday flavor. Christmas music bounced and thumped. There was lively conversation and eating. A tall, majestic tree blazed with Christmas lights, and kids circled it, laughing and playing. A long table, covered by a white tablecloth and decorated with poinsettias and holly, displayed ham, fried chicken, pot roast, pasta, hot dogs and hamburgers. There were luscious cakes and pies, and mounds of brown biscuits, freshly baked breads, and crusty muffins.

Juliet scanned the room, looking for Paul. She didn't see him. She and her mother stepped over to the table and delivered their goods to two friendly middle-aged women, who identified themselves as Paul's high school music teacher and his Aunt Ruby.

"He couldn't sing one note in tune," the teacher said, laughing. "I'd hit middle C on the piano, and he'd sing a D or B flat."

"Everyone in our family is tone deaf," Aunt Ruby added.

The spirit of Christmas swept through the room in bursts of laughter, singing and dancing. Cellphones snapped photos, the punch bowl was whisked to the table and sweet and savory smells lifted noses and widened curious eyes.

Anne found friends and fell into easy conversation. Juliet drifted, searching for familiar faces, unable to find any. She continued to search for Paul and asked a fresh-faced waiter if he knew where he was.

"He ain't back yet. Had to go home to get Amy, his daughter."

Juliet nibbled on fried chicken and sampled the "adults only" punch. It was sweet, with hints of rum, orange, and pineapple.

By eight o'clock the restaurant was stuffed with people, overflowing with expectation and joy. Who would win the restaurant name contest?

Sheriff Hansel caught Juliet's eye. She waved at him, picking her way through the crowd to meet at the food table, where he was piling on ham, sweet potatoes, biscuits and pumpkin pie.

"I'm not taking any chances on missing that pie," he said. "Not much left of the apple and pecan already. How are you, Juliet?"

"Good. Everything's good."

"I never did get that phone call from you," he said, balancing his plate in his left hand and leaning to snatch a cookie with his right.

"I was going to call you after Christmas and tell you all about it."

"Everything work out okay?" he asked.

"Yes. Thanks for your help. It worked out great."

She kissed him on the cheek. "Merry Christmas, Sheriff."

He pointed a finger at her. "You call me now, okay? I want to hear the whole story."

He flashed a little grin and went back to searching for food.

Juliet saw Karen and recognized that she was with her ex-husband, Dave. Surprised, she threaded a path over to them. Dave shyly looked down and then backed away toward the punch bowl.

Juliet faced Karen, bewildered. "What was that all about?"

Karen shrugged. "He's all shy and weird right now. You know how crazy guys are. We're trying to work things out."

Just as Juliet opened her mouth to speak, she saw Paul enter with Amy and a tall, sexy blonde. The room burst into sudden applause. Juliet's face fell. She saw Amy dash off toward the Christmas tree to play with the other kids. The blonde hung on Paul's arm. She was alive with blonde gestures, blonde talk, and blonde laughter.

The room rushed in toward them and Paul motioned, with both hands, for the servers to bring out the champagne. An anxious crowd circled Paul, waiting for the announcement. The music was switched off and the room slowly gathered into a hush.

Juliet looked on, assessing Paul's relationship to the blonde. New girlfriend? Old girlfriend? Paul was never more handsome, dressed in a powder blue shirt, with a dark blue sport coat and gray slacks. The blue set off his happy, glittering eyes. Juliet edged forward, drawing close so he could see her. He seemed to be ignoring her.

Paul cleared his throat. "First, let me say how happy I am that you all came—especially on Christmas Eve. Second, I'm not going to drag this thing out. We received about four hundred entries, which is just incredible. Now please understand, we could only choose one. So, I don't want to receive a bunch of angry emails after Christmas, okay!?"

There were shouts and whistles and applause. "But before I say anything else, I want to let you all know that all of this happened because of one person. All this was Juliet Sinclair's idea."

Paul indicated toward Juliet. All heads turned to face her. There were more whistles and applause. Juliet, now stunned to be the center of attention, grinned meekly. She noticed the blonde's face had slackened into a brooding darkness.

"So, without any further babbling from me, here it is. The winner is... Nickie Patterson! And the new name for the once No Name Restaurant is now The Good Gravy Café!"

Nickie shrieked out surprise and glee just as the champagne corks popped. Glasses were raised, champagne was poured, and music jumped from the speakers. The room erupted into dancing. The blonde seemed to disappear when Brenda Lee's Christmas song, *Rockin around the Christmas Tree,* closed her in a circle and yanked her away.

Paul called for Juliet, reaching out for her. She pushed forward to meet him.

"What a night!" Paul yelled. "What a great night. Thank you."

"Who's the blonde?" Juliet asked.

"Who? Do you mean Courtney?"

Juliet's eyes enlarged as if to say, "Who else?"

"My cousin. You'll like her."

"I want to talk to you," Juliet shouted.

He shook his head firmly. "No."

"No?" Juliet said, surprised.

"Absolutely No. No more talk! I'm done with talking for now."

Paul grabbed Juliet's hand and dragged her through the surging crowd, through the bustling kitchen and out the back door into the cold, chilly night.

"No more talk," he said. "I've had it with talk."

Juliet opened her mouth to speak. Paul leaned in and kissed her, long and warm. He grabbed her shoulders and drew her in close. At first, tense with surprise, Juliet quickly felt a sudden and aching excitement, and she relaxed into his chest. Their lips explored and searched. Their arms enveloped, bodies moving into a slow, easy rhythm, with gentle grasps of hands. And then came the sighs and the play of tongues and the cessation of thought, as they swayed in a rebirth of love and sensation. They surrendered to each other. Snow settled on their hair and shoulders, and kisses expanded; they became wild and tender.

Slowly, reluctantly, they awakened to the returning sound of the wind through the trees, and the singing and conversation coming from inside the restaurant. They heard the distant moan of a train whistle.

Juliet opened her eyes, still in a kind of dreamy trance, and she looked up into Paul's magnificently handsome face. "Wonder where that train's going?" she asked.

"To New York?" Paul asked. "Then maybe on to London?"

Juliet smiled, stood on tip toes, and kissed him again. "No... I don't think so. I think it's returning home, after a long, long journey."

EPILOGUE

On Christmas Day at the Sinclair house, when there was great food, good conversation and high spirits, Anne found Juliet and Paul sitting near the fireplace, playing with Amy and her new toys.

"What a delightful Christmas," Anne said, happiness all about her. "Oh, how I wish Rad were here. He would have such a good time."

Juliet took Paul's hand and turned to look outside at the wet silver sky and falling snow. "He's here, Mom. Dad is definitely here."

At that moment, down at the pond, a skiff broke free from the dock. It drifted aimlessly across the water, pushed by a gentle wind, barely visible in the haze of falling snow.

Thank You!

Thank you for taking the time to read *Christmas for Juliet*. If you enjoyed it, please consider telling your friends or posting a short review. Word of mouth is an author's best friend, and it is much appreciated.

Thank you,
Elyse Douglas

The Christmas Diary
The Christmas Diary – Book 2 - Lost and Found
Christmas for Juliet
The Christmas Bridge
The Date Before Christmas
The Christmas Women
Christmas Ever After
The Summer Diary
The Summer Letters
The Other Side of Summer
Wanting Rita

Time Travel Novels
The Christmas Eve Letter (A Time Travel Novel) Book 1
The Christmas Eve Daughter (A Time Travel Novel) Book 2

The Christmas Eve Secret (A Time Travel Novel) Book 3
The Christmas Eve Promise (A Time Travel Novel) Book 4
The Lost Mata Hari Ring (A Time Travel Novel)
The Christmas Town (A Time Travel Novel)
Time Change (A Time Travel Novel)
Time Shutter (A Time Travel Novel)
Time Sensitive (A Time Travel Novel)

Romantic Suspense Novels
Daring Summer
Frantic
Betrayed

www.elysedouglas.com

Editorial Reviews

THE LOST MATA HARI RING – A Time Travel Novel by Elyse Douglas

"This book is hard to put down! It is pitch-perfect and hits all the right notes. It is the best book I have read in a while!"
5 Stars!
--Bound4Escape Blog and Reviews

"The characters are well defined, and the scenes easily visualized. It is a poignant, bitter-sweet emotionally charged read."

5-Stars!
--Rockin' Book Reviews

"This book captivated me to the end!"
--StoryBook Reviews

"A captivating adventure..."
--Community Bookstop

"...Putting *The Lost Mata Hari Ring* down for any length of time proved to be impossible."
--Lisa's Writopia

"I found myself drawn into the story and holding my breath to see what would happen next..."
--Blog: A Room Without Books is Empty

Editorial Reviews

THE CHRISTMAS TOWN – A Time Travel Novel by Elyse Douglas

"The Christmas Town is a beautifully written story. It draws you in from the first page, and fully engages you up until the very last. The story is funny, happy, and magical. The characters are all likable and very well-rounded. This is a great book to read during the holiday season, and a delightful read during any time of the year."
--Bauman Book Reviews

"I would love to see this book become another one of those beloved Christmas film traditions, to be treasured over the years! The characters are loveable; the settings vivid. Period details are believable. A delightful read at any time of year! Don't miss this novel!"
--A Night's Dream of Books

THE SUMMER LETTERS – A Novel
by Elyse Douglas

"A perfect summer read!"
--Fiction Addiction

"In Elyse Douglas' novel THE SUMMER LETTERS, the characters' emotions, their drives, passions and memories are all so expertly woven; we get a taste of what life was like for veterans, women, small town folk, and all those people we think have lived too long to remember (but they never really forget, do they?).
I couldn't stop reading, not for a moment. Such an amazing read. Flawless."
5 Stars!
--Anteria Writes Blog - To Dream, To Write, To Live

"A wonderful, beautiful love story that I absolutely enjoyed reading."
5 Stars!
--Books, Dreams, Life - Blog

"The Summer Letters is a fabulous choice for the beach or cottage this year, so you can live and breathe the same feelings and smells as the characters in this wonderful story."
--Reads & Reels Blog

Made in the USA
Las Vegas, NV
16 January 2023